MW00760213

# The Alto wore Tweed

A Liturgical Mystery
by Mark Schweizer

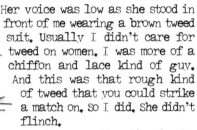

Her voice was low as she stood in front of me wearing a brown tweed suit. Usually I didn't care for tweed on women. I was more of a chiffon and lace kind of guy. And this was that rough kind of tweed that you could strike a match on. So I did. She didn't flinch.

She was attractive in the sort of way that some heavy women with very short hair and no makeup, wearing a three piece brown-tweed suit with wingtips and smoking a cigar can be called attractive. She reminded me of my Aunt Mable. Or Winston Churchill.

Pulling up a chair, she sat down gracefully, crossing her tweed-covered legs with an elegance belying the sound of tweed-on-tweed, a sound not unlike forty Amish farmers shucking corn. "I heard you were good with altos and I need some advice. My name is Denver. Denver Tweed."

"It'll cost you."

I could tell she wasn't put off a bit as she dropped two C-notes on the desk in front of me and pulled a meerschaum pipe from her pocket. Somehow I wasn't surprised. Tweed and meerschaum. What next?

"Someone stole my elbow patches."

Like I said before, I wasn't surprised.

St. Germaine is a quiet little town in the mountains of North Carolina. Quiet until full-time police detective, part-time Episcopal choirmaster and aspiring whodunit novelist Hayden Konig begins his opus amidst murder and hilarious mayhem at St. Barnabas Church. "It's like *Mitford* meets *Jurassic Park,* only without the wisteria and the dinosaurs."

224 pages • $10.00

*get your copy at sjmpbooks.com*

No Regrets
Copyright ©2003 by Paul J. Heald

Cover Illustration by Wendy Giminski
wgout@uga.edu

Published by
**St. James Music Press**
www.sjmp.com
P.O. Box 1009
Hopkinsville, KY 42241-1009

ISBN 0-9721211-1-0

First Printing, December, 2002

**Acknowledgments**

Sally Coenen
Jill Crandall
Paul De Angelis
Christopher Guthrie
Rosemary Hathaway
Laura Jackson
John Miller
Melinda O'Neal
Rick Powers
Phil Williams

NO REGRETS

*For Marilyn*

# WARM-UPS


(July 1989)

*1*

## A Character Study

Dorothy Henderson was the only woman in Clarkeston who could tolerate Doc Burton as her physician, but even she was startled by the directness with which he pronounced her death sentence. She watched his humorless brown eyes flick back and forth from her shoulder to the lab report in his hand as he explained in an even voice that her cancer was back, wrapped so extensively around her collar bone that no operation could possibly eradicate it. Only his rigid posture and the thin sheen of sweat glistening on his forehead betrayed that his diagnosis was anything more serious than the discovery of bursitis or strained ligaments.

"We both knew this might happen."

Dorothy ignored his accusation and studied the unframed prints of World War I biplanes tacked to the wall over his shoulder. An old-time aviation buff, he liked to talk about the joys of restoring the only Fokker Series II fighter in the state of Georgia and had once offered to take her for a ride. Although she frequently visited his office, she found herself for the first time distracted by the figures locked in combat in their fragile planes of cloth and wood. The glare from the fluorescent lights in the examination room obscured large sections of the prints, leaving her to guess whether the Germans or English were winning.

"Dorothy, is there anyone you can talk to about your breast cancer coming back?" She turned her attention back to him, surprised by his reference to breast cancer when he had already taken her breast years before. She looked down and concentrated on buttoning her blouse.

"I suppose I could tell Beverly." She finished the task without fumbling and slid off the examination table hoping to end the interview without further awkwardness.

"Well, it's important for you to talk to somebody. I don't want to be treating you for depression in addition to the cancer."

"No, I don't suppose you do."

"Alright then. I've got several other patients to see this morning. Make an appointment with Sparkie to come by again next week--that will give me time to call our oncologist in Atlanta and develop an appropriate

1

protocol for your situation." Having steered himself back into familiar clinical waters, he gave her a brief nod and slipped quickly out the door. "Remember what I said about talking."

"Like hell I will," she hissed at the pilot of a yellow fighter plane spiraling down into No Man's Land.

When she was diagnosed with an advanced case of breast cancer five years earlier, she found the response of her students and colleagues in the music department of Clarkeston College unbearably intrusive. She had wanted to keep the surgery secret, but she was told that the surgical scars would have to heal fully before she could wear her prosthesis for the first time. The resulting lack of symmetry in her torso would have been obvious the moment she returned to the chorus room, so she had no choice but to inform the head of the music department that she was having a mastectomy.

The subsequent outpouring of sympathy had been frightful. Everyone on campus, half the town, and most of her former students sent flowers or cards or left embarrassing messages on her answering machine. The constant nausea from the weekly rounds of chemotherapy prevented her from openly rebelling against the invasion of her privacy, although she did manage to leave a vengeful load of bile all over the top of her department head's antique desk.

This time she was determined not to tell anyone. According to Doc Burton, no surgery was possible and she planned to refuse any chemotherapy that might prolong her life for a few insufferably queasy months. She fantasized about hiding her illness and collapsing dramatically at the final curtain call of the December concert. She could not halt the course of the disease, but she wanted to avoid being the object of everyone's pity until the very end. As she rolled her car out of the parking lot across from the medical complex where Doc Burton kept his office, she vowed that tears would not give her secret away.

She had covered half the distance back to her home on the edge of the campus when a question struck her: Had the last five years been so good because she had already accepted that she was going to die? Her musicianship had surely improved since she first fell ill. As popular as she had been with prior generations of students, the last several years had seen her direct the best performances of her career. The previous fall's performance of the Fauré *Requiem* was so well received that the chorus had sung it with the Atlanta Symphony after a Russian choral group was forced to cancel its appearance. Even the quirky little production of Honegger's *King David* staged in the spring had been wonderful. In a market with no great recordings of the work, a minor record label had asked permission to market a compact disc of the performance.

The true test of her resignation would come when she fully understood that the recurrence meant an end to music making. If the first cancer improved the music, she thought, the second was going to kill it. She gripped the wheel hard and drew a deep breath, but she refused to cry as she drove slowly through her leafy neighborhood, past rows of familiar brick bungalows and well-manicured lawns.

When she had moved back to Clarkeston twenty-five years earlier, she could have afforded one of the stately, white frame houses that graced the old section of town on the north side of the river, but she saw no need to maintain four or five thousand square feet of living space just for herself. The sudden end of her relationship with a fellow graduate student in Illinois had left her a confirmed single woman, and she was content with renting and then purchasing a three-bedroom, red brick house in the "new" neighborhood on the other side of the river, just south of the college.

Newcomers to town were amused that a subdivision from the 1920's could still be described as "new," but unless one had grown up in Clarkeston it was difficult to appreciate just how long political and economic power had been concentrated in the antebellum mansions regally situated in the neighborhood surrounding the downtown courthouse. She had grown up there, her father a prominent attorney, but the rebellious streak that led her away from Clarkeston to get her education (and that later produced the most controversial musical events in the town's history) had also pushed her away from her childhood streets. For more than thirty years, she had instead lived in this unremarkable section of town built just after WWI for a swelling population of successful merchants and educators. The house was just the right size for her, shaded by big oak trees and surrounded, as were all the houses in the area, by dogwoods and redbuds. Surely, Clarkeston Hills was the most colorful place in town in the spring, when the trees were blooming and everyone competed to see who had the most impressive display of antique tulips and daffodils.

Clarkeston Hills was also practical. It took Dorothy less than twenty minutes to walk from the house to her office in the music building on the far south end of the main campus quadrangle. Some of her most inspired ideas had come as she walked to work each day, pleasantly oblivious to summer's swelter or the occasional damp chill or cold rain of winter mornings. The house itself suited her solitary life; she had converted the dining room into a music room and used one extra bedroom as a study. The other bedroom was for old college friends or for visiting colleagues that the chronically under-funded music department refused to

3

accommodate anywhere else but the dismal Suburban Lodge motel on the edge of the bypass.

She sat in the small alcove off the back of her kitchen and finished a leftover portion of chicken salad she found in the ancient refrigerator that dominated the room. As she added more salt and pepper, she heard movement in the music room.

"Beverly, is that you?"

A tinkling of the piano keys confirmed the presence of her friend.

"Doc Burton told me today that I'll be lucky to see Christmas . . . What do you think about that?"

Silence.

"Are you gonna stick around to help me through?"

Suddenly, Beverly bounded into the room and jumped up on Dorothy's lap, purring loudly, and pleased with the restraint she had shown in not greeting her mistress the moment she entered the house.

"You promise not to tell anyone, alright? I want to be able to reflect on my life in peace. I know it sounds selfish, Bevy, but I don't want to spend my last semester comforting all the people who have trouble coping with my mortality. I just want to climb into my music and fade quietly away. Is that too crazy?" The cat put her shoulder against Dorothy's chest and rubbed its head under her chin. "I don't think so either."

Dorothy finished her lunch with one hand and kept the other free to scratch behind Beverly's ears and fend her luxurious tail off the food. When she was done, she stared for a moment at the jungle of her backyard, absent-mindedly grooming the contented creature in her lap. The noisy hum of the refrigerator prompted her to check her watch.

"You go talk to Kathleen and Luciano while I freshen up and get out of here." She nudged the cat off her lap back in the direction of the music room, and she made her way to the bathroom.

When she had pulled her hair back into a bun, she cast a critical glance at the mirror. She noticed the wrinkles drawing attention to her bloodshot eyes but did not bother reaching into her sparse collection of make-up for camouflage. As she forced a smile, hints of a youthful beauty returned, a sparkle in her large green eyes, a flash of sensuality in her lips. Her once lustrous brown hair, however, was shot through with gray, and the years past forty had made the intriguing angularity of her features more severe than striking. For the first time she looked all of her sixty years.

"The young boys will just have to downgrade their fantasies this afternoon, Placido," she commented to a small calico as she slipped out the front door.

During the walk to her office, Dorothy pushed her health problems to a remote corner of her mind and focused on her afternoon lecture. Teaching music history to summer school students demanded little in the way of formal preparation, especially when she had already taught the course fifteen times and at least half of the class was spent playing excerpts from compact discs. With summer winding down, the course's focus was on the twentieth century, and as she walked under the leafy canopy of the neighborhood toward campus, she tried to formulate a comprehensible explanation for the breakdown in tonality and form in the group of modern recordings that the students would be moaning and groaning about for the next three weeks. She entered the music building with a nod at a departing colleague and made her way up the three flights of stairs to her office. Pausing to catch her breath at the top of the landing, she noticed a young man with closely cropped hair sitting outside her office.

"Dorothy?"

It took her a moment to recognize him. She was thrown off by his tight-fitting black t-shirt, faded jeans, and MTV haircut. His thin smile, though, recalled the more formally attired interviewee who had entranced most of the music faculty during his visit that spring. Only she, and two others, had cast votes against Evan Roberts, preferring a young woman from Florida State over the flashier Juilliard graduate.

"Mr. Roberts, how nice to see you again." She greeted him with a gracious smile. "When did you arrive in Clarkeston?" Although she was an unconventional Southern woman in many ways, only with good reason did she drop the facade of gentility that kept peace among the various personalities at the College and in town. She redoubled her resolution to be polite. The faculty meeting at which his candidacy had been debated was one of the few occasions when she had cast aside her outward civility as she joined the fray over who should become the college's second professor of choral music.

"We got in a couple of days ago and have been busy fixing up the bungalow we rented. Do you know Clarkeston Hills?"

"Yes."

"We've got a crappy little starter home there. But at least we're fixing the place up--half of the neighbors' houses could use a paint job bad. We'll see if we can move somewhere better next year."

"How lovely. . . . were you waiting for me?" She suppressed her annoyance at the put-down of her neighborhood. "Sit down for a bit then. I'm just about prepared for my 2:30 class."

He followed her, but instead of sitting down in one of the two chairs facing her desk, he perused the stacks of sheet music scattered across the small piano blocking her bookshelves.

"Are you a big Vaughan Williams fan?" he inquired with a score in his left hand and an amused grimace on his face.

"We've done a good bit over the years."

"Accessible, but a bit schmaltzy, don't you think?"

"Mr. Roberts," she smiled again to signal that her impending sarcasm was meant to be playful, although in reality her patience was being stretched, "I'm sure you didn't interrupt the rehabilitation of your *starter* home just to come here and criticize my taste in music. Is there something that you wanted to discuss?"

"Yes." He laid the music back down on the piano and noticed the brand name for the first time. "Damn," he exclaimed, distracted once again from the point of his visit, "they gave you an even shittier piano than they gave me! Whoever is in charge of purchasing instruments must be a complete moron. That company made nothing but junk until they went out of business twenty years ago."

"It was my mother's, Mr. Roberts."

"Oh."

"My mother bought it, and I use it for sentimental reasons, although it does need to be tuned more frequently than the others in the building." Now she was seething. "Do you think you could come to your point?"

"Yes," he nodded shamelessly, finally sitting down and focusing his attention on her. "In fact, I've got a big favor to ask you." Were he less brimming with nervous energy, less intense and obnoxious, if some manner of playfulness had infused his demeanor, then his dark eyes and narrow face might have been described as interesting, even handsome. As it was, Dorothy could not help but think that his under-shaven jaw line, pinched features and narrow shoulders would not quickly enthrall the women of Clarkeston.

"A favor? You might think about improving your technique of buttering people up." When he laughed, she almost recognized a likeable young man behind the offending exterior.

"I'm afraid you may be right. Even in New York I tend to put people's backs up, and that's saying something," he explained with another nervous burst of laughter. After a brief glance outside the office window, he forced himself to come to the point.

"Our department head, Dr. Sanders," he gave Dorothy a look that clearly questioned the fitness of a musician who insisted on colleagues calling him *Doctor*, "has told me you have not exactly been one of my biggest supporters."

6

"Please remind me to have yet another talk with Dr. Moron about his big mouth." She sighed with exasperation and pushed her chair back so she could take in the placid expanse of the main quadrangle and still make eye contact. "Evan--and please call me Dorothy--don't let my preference for the other candidate we interviewed bother you. She stayed at my house during her visit and we hit it off really well. I'm sure that you will be a fine addition to our faculty." She gave him a brief smile, leaving unspoken the fact that his arrogance had been the main motivation for her vote. "And now, tell me what you need, then leave me a couple of minutes to think about what I'm going to say to my little collection of distracted summer school students."

"Okay then, here goes . . . this fall I would like a chance to show you--and any other folks who doubt my ability--what I can do with a choir. I was hoping that you'd let me borrow the College Chorus for a big production at the end of the semester."

"Why not use the Men's Glee Club?" she asked as calmly as she could. Everyone in the department had agreed that he would start out working with the Men's Glee Club and the music school's small baroque ensemble, while she would continue to direct the Chorus and the Women's Glee Club until she retired. Whatever the reasonableness of Evan's request, this fall was the one semester she could not accede control over her best group. Not only is the chorus my only child, she thought, this is my last chance to make music with her.

"I'd like to do something big that requires men's and women's voices--something like the Beethoven *Mass in C* or the Brahms *Requiem*. I asked Sanders, and he said that neither had been performed here in the last couple of years." He was getting excited now, envisioning a triumphant debut before an appreciative audience, anticipating her acquiescence as a good-will gesture.

"You've already talked to Sanders about this?" she sputtered, barely able to get out the name of her chief antagonist.

"I just wanted to run the idea by him--"

"--and what did His Eminence say?"

"He thought it was a good idea and even seemed to think that you'd be pleased." Dorothy's glare threatened to melt Roberts into a small puddle on the floor.

"One thing you will learn very quickly is that Stan Sanders's notions about what is a good idea seldom coincide with anybody else's." She tried not to blame Roberts for going over her head, but the mere thought of the two men discussing the business of her chorus--especially on the day Doc Burton had made it clear to her that the group would soon be theirs anyway--was too much for her to take.

7

"Professor Roberts," she continued, "it's impossible; I must work with the chorus this fall. I'm quite sure, however, that you will be able to work with them in the spring. Until then, I'm certain you'll have a *very* special time with the Men's Glee Club."

"But this isn't just about my being able to put on something for the faculty," Roberts pleaded, a fresh urgency in his voice. "I still need to complete a major conducting project to finish my Ph.D. requirements at Juilliard. My major professor told me that he'd be willing to come down here and evaluate the performance of a significant work."

"So have him come in the spring."

"He spends every spring in England as an artist-in-residence working with some of the Cambridge College choirs."

"Then send him a videotape--"

"--I don't think that would be acceptable." This response cracked the remaining facade of Dorothy's southern politeness.

"What is not acceptable, Mr. Roberts, is your marching into my office demanding to use my choir to complete work that should have been done last year in New York," she paused for a moment and stared a hole through his forehead. "In fact, I remember the hiring committee last spring assuring the faculty that you would arrive here with all your requirements satisfied and credentials in hand. Well, if there's a bright side to all this, I guess it's nice to be proven right." She turned dismissively and studied the students drifting out onto the quad as the day's fifth period concluded. Their summer attire spun kaleidoscopically through the gaps of the tree branches arching over the sidewalks.

"Now, I really do need to look at my notes," she said as she swivelled back in her chair, but Roberts was nowhere to be seen. "Shit," she whispered under her breath, wondering if the day could get any worse.

# 2

## The Clarkeston Blues

"What an incredible bitch!" Evan Roberts leaned against the kitchen doorframe, fuming at a sandy-haired man who stood covering a row of smudgy cabinets with a coat of cool green paint. "John, I let her know exactly why it's so important for me to work with the chorus this fall, and she turned me down flat." He slapped the door to emphasize his point and then hopped onto the kitchen counter. He leaned forward, arms locked at the elbows, cantilevering himself over the stained linoleum floor. "She's worked with them every semester for the last twenty years, and she's still not ready to let anyone else have a chance."

"Well," John replied calmly without interrupting his work, "maybe the twenty years are why she finds it so hard to let someone else direct them. They're her babies."

"Her babies? No way. Creatures like that eat their young." Evan hopped down and began to pace. "No, she just doesn't want any competition. She's been running the show for so long she can't bear the thought of someone else getting noticed. That's the kind of bullshit I used to see in New York all the time. I don't know why I thought things would be any different down here."

"Musicians are the same everywhere," John, a computer technician, replied. "They just can't govern themselves. I've been around you long enough to know that if you leave musicians alone, eventually you'll find them dancing naked in a circle, shaking wooden spears and chanting, *Piggy, Piggy*, just like in *Lord of the Flies*."

He had heard that barb before. He picked up a brush. "And where does that leave me? With one year longer to spend in this stinking backwater until I finally finish my degree."

"It's not that bad here," John said, looking over his shoulder to gauge how upset his lover really was. "And you know how glad I am to get out of New York. If you give it a chance, you'll see that this might be a really good place for us to be."

Evan offered an incomprehensible grunt in reply, and they painted together in silence for a few minutes as Evan calmed down.

"Now, are you ready for some good news?" John asked.

"Always."

"I interviewed with the administrator of the federal courthouse today, and he wants me to set up their computer network. They need someone to order new equipment, hook up the system, do some personnel training, and keep them generally up-to-speed on new technology. Officially the job's only temporary, but once I get the system up and running, I'm sure they'll want to hire someone to maintain it. Best of all, the feds pay way better than the city or state."

"Why not find a business job?"

"Nobody else in town is big enough to need my talents."

Evan thought of a salacious comeback, but let it go. Toning down his mouth was one of several concessions he made to living with his maddeningly conventional and sometimes downright prudish partner.

He reflected on how things had changed over the last two years as he put a layer of paint over the dingy walnut panels. Probably for the better, he concluded. Although he was no longer hitting trendy clubs in Manhattan and partying until the wee hours of the morning, he was forced to conclude that he was fortunate--even if he was stuck in rural Georgia with June Cleaver. A serious technocrat with *SAFE* stamped on his forehead, John was the most attractive man Evan had ever been involved with but also the one most likely to share an opinion with Evan's parents. Even so, the promise of monogamy John had extracted from him had been easier to keep than expected, although he still sometimes resented having to make it.

The phone rang, startling Evan into painting the edge of a burnished brass door hinge. John answered while he wiped away the mistake. "Yes, he's right here." John covered the receiver and mouthed the word "Mom" before handing over the phone.

"Yeah, we're settling in okay . . . sort of . . . kind of a pit actually, but John's been working his butt off all week painting and working on the floors . . . uh, huh . . . yeah Christmas should work . . . okay . . . bye." He hung up the phone and turned around.

"What do you think about having my folks for Christmas? Is four months enough time to whip this place into shape?" Evan picked up a brush again and saw that the persistent dark stain had already started to seep through the cabinet door he thought he had finished. "Goddamn, how many coats are we going to have to put on these things?" He laid on an extra thick coat and looked at John. "What about Christmas dinner with my parents, oh strong silent one?"

"That'll be great."

"Then why the glum demeanor?"

"I was just thinking how nice it would be to have my family here sometime."

"What!" Evan exclaimed, "I can hear the introductions now: *'Mom, Dad, this is Evan. He's my tender love slave.'*"

"Hah, hah."

"John, you're going to have to tell them some day. When I was twenty-six, my folks had already known for seven years that I wasn't the All-American boy." He stopped painting again and lectured his lover directly. "You know, studies show that people have difficulty dealing with problems they think result from bad choices. Volunteers would rather read to the blind than the illiterate, for example. So, just tell your folks that your sexuality is hardwired--immutably written into your genes. They won't like to hear it, and they'll still freak out, but eventually they'll let you back into the family fold."

"That's easy for a precious only child to say. You could've announced that you were an axe murderer, and your parents would have said, *'That's nice dear, please pass the carrots'*."

"Touché," Evan conceded as he pulled the paint can closer and went back to work on the stubborn cabinet door. "Besides, your brothers and sisters already know, and they've undoubtedly been preparing your mom and dad for the big blow."

"They don't know anything!"

"Oh, yes, they do. You think your sister buys your *this-is-my-roommate* story?" John ignored the question and kept on painting. "You know that night last fall when she stayed with us in New York and we all got drunk at Gino's," Evan continued, "and you went to bed early? I told her you were gay."

"Bullshit." John whipped around. His blood ran cold with excitement and horror as he dripped paint onto the yellowed vinyl floor. "What did she say?"

"Let's see if I can quote her accurately. I believe her exact response was, *'Duh!'*"

"Bullshit."

"I'm not kidding. Jessie, Susan, and Josh figured this out years ago and, if I know your learning curve, probably long before you did." Judging from John's reaction, he knew that he had struck a nerve. "Now, you just have to figure out a way to break the news to the folks. We shouldn't have to pay for two separate phone lines forever. And now that we're out of the evil city your parents would never visit, you can expect them to come observe you in your natural habitat."

John gave his friend a reluctant smile. He was almost six feet two inches tall with broad shoulders and moist brown eyes. Only his

11

prematurely receding hairline and careless posture prevented him from being movie-star handsome. His smile was one of the few things in the world that could coax Evan from the cynical to the romantic. It was also responsible for John's first steps taken out of the closet, because revealing his secret had turned out to be the gentlest way to let down the young women who turned to mush when he made eye contact and his face broke into a shy smile.

"What did you tell your mom and dad?" he asked Evan.

"You've already heard how I came out to my folks."

"Yeah, but you just told me their reaction and the fallout and all that stuff. You never told me exactly what you said."

Evan set his brush on the lip of the paint can and crossed the kitchen to grab a beer out of the refrigerator. He leaned back against the counter.

"Actually, I told them the truth. I explained that when my seven and eight-year-old friends played spin the bottle, we didn't discriminate between the sexes and the spinner had to kiss whoever the bottle pointed to. I discovered early on I enjoyed kissing the boys more than the girls. As it turned out, one of my friends did too, and we started to explore things when no else was around." He took a long swig from the beer bottle. "It helped with my parents that I'd dated a couple of girls in high school, so I had some credibility when I told them I preferred men to women. And I also waited until after I'd been in college for a year, out of the house and out of their control. I told them my experiences in college confirmed who I was, so I presented the fact as a done deal." He punctuated his statement with a flourish of the bottle.

"That doesn't help me much, I'm afraid."

"You could just tell them that you were totally straight until your high school sex education class, when your liberal, secular humanist teacher presented homosexuality as an alternative lifestyle and you couldn't resist the temptation to partake."

"That's it! I love it!" John laughed. "I'll blame the public school system. My folks love all those *Why Johnny Can't Read* news stories."

"Our headline tonight: *Why Johnny Likes Jimmy*. Film at eleven." After they finished laughing, they worked quietly together until Evan headed back to the college to continue the process of moving into his office and preparing for the upcoming semester.

*3*

### A Music Lesson


After struggling for a couple of minutes to collect her thoughts, Dorothy gathered her books, picked up a cup of coffee from the communal pot in a hallway alcove, paused for a moment to swallow two more aspirin, and then walked down to the first floor where her classroom was located.

Most of the thirty students who sat waiting looked hung over, bored, or both. The more motivated students at the college found interesting jobs or internships over the summer vacation, or convinced their parents to finance a tour of Europe. Those who hung around Clarkeston in the summer set more modest goals: work on a tan, drink at least a six-pack of beer every night, sleep until ten every morning. Still, she thought, as she entered the room and saw the class straighten up a little, maybe she could slip something past their apathy.

"Well, what did you think about the listening selections for today?" During the school year, she called on her students by name and grilled them as rigorously as a law professor might, but that was usually counterproductive during the summer session. She set her folder down on the table and sat on the desk at the front of the room, hands temporarily folded in her lap. "Come on, don't tell me that you all liked this modern stuff?" Several students screwed up their faces and a short blond boy muttered something that sounded like "crap."

"Aha!" she exclaimed with delight. "By sheer coincidence, I looked up 'crap' in Grout's *History of Western Music* last night and, lo and behold, right next to it was a picture of Anton Webern, whom you've just been listening to . . . Any guesses as to what the entry read?" Silence. "Using some musical terms," she rephrased her question with a mischievous smile, "what makes music around the turn of the century sound so different from what comes before it?"

The blond student raised his hand. "There doesn't seem to be any real melody. The music wanders all over the place; it's ugly. It just doesn't sound like music--half the time it sounds like an orchestra warming up and never getting to the piece it's supposed to play."

"That's actually a pretty good paraphrase of what Grout says about Schoenberg, Webern, and Berg," Dorothy exaggerated strategically. "After we listen to a few more selections this afternoon, we can start to analyze the technicalities of what these composers were trying to do with musical form, but before we get to that, I did want to ask you another question." Her expression was more serious now, and the class appeared relatively attentive and curious.

"Why? . . . Why do musical tonality and form break down so completely at the end of the nineteenth century? What's going on here?" Most of them seemed interested in the question, but no one was willing to offer any theories. She pursed her lips and made eye contact with a couple of the better students, then went over to the stereo and played an excerpt from the beginning of Stravinsky's *Rite of Spring*.

"Now we'll see who did the reading," she asked with a grin. "When was the premiere of the work?" As she loaded another disc into the player, she heard the shuffling of pages followed by the exclamation, "1913."

"Very good. Now, the *Rite of Spring* is not nearly so atonal as Schoenberg's later stuff, but it sure isn't Beethoven, is it?" She leaned forward and finally pressed them for an answer. "What else is going on in Europe at this time in terms of history, culture, and art? Does this music fit in or are its composers out of step with their contemporaries?"

A well-dressed girl in the front row whom Dorothy knew was taking a modern history course raised her hand. "Didn't World War One start in 1914?"

"Very good," she responded, keeping most of the sarcasm out of her voice. "And did that conflict come right out of the blue, without any warning?"

"Professor Kennedy says that the countries in Europe were getting ready to fight for years before that guy was assassinated in Sarejevo. He says it was like they'd already decided to go to war and were just lookin' for an excuse to fight each other."

"Wonderful," she said, turning her attention back to the whole class. "In 1913, Europe stands on the brink of self-annihilation. I hope Professor Kennedy gave Ms. Minton some idea of the scale of combat to come. Millions of men sat in trenches for months, stood up, took three steps out of them, and were instantly cut down. In the second battle of the Somme alone, there were two million casualties."

She slid off her desk and felt her shoulder twinge. For a moment she was back in Doc Burton's office. "Imagine being a pilot looking down on the carnage and unable to do anything about it, knowing that your own life expectancy is measured in weeks.

"I think artists and writers understood early on where the arms build-up in the twenty-five years prior to Sarejevo was leading. It shouldn't surprise us that political breakdown is reflected in the breakdown of form in artistic expression. It is during this era that abstract art is born, that a novel can be nothing more than an unpunctuated stream of someone's consciousness, that all previously established musical rules, as we've been hearing, seem made to be broken."

She looked around the class. As usual, she had lost a couple of those who had stayed out late the night before, but for the most part, the students seemed to have followed her. One disheveled boy in the back of the class stared at her with a particularly troubled look on his face. She avoided his eyes and turned to play the next selection.

"Now, we've just told one possible story about the genesis of twentieth century music; others are certainly plausible." She got up and pressed the play button on the compact disc player. "Imagine if you were a composer with the vision of a pilot flying over Flanders fields. You might find that old Romantic forms no longer suffice."

*4*

## Another Character Study

The fall semester began just as Evan finally finished painting the house and moving into his office. Despite a shortage of preparation time, his first day of class had gone fairly well. The students had not been brimming with questions, but that was to be expected. The worst I will ever be in the classroom, Evan thought, is boring, and there are far worse pedagogical sins than that.

Wednesday afternoon of the first week found him pacing nervously inside his office, craving a cigarette and cursing the idiot who had taken the last cup of coffee from the faculty lounge without making a new pot. He had been calm for the first two meetings of his introductory music history course, but the upcoming meeting with the glee club presented a more fragile situation. The safety valve of lecturing or putting on another CD was not available. Lengthy explanations just did not work to improve a group's sound. A director had to develop some degree of rapport and trust with the singers before any real work would get done, and the moments before a connection is established could be terrifying.

What if they just stare at me like well-bred cows? Evan asked himself. What if they sound like shit and none of my suggestions improve the sound? He had been very effective with every choir he had ever worked with, even a prison group he volunteered to coach one summer, but that fact did not relieve the pressure of a first-time meeting. He paced in the small confines of his windowless office. And why did I let John convince me to give up smoking?

At five minutes to four, he picked up his music and locked his door. Stopping at the men's room on the way, he splashed cold water on his face, wiped it off with a brown paper towel, and pasted on an exaggerated smile. "Show time," he cried aloud to the manic visage in the mirror. He turned abruptly and left, unconsciously drawing a deep breath as he approached the door marked "Stuart Rehearsal Hall."

As he entered and set his music on the podium, he heard a couple of suppressed laughs from the back row of the risers, but when he glanced up, he could not locate their exact source. Looking more carefully at the group, he was taken aback by the antagonistic expressions on some of the faces in the group of fifty young men. I haven't even opened my mouth yet, he thought, and I'm already getting a lot of attitude. Had Henderson said something to her former students?

"Good afternoon, I'm Professor Roberts, and I will be directing the Glee Club this semester. Professor Henderson provided me with a tape of your spring concert, and I really liked what I heard. I'm very excited about the prospect of working with such a well-trained group of voices." He looked around the room as he talked, making eye contact with all those in the group who would let him. He wondered why, in spite of his praise, several of the boys were leaning back insolently in their chairs, eyeing him with distaste.

"We've added some new members this fall, so let me hear what you sound like today." Having not yet found an accompanist, he played an A flat on the grand piano in the corner. "Let me have an 'ah' on that note." The sound he heard was basically rich and warm, but several of the voices screeched in an annoying nasal register and a few others were clearly under pitch.

"Okay, let's sing with a nice open mouth. Support your breath down here," he said, indicating his abdomen with his right hand, "and drop your jaw." Unfriendly snorts of laughter erupted again from several of the singers. He let the uneven sound go on for a few seconds and then cut them off with an authoritative flick of his right hand. He gathered himself for another try at getting the group to sing with one voice. Now I can see why sweet Dorothy was so happy to dump them off on me, he thought. Oh well, nothing like a challenge to sharpen one's technique.

As he turned to the blackboard to write the list of five pure vowels that he wanted to hear in the next warm-up exercise, he realized with dismay that the challenge was going to be harder than he had imagined. Much harder. In the upper right-hand corner of the otherwise pristine chalkboard he saw it: *FAGGOT*.

Had he not paused, he might have been able to ignore the slur and through sheer determination plow through the rest of the rehearsal. But he froze momentarily, taken aback by the violence of the scrawl. When the class saw that he had noticed, most of them shifted uncomfortably, but the same voices that had laughed earlier and twanged flat during the attempted warm-up hummed snatches of *YMCA* in the background.

He stepped back from the blackboard and continued to stare at the word. In for a penny, in for a pound, he thought. Unlike John, who had once quit a job when his boss suggested that his sexual orientation might make his co-workers uncomfortable, Evan's response to prejudice, sharpened through several nasty encounters in the dormitories at the

University of Michigan, had always been far more confrontational. Running from the rehearsal room in tears was not an option; neither was ignoring an insult when he had been deliberately goaded. Too bad it doesn't say *FAGGOTS*, he thought, then we could pretend it was a general insult to guys who enjoy singing even after they're in college. Glee, after all, was not exactly a macho concept.

Without an *S*, however, the option of pretending *we're all in this together* was impossible, and Evan remained focused on the blackboard, adopting a Jack Benny chin-on-left-hand pose as the class grew increasingly anxious. Good, let 'em all squirm for a bit longer, he thought. Probably only two or three of them were in on writing it, but all of them are guilty of not erasing it before I got in. Shit, there's nothing more macho than straight male singers and ballet dancers. The tension continued to grow behind him, thickening in the nervous atmosphere like a huge soufflé. He turned calmly and began to stomp it flat.

"First of all," he said, leaning casually against the podium and looking one by one at every member of the chorus, "and in case there is any doubt in your mind, I am indeed a faggot and intend to remain one for the foreseeable future. If that's a problem for any of you, please leave now and don't undermine the work of the majority of you who, I am quite sure, could not give a shit about my private life." Nobody moved to leave. "Second, I live with a gorgeous hunk named John, so you can rest assured that the chances of my showing a prurient interest in any of you is quite remote. And third, we will NOT be singing any Judy Garland tunes this fall."

He could tell by the smiles in the audience that his speech had won over some of them, but when he saw a bullet-headed boy in a fraternity t-shirt giving a blow-job to his bottle of Mountain Dew, he decided to escalate the confrontation. He strode back over to the piano.

"Alright, let's have *FAH* on this note. Pianissimo first . . . listen to your neighbors . . . keep it in tune . . . good." Some were still purposely singing off-pitch but fewer than before. "Now, crescendo . . . more . . ." As the sound crested toward maximum volume, the sour notes were overwhelmed. Evan moved back toward the center of the room nodding his head and indicating with precise hand gestures the shape of the sound that he wanted.

"Good. Now, down the scale four notes . . . keep it in tune . . ." He moved back to the piano and signaled that he was about to give them the final pitch on a new syllable.

*"FAH."* He sang clearly on the note just before he played the tonic note on *"GOT."* A third of the choir sang strongly with him, not realizing the word they had just completed. Another third sputtered out the *GOT*,

a machine burst of final *T*'s splatting around the room. Another third just stood in stunned silence.

"No, no, no, that was a horrible cutoff. Everybody needs to be on the same *T* and I need a rounder *O*. Let's try an arpeggio this time. *DO, ME, SO, DO* on *FAH, AH, AH, GOT*." He demonstrated what he wanted to hear and then gave them the initial note on the piano. "Don't hesitate. Let me hear what you can do . . . now forte." He beat them through the exercise twice until all but two or three were following his directions, enjoying the bizarre new director and savoring the opportunity to show off their voices at maximum volume. Only a couple in the back had not given up the hope of driving him away. When they began whispering to their neighbors, Evan concluded it was time for drastic measures. He cut off the sound; this time each *T* sounded together.

"Still not quite there yet. Let's try *AH* on this note . . . good . . . now everybody up a third on *YAH* . . . good, crescendo slowly . . . up another third on *MAH* . . . excellent . . . now on *FAH*." He gave the troublemakers in the back a demonic smile, hinting at what sound he was going to call for next and daring them to complete the phrase, *AH, YAH, MAH, FAH . . .* As he opened his mouth to provide the punch line, two of them picked up their book bags, hopped off the back of the risers and stormed through the doors. Score that faggot one, assholes nothing, he thought as he brought the exercise to a close.

"*FAH . . . NNN . . . OF BAR-OQUE QUAR-TETS*," he sang, each syllable moving stepwise upward until he and the group landed together back on the tonic, holding the note while several of the stronger singers harmonized to the emphatic cadences Evan provided on the piano. Finally, he cut off the frenzy of sound with a wave of his hand and erased the writing on the board.

"Now, let's get down to work."

\* \* \*

Immediately after the rehearsal, Evan stormed upstairs to find Dorothy. A *very special time with the Men's Glee Club* was what she had promised, and he suspected she had told some of the singers about his sexual orientation. He had never intended to keep it secret; that would have been impossible in a small southern town. But he did not want the issue to arise until he had established himself as a competent director. Once a rapport with the singers was developed, they would be more likely to ignore the fact he was living with someone named John instead of Jessica. As it was now, he would face an uphill battle to win their trust.

When he reached the corridor in front of her office, he saw that the door was shut and her light off. He stood outside for a moment, trying to see through the old-fashioned smoked glass panel onto which she had taped promotional materials from the previous spring's concert and cutouts from a few comic strips. A yellowed three-by-five card on a small corkboard to the left of the door invited him to leave a note, and he considered the wisdom of doing so before his temper cooled down. You'll regret it if you leave a note now, he warned himself. You've learned your lesson many times before--keep your mouth shut until you've calmed down, especially when the matter involves colleagues who have the power over your tenure. The absence of thumbtacks finally turned him away.

He walked slowly back toward the stairs, but his show of restraint was fragile. When he saw some tacks on the secretary's desk in the vestibule, he sat down and composed a short note, dripping with sarcasm but falling short of expressly accusing her of spreading gossip.

Dr. Henderson,

We had quite an interesting practice today. You certainly had them ready for me. I'll let you know how long it takes to undo the damage.

E.R.

# 5

## A Stray Memory

Dorothy eventually accepted the minimal radiation therapy that Doc Burton offered after he convinced her that she would not survive the autumn without giving her body some help in slowing down the disease. She had decided to conduct a secret requiem mass, the Beethoven *Missa Solemnis*, at the end of the semester, and if she could not hang on, then there would be no closure, no final triumph, no farewell to the stage that she had dominated for thirty years. When he met with her in early September, Burton had argued for more than mere radiation, advocating a complex regimen of intravenous and pharmaceutical chemotherapy with an earnestness distinctly out of his normal character.

"I'm not going to spend this precious last bit of my life puking my guts out," she spit at him with a vehemence that left him temporarily speechless. "Been there, done that, and you know something, even when I was done with all those drugs the first time--when I thought I might be cured--I wasn't entirely sure it was worth it."

"You know, they've come up with some good, new anti-emetics in the last five years."

"Will they totally eliminate the nausea?"

"No, but three quarters of the patients in the trials reported some relief in their symptoms."

"Some relief?" She prepared to deliver another broadside but was momentarily tempted by a vision of cancer-killing chemicals coursing through her veins while she went about her daily business, blissfully unaware that her system was full of beneficial poison. "And what are my chances if I go through chemo again and the drugs are effective?"

"Dorothy," he said, demonstrating the equine snort that had cost him dozens of patients over the previous twenty-five years, "we've already discussed this . . . the tumor has already corrupted your collar bone. Your scans are horrible. We could shrink the tumor to the point where it doesn't pose an immediate threat to your arterial system, but at most we can buy you nine months to a year."

"And then I die of bone cancer instead of the tumor."

21

"Probably."

"Damn it, Doc, it's a good thing you never tried to make a living as a salesman." She gave him the look of disgust that had cowed two generations of choristers at Clarkeston College, and he responded by laying out the radiation option, a treatment that would leave her feeling weak but able to finish out her last term as a director with some dignity.

When she got back to the music school, she picked up her mail in the departmental office and avoided a confrontation with Sanders by ducking into the photocopy room as he exited his office with one of her colleagues. She waited a moment, then retreated to her office to be alone with her thoughts. After plodding slowly up the stairs, she was disappointed to find that someone was waiting outside of her office door. She recognized him as one of her former summer school students, a slovenly boy who had stared at her intently during her lectures. He was ferociously nibbling at the knuckles of his right hand.

"Are you waiting for me, Mr. Coates?" Unlike most of her colleagues, Dorothy memorized the names of her students within the first two weeks of each semester. She also deliberately maintained some professional distance by only using their surnames. Sanders criticized her manner as pompous and Kingsfieldian, but he grudgingly admitted that she had the respect and affection of her students just as the mythical law professor did.

"Yes, ma'am." He stared at the floor as he spoke. It looked to Dorothy as if he had slept in his clothes and had not washed his hair for several days.

"Well, come on in." She pushed open the door and placed her mail on her desk. Although it was almost five o'clock, the July sun was still pouring down on the quadrangle outside her window. She slid behind her desk and found that Coates was still standing, waiting for her permission to sit.

"Please, just throw those scores off the chair and sit down." She folded her arms and set her elbows on her desk. "What can I do for you?"

"Uh, ma'am," he squirmed uncomfortably in his chair, "I really liked your class this summer." His voice was infused with a slightly nasal quality that marked him as a Midwesterner. He paused and she watched him struggle to come to his point. If he even has one, she thought, wondering how such a confused and unkempt young man had found himself within the generally confines of Clarkeston College.

"I didn't know how bad World War One was," he said with difficulty. She was momentarily confused, but then remembered the historical bent her class had taken during the last weeks of the summer session.

"Well, it was seventy years ago, and since the U.S. fought in France for less than a year, World War Two tends to get top billing."

"I don't know any of that stuff," he admitted. "Our high school history classes never got past the Civil War." He looked up briefly, then went back to studying the books on his lap.

"You should take Professor Kennedy's modern European history course."

"I don't have time for it."

"Why not?"

"My mother has already picked out all of my classes. I'm a piano major, and most of my electives are going to be music courses." He continued to stare at the floor.

Something in the way he referred to his mother deterred Dorothy from attempting to convince him that a change in curriculum might make him a better musician. He seemed cowed enough without another authority figure dictating a new course schedule to him.

"I'll tell you what, Mr. Coates," she said in an artificially light-hearted voice, "go down to the library and check out *All Quiet on the Western Front*. It's not that long, and it'll give you a very accurate picture of how western civilization destroyed itself from 1914-1918.

"As to the rest of world history, you'll just have to convince your mother that a great musician can't perform in a cultural vacuum. Tell her the director of the Atlanta Symphony Chorus has degrees in religion and literature, not music."

"Yes, ma'am." Something that might have been a smile flickered across his face, and she made a mental note to suggest Coates as possible accompanist for Professor Roberts's glee club. That might be interesting, she thought. When he finally realized that she had nothing more to say, he got up quickly and bolted from her office with a furtive glance back at her desk.

*Okay, that was weird.* Music was interwoven into the fabric of Dorothy's life, and she was usually gratified when her students looked through the lens of history with her and saw its themes threaded through each upheaval and turning point. But Coates's intensity and disconnectedness had been disturbing. *He's like a screwball version of Gordon,* she thought to herself, drifting back to her days in graduate school and her intense young lover. Gordon had been a fanatic, seeing musical parallels in every historical movement, philosophy, and art form. But, of course, he had been handsome and articulate in his passion.

She shook her head. I came up here to think about the future, she chided herself, about the *Missa Solemnis* and the choir, not to dig up the past. She was surprised Gordon still lurked in her thoughts. Speculation about *what if* had ended long ago, but she had never been comfortable with the pain she must have caused him at the end.

## Regrets (Part I)


Gordon Samuels also sat in his office, nearly a thousand miles away, talking to a student. "Evan," he inquired, "how are things below the Mason-Dixon line?"

"A bit rocky at the moment to tell you the truth."

"You know, I'm not worried about you finishing your final conducting project. I figure getting the Ph.D. is enough motivation without me pestering you, but I wanted to give you a ring before scheduling my flight to England this December. I'd hate to buy a ticket and then have you call to tell me that your performance will be the day after I leave."

"Don't worry about it."

"Oh?"

"The old hag who runs the department down here refuses to let me direct the college choir until the spring semester--"

"--when I'll be in Cambridge."

"Yes, I know that, and I told her too. She's stuck me with the Men's Glee Club, and there's no way I can whip up a serious orchestral work for us to do before December. How'd you like to come down and hear our concert of *Songs of the South*?" Evan asked facetiously.

"I'm sure it will be quite good, Evan."

"Actually, it's not going to be too bad. I figured I'd stay regional with the repertoire until they trust me, but this concert is going to be a stretch." He forced a laugh. "This is not quite why I got into directing."

Gordon smiled to himself. He had always liked the young doctoral candidate. Even though he had a magical knack for saying the wrong thing at the wrong time, he always had a fresh perspective to offer on Gordon's colleagues or on the way the school was run. Most of all, his enthusiasm reminded Gordon of a younger version of himself, career first, everything else second.

"Who's giving you so much trouble down there, anyway?"

"A local legend named Dorothy Henderson. She's Ms. Choral Music down here as far as I can tell."

A long pause. "I didn't know she was still there."

"You mean you know her?" Evan replied, disappointed that she had a reputation outside of Georgia.

"You might say that," he said under his breath. "Yes, I know her rather well. If memory serves me correctly, she can be quite single-minded."

"Unreasonable would be a better word. But in any event, it looks like I'm screwed until next year," he sighed. "Just make sure your plane stays in the air. I'd hate to start over with another advisor."

"I'll be sure to pass that cheery thought on to the pilot. Talk to you later."

Gordon put down the phone and realized that at some point in time he would be making a trip to Clarkeston for an unanticipated reunion with his former lover. He found himself shrinking from the thought. He was not afraid to see her, but he preferred to retain the memory of her as a young woman, not the reflection of himself as an aging man. He shook his head and for the hundredth time in thirty years wondered how they could possibly have come to live their lives apart.

* * *

He had first seen Dorothy Henderson as she slipped late into the back of a classroom on their first day as graduate students at the University of Illinois. The look of embarrassment on her face suggested that she was usually a punctual person. The hint of color suited her somewhat sharp features nicely, he thought. Uninterested in the professor's droning about the complexity of fugue form as practiced by J.S. Bach, he wondered what might have made her late and daydreamed about a conversation with her after the class. He stole a look over his shoulder at her. The intense young woman was taking notes with a pencil so deeply chewed-upon that her dentist could have made a set of dentures from it. He decided impulsively that talking to her might be worth the risk of embarrassing himself.

Although Gordon Samuels in his twenties was quite a handsome young man--broad-shouldered, tall, with a squarish face topped by an unfashionably thick mop of sandy-colored hair--he usually talked himself out of approaching attractive girls rather than plotting to capture their hearts. His tentativeness with women sprang from his tendency to quick infatuation that made initial overtures awkward and unnatural. *Would you like to go to the movies Friday night and then talk about where we should honeymoon?* Resolving to spend his graduate school years dating women rather than merely pining for them, he walked out of the classroom after Dorothy as soon as the lecture had finished and positioned himself at her side as they both headed toward the Student Union for lunch.

"Hey, we're in Schmidt's class together," he said as nonchalantly as he could. "Are you new here too?"

"Yes," she said, casting a curious glance at the earnest young man bobbing and weaving in between the clumps of students hurrying to their midday classes, "I just got here from New Jersey."

"You don't sound like you're from New Jersey," he exclaimed with a broad smile. He was from Chicago and not particularly well traveled, but he could recognize a cultured southern accent when he heard one.

"How can you tell?" She smiled back, and he saw for the first time how any sort of animation, whether laughter or surprise, could transform her face.

"Well, for one thing, you don't say *New Joisey*."

"And if I ever do, shoot me . . . what's your name?"

"Gordon."

"Mine's Dorothy." She offered her hand. "Gordon, if I ever show signs of changing from a charming southern belle into a pudgy Italian mother of eight, you have permission to report me to the national office of the Daughters of the Confederacy."

"Where are you from originally," he asked, "and how do you like the land of the endless corn?" She looked at him with narrowed eyes, as if she were wondering how much criticism of his home state he would be able to take.

"I'm from Clarkeston, Georgia, and I'm sorry, but this is the most boring place I've ever been in my entire life." He held open the door as they entered the Union. "I spent the last four years in northern New Jersey going to school, just a short train ride from New York City, and we never ran out of things to do or great music to listen to." He slid into line behind her in the huge cafeteria in the basement of the student center.

"Of course, you're right. Central Illinois can't compare to New York for music, but maybe I could take you to Chicago sometime and we could hear some jazz downtown or go to some of the blues clubs in Hyde Park."

"Hmmm," she offered a smile to acknowledge his offer. "I'm sure we'll be able to find some things worth listening to on campus later in the fall."

From Gordon's point of view, the hint of future rendezvous made the impromptu lunch an unqualified success, and he spent the rest of the meal telling her all he knew about the university and town that had grown up together in the middle of the flattest and most fertile portion of land on the planet. Several of his friends had been undergraduates there, and their reports and his own weekend visits helped him piece together for her a fair picture of life in the farm belt. As a native Chicagoan, he offered a critical perspective that fit her mood.

"So, why are you here, if you think Chicago is so much better?"

"Three reasons," he answered, counting the familiar rationalizations on his fingers, "this is better than any music school in Chicago, the department gave me an assistantship in choral conducting, and my parents are tired of paying for my schooling . . . maybe that's just two reasons." His face split into another easy grin. "And why are you so far away from home, deep in the land of Yankee vermin?"

"I'm in the directing program, too," she explained, dark eyes dancing over him. "All the other schools I applied to wanted to put me in their music education program. Since I have no desire to spend my life babysitting some junior high school choir, here I am." She stared at him over her coffee and dared him to suggest that she belonged anywhere else than behind the podium in Carnegie Hall.

He shook his head enthusiastically, not out of some proto-feminist commitment to gender equality, but because he was already half-smitten with her. For someone who could fall deeply in love with a girl who had just sat across from him in the library, waiting until the middle of lunch before making a romantic commitment to Dorothy constituted a slow developing crush. By the time they parted, he was already imagining what their children might look like.

As he walked out into the huge quadrangle dominating the middle of campus, he avoided the bustling sidewalk and charted a meandering course through the graceful Dutch Elm trees shading small groups of studying and dozing students. He could not get her face out of his head. She was not classically beautiful--her nose was too long and her chin too pointed--but her eyes pierced him through, and her short dark hair framed an endlessly interesting face. When he remembered her willowy figure and how snugly her calf-length, plaid skirt fit around her waist, he wondered whether he should ask her to a concert or a movie on the weekend.

As he walked to the library and visualized asking her out, he began to feel nauseous. He had never dated a woman he was attracted to. In college, he had asked out a couple of cute sorority girls, but they both pleaded existing boyfriends. His only dates had been matters of convenience so he could attend a fraternity dance or some other event. His first college date was just to show his fraternity brothers that he wasn't gay. Gordon sat staring at his book, wishing for the thousandth time that he had not graduated from Oberlin College with his virginity intact.

* * *

Dorothy skipped their next class, but Gordon saw her in the windowless halls of the music school later that afternoon. "When are we going to see you *Bach* in class?" He sidled up to her as she pushed a fistful of sheet music into her locker.

"Ugh, that's awful. I'll be there next time for sure. This morning I had to wait forty-five minutes to get a practice piano, and I wasn't about to let go of it until I finished arranging this piece for the Women's Glee Club." She held up the annotated score that justified her absence. "I wouldn't mind borrowing your notes, though, if you're in a sharing mood."

"I'd be happy to let you borrow them." Then he impulsively decided to capitalize on the opportunity, "Maybe right before a movie on Friday night?" As soon as he spoke, he realized that he did not sound breezy and devil-may-care, but somehow presumptuous and demanding. Or at least he thought he did. When she did not immediately answer but looked at him with unblinking, expressionless eyes, he sputtered on, "I mean, I'd be happy to let you have them now, but I thought it would be nice to get out this Friday and do something. You know, all work and no play . . ."

She did not exactly smile, but a faint hint of amusement traced itself on her face. "Okay, why don't you pick me up at the women's grad dorm around seven o'clock?"

"Great," he replied with a sudden sense of unease.

* * *

He picked her up on time and immediately noticed how distracted she was, preoccupied and uninterested in his movie suggestions. The only theaters within walking distance of campus were playing mindless paeans to Eisenhower America, and fifteen minutes after the Bugs Bunny short ended, he realized he should have made his move later in the semester when the music groups on campus were ready to give their first round of fall performances. Mendelssohn, followed by coffee and conversation would be far superior to Rock Hudson, soda and popcorn. He did not dare snake his arm behind her until the last half-hour of the movie, where it

29

rested stiffly, numb and tingling against the hard wooden curve of the back of her seat.

As the movie mercifully concluded, Dorothy pleaded a headache and declared she needed to go home. At this point, Gordon should have cut his losses, apologized for the lameness of the film, and tramped his way across campus. Instead, he walked her back to the dormitory and eventually found himself standing next to her in the empty lobby of the building. Countless images from movies and books had taught him how a modern American date should end, so he leaned forward in a clumsy attempt to give her a goodnight kiss. Her reflexes were Olympic quality and she eluded him, his lips missing her right ear by a millimeter as she spun neatly and headed up the stairs with a wave and a faint call of goodnight.

He remained still for a moment, face tinged with crimson, too embarrassed to return her wave or offer some light-hearted reply. He jammed his fists into his pockets and tumbled out into the night, grateful for the anonymity it provided on the long way home. He walked quickly, and as his shame gave way to anger, he cursed his lack of judgment and stubborn commitment to force the date into a conventional mold that had never worked for him before.

Gordon focused on his classes the rest of the semester and prepared a small non-auditioned undergraduate choir for its fall concert. He and Dorothy were cordial, but she never referred to their date and seemed perfectly willing to fix their relationship as a series of formal greetings and musical shoptalk. Two months into the semester he saw her speaking animatedly over lunch with a young assistant professor and assumed that she had finally found someone who interested her. Safely untouchable once again, she invaded his fantasy life, a melancholy symbol of the heights of adulthood he had yet to survey. He finished the semester immersed in his work, delaying his vacation in order to complete a final project for Professor Schmidt.

* * *

Thirty years later, Gordon stared at the phone on his desk, suddenly aware that he could use it to bridge a gap of time and space that had come to define how he looked at the world. He paused for a moment and then called his travel agent to book a December flight to London.

# 7

## A Friend Intrudes

"Damn it Beverly! Get off the piano!" As Dorothy charged into the living room, the cat leaped off the instrument with a squeal and kicked three more scores into the dusty recesses next to the wall. "I need that music, you stupid fur ball."

Her arm was not small enough to slide back to where the papers lay, so she tried to push the piano back, but the carpet underneath it offered far too much friction. Even if her shoulder were well, she knew that she lacked the strength to lift it and move it over. She slumped against the wall with a frustrated groan while Placido and Kathleen comforted her, rubbing the corners of their mouths and whiskers against her ankles and purring loudly.

She tried fishing the scores out with a long ruler, but when she ripped the nearest one, she decided that she would have to give up and ask for help moving the piano. Lord knows what I'll find back there, she wondered, twenty-year-old pencils, more music, and massive dust bunnies. Help in the form of Evan and his roommate was just a couple of blocks away, but the last thing she needed was another dose of her colleague's paranoia. Just the day before, an innocent question about a cryptic note he left on her office door had prompted the accusation that she had told the Men's Glee Club that he was gay!

"So you deny telling anyone about me?" he asked in disbelief.

"Not only do I refuse to gossip in general," she said calmly, "but I wouldn't tell anyone even if you were my worst enemy, which, by the way, you seem determined to become. So, why don't you leave my office and go yell at someone else." After he left, she promised herself to avoid him whenever possible and blocked out the grim thought that he was soon to be her successor as the senior director at the college.

Apart from Evan, her neighbors were mostly of her age and unlikely to be of much help in moving heavy furniture. She refused out of principle to call any of her students for help. She would not ask them for one simple reason--if she kept them at a distance, they sang better.

The sort of challenge she presented to them, occasional tongue-lashings included, could not come from an authority figure who buddied up to her young charges. Her worst experience as a choir director came shortly after she returned to Clarkeston and agreed to serve as the interim director at the large downtown Episcopal Church which she had attended as a child. The church choir had some fine voices in it, but she was completely unable to get any sort of acceptable sound out of them. She knew too many of the singers. Their familiarity with her made it impossible for her to divest them of their bad habits. Every time she tried, the choir got hostile and she became frustrated. At the end of six trying months, both the choir and Dorothy were happy to part ways.

While she contemplated the inaccessible scores, she decided it would be safe to give Arthur Hughes a try. He was not one of her students at the school, but one of the voices (inevitably a tenor or high soprano) that she sometimes recruited from the community. He was older and had already, in a strange way, bridged some of the distance between them. Once she had asked the choir in an offhand way about a folk singer she was interested in, and afterwards he had slid under her door an original short story about the singer's death, a very odd response to get from someone who worked for a federal judge. Although she did not know quite what to make of the young man, letting him into her house seemed unlikely to disrupt the karma of the choir. He was already a wild card, the kind of small town eccentric one finds in the South.

She got up off the floor, took three aspirin and called him, apologizing for bothering him at home. He promised to come over within the hour, and while she waited she straightened up the front room and put on a fresh pot of coffee in the kitchen. Placido and Beverly raced her to the door when the bell rang forty minutes later.

"Hey, what nice kitties," Arthur said as she opened the door to reveal her tenor and a sturdy looking young blond. "This is my partner in the piano moving business, my sister Terri. She's running away from her fiancé in Iowa."

"Arthur!" She elbowed her brother. "Nice to meet you, Ms. Henderson."

"Please call me Dorothy." She studied the pair as she moved aside to let them in and could see immediately that they were related. The two siblings shared the same aquiline nose and naturally graceful sense of movement. A former cross-country runner, Arthur was the more sinewy and athletic of the two, but Terri's complexion glowed with equally robust health. Although his face was framed with wavy dark hair and hers with a thick shock of straw-colored blond, the same piercing eyes searched the living room for the piano.

"It's over here in the dining room." Dorothy led them to the scene of the feline prank. "Don't hurt your backs trying to move it. If you can just slide it forward a couple of inches, I can reach my hand back there and get the scores."

When Arthur and Terri coordinated their lifting on the third try, they finally managed to the move the old Baldwin six inches away from the wall. She began to tell them that it was enough, but her shoulder started to tighten and the words would not come out.

"Are you alright, Ms. Henderson?"

"Yes," she said in a voice just short of a gasp, "but why don't I sit on the sofa and see if you can't get my scores." He reached his hand around the piano and began to retrieve the papers for her.

"Let's see . . . here's your full orchestra score for the Beethoven *Missa Solemnis*. Duruflé, Fauré, Poulenc . . . I guess the cats attacked your French pile." He looked over and smiled at her, but she managed only a tight-lipped grimace in response. "Ah, the Honegger, I recognize that one! Here's one more." He scrutinized a collection of Mozart opera arias. "Professor Henderson, Barry Manilow sings Hawaiian love ballads? Shame on you! And what's this?" He pulled out a dusty picture frame and handed it to her. "Some picture of a slicked-up dude taken when cars still had huge tail fins."

For a moment the world around her slowed to a stop and she was aware only of the figure standing in the long-forgotten picture. She could not take her eyes off of it. The photograph has been back there for twenty-five years, she realized with a slow shake of her head. She suddenly remembered their final phone conversation, one last unproductive argument, an unmerited insult, and a well-thrown shoe condemning the picture to its shadowy jail.

"Professor Henderson, are you alright?" Terri interrupted her reverie in a quiet voice.

"Oh, I'm fine," she said, forcing a brittle smile on her face. Just look at that old picture! It must have fallen back there years ago . . . I don't know how to thank you two for coming over and helping me."

"No problem," Arthur said lightly, "when my hernia pops back in, I'll be as good as new."

"Why don't you both stay for dinner?" She made the suggestion without really thinking, perhaps prompted by the same shock that had chased the pain out of her shoulder, perhaps by her sudden desire not to be left alone. "I've got some kidneys soaking in the fridge and plenty of

33

egg noodles to go underneath them." They hesitated, perhaps because the image of marinating organ meat did little for their appetite. "Don't be afraid," she laughed, "it's a recipe I picked up in Paris. You soak the kidneys in vinegar overnight and it takes all of the strong taste away. It's really quite a delicate meal."

"We'd love to stay," Arthur replied when he saw his sister nod her approval.

"Wonderful! Arthur, why don't you find something nice to put on the stereo while I open a bottle of wine and get dinner started?"

The meal was splendid. She had not had guests over since the summer, and the siblings were delightful company. Ever since Doc Burton had told her that the cancer was back, she had coveted her privacy, spending most nights at home in a painkilling cloud of music. She could not avoid death through her stereo; she could listen carefully to what the world's greatest musicians had to say about it. But the impromptu dinner was a reminder that conversation had an important rhythm and timbre of its own. Not long after dessert, however, she felt her shoulder begin to throb. Before she faded completely, she thanked them again for coming and surprised herself by asking her second impulsive question of the evening.

"Terri, did you say that were going to be visiting here for a while longer? I was wondering if I could hire you to spend a couple of afternoons helping me organize all the musical junk I've got scattered around the house. I couldn't pay you more than a pittance, but I've been feeling my age lately--" she waved off Arthur and Terri's exclamations of how young she looked "--and would really like to get my life organized a little. I need to catalog all the music I have lying around, and I inherited a collection of hundreds of old-time hymnals and church song books I need to organize and get appraised."

"Just tell me when you need me," Terri said with genuine enthusiasm, "and I'll help you with anything you want." Her acceptance provided a fine ending to the most enjoyable evening Dorothy had spent in months. They parted company shortly thereafter, and she hummed quietly to herself as she carried the dirty dessert plates back to the kitchen.

* * *

Terri returned the following Saturday with a bright red handkerchief holding back her hair to begin the task of sorting out the collection of music. After making small talk over coffee in the kitchen, they started to plan the work.

"As I see it, we've got three different jobs," Dorothy said. "We need to catalog my records and c.d.'s by title, composer, performer, and director and then do the same with my loose sheet music and folios."

"That shouldn't be too bad."

"Except for one thing," Dorothy took a sip from her coffee.

"What's that?"

"I've got over three thousand records and I don't know how many thousand pages of sheet music." She was glad to see Terri's face register more awe than horror. "And that leaves out the four hundred hymn books, but all we need to do with them is list the title and the condition they're in for the appraiser."

"This might take a while."

"Don't feel like you have to help. You see, I'm not horribly organized, and I've been putting this off for twenty years." She put her cup in the sink, and then she said something she had not uttered to anyone except her cats in a long time. "It would be nice to have a little bit of company while I do this."

The two women spent the rest of the day gathering sheet music and hymnals from every corner of the house and attic, creating huge piles that covered most of the floor in the living room and threatened to break the springs of the sofa. After hauling out a couple dozen records, they decided to reverse course and catalog the discs where they lay boxed in the guest bedroom and attic. If the music school wanted to accept her donation, it could come and haul the boxes away itself. It was hard work, but Dorothy made it clear they were not in a hurry and insisted on frequent breaks to guard her strength. She noted with growing pleasure that her estimate of a couple of days of work was ridiculously low and she would have an excuse to ask Terri back again.

"So what brought you to Clarkeston? Arthur indicated last night that it wasn't just to visit him."

"I had a huge blowout with my fiancé. In fact, he threatened to kill himself if I left him." Terri's voice was filled with disbelief as she recounted the circumstances that had brought her from rural Iowa to her brother's adopted hometown. "He was hysterical, grabbing at the side of my car while I was trying to get away from him."

"What did you do?"

"I leaned my forehead against the steering wheel and started to cry, but then I heard him begging again and I finally cracked. I just exploded." She picked up a small pile of music from the floor in Dorothy's spare room. "I swear I'm a nice person, Professor Henderson, but I told him he didn't have enough guts to kill himself!

35

"I slammed the car door, flew away from his parent's farm in a cloud of spitting gravel, went home, packed, and didn't stop driving until I hit Tennessee."

"Good lord." Dorothy's eyes flashed and she leaned forward in her chair. "Why did you break up with him?"

"We'd been saving money to buy a house, you know, clipping coupons, buying generic food and having each other over for dinner instead of eating out. Two weeks before the wedding, he suggested that we move in with his parents afterward instead of buying our own home. He wanted to pour all of our money into reviving his family's money pit of a farm. He said he'd inherit it when they passed away. Professor Henderson, his parents are only sixty-two or sixty-three! I couldn't believe he was asking me to live with his mother. She can barely stand me. Not to mention breathing his father's cigarette smoke. He wanted me to hand over thirty-thousand hard earned dollars so his parents could replace their rusty combine!"

"Surely it's not a crime to make a stupid suggestion?"

"No, it's not. His plan was merely ridiculous. What hurt was his assumption that I'd go along with it. He was truly shocked when I wouldn't. After seven years of dating, he still had no clue who I really was." She shook her head. "Do you think that people ever really know other people? I mean really deep down?"

"I don't know," Dorothy replied carefully. "Surely it must happen sometimes." She thought about her own life. Her choirs loved her, but she doubted their devotion was inspired by a knowledge of her inner-nature. And her colleagues certainly were clueless.

"You must be right. My brother's madly in love with this widowed mom he met when he was clerking for the Judge. He was all set to go to Washington, D.C., and work for the Justice Department when his clerkship was over, but instead he calls me up out of the blue and tells me he's going to be a history instructor at Clarkeston College. That was nothing compared to the news that Suzanne was pregnant, and he was moving in with her and her daughter!"

Dorothy raised her eyebrows and offered a nonjudgmental grunt, but inwardly she was amazed. She knew there was more than met the eye with Arthur, but did not expect he had a romance epic in him.

"You really should come over for dinner sometime." Terri suggested. "They live in this huge old house on Oak Street."

"That would be nice." Her own childhood home had been on Oak Street, and she remembered Suzanne's father, a prominent local attorney who had passed away years before.  Suddenly she felt less content with her isolation.  "Yes, I'd love to come."

## 8

### Louis

The last thing on Louis Coates's mind at the start of the semester was responding to the plea for an accompanist posted by Professor Roberts on the Music School bulletin board. Instead, he followed Professor Henderson's advice and immersed himself in history, starting with *The Guns of August* and then other histories of what took place in the fields of France and Belgium from 1914-1918. He swallowed Manchester's history of the House of Krupp in a single weekend. He intended to read Churchill's multi-volume treatise on World War II, but after devouring Shirer's *The Rise and Fall of the Third Reich*, he skipped backward into the nineteenth century, searching for clues as to how the course of world affairs had come to such total disaster in the first half of the twentieth. The second half of the century was frightening too, he reminded himself with a shiver, considering the possibility that one fanatical Russian could have probably started Armageddon.

His days were filled with almost nothing but reading and practicing. The courses he took were just distractions--his memory was so formidable that even when his attendance was spotty, he still got A's in all his music classes, and A's and B's in the rest. He arrived at the music school at seven-thirty every morning to secure a seat at the best piano in the building and played until ten-thirty. He went to class or read until three-thirty when he began another three-hour practice session. He ate alone at the student cafeteria before it closed at seven and walked back to his apartment where he would often read until past midnight. He went entire days without talking to anyone. Apart from his occasional visits to Dorothy's office, his only regular conversation occurred during his piano lessons with Herr Gabel, when he soaked up everything the aging Austrian knew about the technique of the great European masters.

Herr Gabel was the reason Louis was at Clarkeston College. When he finished high school in Nashville, his private piano teacher convinced his mother that the prestige of the institution Louis would attend was secondary to the quality of the instructor in whose studio Louis would be taking lessons. During the fall of his senior year, Louis and his mother embarked on a tour of music schools around the country and interviewed piano faculty, but no one impressed Mrs. Coates more than Herr Herman Gabel, an imperious old-school technician who had been driven out of Vienna during the post-war Russian occupation. One of the better-known performers of his generation, he established a solid reputation in the United States before retiring from the stage and accepting an offer to teach in Clarkeston. After a year as a visiting professor, he stunned many academics by turning down an offer from the Eastman School of Music in Rochester, New York, to stay in the warmth of the south. In reality, the mediocrity of his peers in Georgia was just as important a reason as the good weather. He preferred being a big fish in a small pond and had spent twenty years swimming in Clarkeston before Louis arrived. He viewed Coates as an eccentric momma's boy whose potential was limited only by his failure to play with adequate feeling.

"Mr. Coates," he said with a sigh as he slumped back in his chair, "I can teach you very little more about the mechanics of playing. Your technique is beautiful. You play even the most complicated runs flawlessly, but you play without any apparent understanding of the meaning of the music." He rapped his knuckles on top of the piano, but Louis did not respond. He never reacted to Gabel's attempts to provoke him. A dissonant buzz from the piano strings reverberated in the room. "No audience is going to pay to see a robot play. Especially not a slovenly robot who can't be bothered to cut or wash his hair." He flinched at his teacher's rebuke.

"Just tell me what to do, Herr Gabel."

"Apart from starting to carry yourself like a concert pianist," he sighed again, "you must somehow develop a musical empathy. You're just seeing notes on a page. The great composers were not mathematicians or accountants interested in putting pretty figures on paper. They wrote because they had to, because they had no better way to express their feelings about the world. When you play, you must bring out those emotions: joy, frustration, despair, rapture . . . ever since you got here in August, all I hear from you is notes."

He stared at the keys of the piano during Gabel's tirade. He heard the words and could have repeated them verbatim if asked, but in reality he was far away, playing a harpsichord for a dozen admirers in a sumptuous candlelit room, in a nobleman's summer residence, somewhere in Germany or Austria or Italy around the turn of the eighteenth century--a fantasy land populated by courtly ladies and gentlemen wearing brightly colored costumes and powdered wigs. It was a place he had discovered years before as his mother yelled at him, a comforting place that he visited frequently amid the unfamiliar environs of Clarkeston College.

"--here, play this for me," Gabel said, unexpectedly placing a piano reduction of the first movement of the Fifth Symphony in front of him. "Fear, despair, conflict . . . show me where we find Beethoven's story in the score. You can't play this like a machine, play it like a man."

Confused and upset, Louis looked at the score and realized he was either the object of scorn or some sort of experiment. Serious practices did not involve playing piano reductions of symphonies. He started playing furiously while Gabel turned the pages. The music did not sing of fear or despair, as the Austrian had asked; instead it rang with Louis's anger. He wrestled the score inside out, not as an artist confronting fate, death, and eternity, but as if he himself rode as one of the horseman of the apocalypse raining death on a doomed generation. He pounded the keys while a sour sweat covered his forehead, his immersion in the music complete, and when he finished, he looked up at his teacher with wild staring eyes that propelled the old man two steps backward.

"Mr. Coates. Do I need to explain to you how inappropriate your interpretation was?" Gabel relaxed perceptibly when his pupil did not immediately jump up and argue with him. "I accused you today of playing robotically, and you have at least shown me that you can play with some emotion, albeit a uniformly angry one."

He sat down again and for the first time demonstrated some compassion for his student. "Unfortunately for you, not much of the world's great music is designed to be performed so violently. But let me make a suggestion, one that I've never made in all of my years of teaching. Our new professor, Evan Roberts, came by my office yesterday wanting me to recommend an accompanist for the Men's Glee Club. I told him that I generally discourage my students from doing too much accompanying because it distracts their focus from the soloist's stage that I'm training them for. You, however, might greatly benefit from interacting with a choir and a dynamic young director like Professor Roberts. He assures me that they will be singing serious music this year, and I think you would benefit from the broadening that such an experience might bring. Please think about contacting him." Coates was looking at the piano keys once again. "Now, could you please let the next student in?"

He opened the door and left without acknowledging the existence of the pretty young girl waiting in the hallway. As he walked, he noticed that some of the central field of vision in his left eye was gone. When he tried to focus on the bulletin boards lining the left side of the hallway, all he could see was a distorted mix of blank space and blurred colors, a sure sign that a massive migraine headache was on the way. The partial blindness no longer frightened him as it had when he was a child, but he dreaded the hammering in his head that inevitably followed. He swallowed four aspirin quickly and found a dark classroom to sit in. He closed his eyes and tried to remember what Gabel had said to him during his lesson. He remembered playing the Beethoven. Beethoven had always been his favorite, an anchor for him when everything else threatened to tear him apart. He remembered humiliation, but humiliation did not stand out anymore.

An accompanist. Gabel wanted him to be an accompanist! His mother would scream bloody murder at Gabel for trying to sabotage her son's career, and at him for not working hard enough to please his teacher. When he tried to figure out why the old Austrian was so disappointed in him, his head began to throb, so he drifted away, back again to the time of powdered wigs and well-mannered aristocrats, when Beethoven was just learning to play. *Play us the Mozart again, Louis.* And he obliged them with a courtly nod, moving his fingers gracefully across the keys of the harpsichord, rocking slowly to keep the beat as the couples in the ballroom spun in perfect time.

He kept his eyes closed and leaned his head back against the cool wall of the classroom until the angry fireworks etched on the interior of his eyelids began to fade. An accompanist. He had seen a note on the bulletin board, but he knew nothing of a new choral teacher at the school. Maybe Professor Henderson had said something in her music literature course in the summer, but he could not remember. She had mentioned that she was conducting the Beethoven *Missa Solemnis* in the fall. Perhaps she needed an accompanist too? That would be better than playing with fraternity boys learning to sing the alma mater. Afraid to get up too quickly, he kept his eyes shut and played one more imaginary sonata before standing up slowly and walking to Dorothy's office.

He found her studying a score at her desk, and he stood in her doorway until she noticed him and invited him to sit down.

"What can I do for you Mr. Coates?"

"An accompanist," he said to his shoes. When she spoke formally, she reminded him more of his mother than the sympathetic older woman who had taught him the previous summer.

"Excuse me?"

"Do you need an accompanist for the Beethoven? Herr Gabel wants me to start accompanying."

"Why?"

"I don't know."

"Debbie Collingwood has been my accompanist for three years, and she's already been working with us for a month. Why don't you try Professor Roberts? I hear he still needs somebody."

"That's what Herr Gabel said. He said I need to be broadened. He said I don't understand the music." He looked up at Dorothy with frightened eyes, pleading for her to help him understand why at the age of eighteen so much of life had already eluded him. She wrinkled her nose; he smelled sour.

"You don't understand the music?" she asked him rhetorically, leaning back in her chair and studying him carefully. "Well, I've known Herr Gabel for a long time and, as you might have noticed, he sometimes has trouble communicating diplomatically. My guess is that he sees a very intense young man whose focus is just a little too narrow. Asking you to accompany some choral group is like sending you abroad to get a different perspective on your music. He might just as well have told you to join the jazz ensemble." He looked unconvinced. "I'm sure he's just emphasizing what I told you last summer about reading some history books. You need to get a perspective outside the music if you really want to interpret it well." Coates shifted in his chair and once again dared to make eye contact with his teacher.

"I've been doing it," he said in a barely audible voice, "reading a lot, I mean."

"Has it helped?"

"I thought about Napoleon when I played the first movement of the Fifth today, but I don't think he liked it."

"Who? Napoleon or Gabel?" She smiled. "Given the amount of death he brought to Europe at the turn of the nineteenth century, I think Napoleon is just the right person to think about when you play the Fifth." She paused for a moment, considering Gabel's advice. "And given your . . . lack of experience, accompanying Professor Roberts might be a really good thing for you to do. For once, I agree with my Austrian colleague."

Although the interview was clearly over, he remained seated, staring vacantly in the direction of Dorothy's piano. Having long ago learned that one of the best techniques for getting students out of her office was simply to stop talking, she relaxed and waited for the silence to drive Coates from the room. Five minutes later, she was still waiting, increasingly fascinated and concerned by the apparent catatonia that gripped her former student.

"Mr. Coates . . . MR. COATES!"

He looked up at her, but gave little sign he recognized who she was.

"Mr. Coates, go see if you can find Professor Roberts now."

"Yes, ma'am." He got up slowly and walked away without a backward glance. It took him almost an hour to find Roberts's office as he daydreamed his way through the music building.

* * *

It was in first grade that people had first noticed Louis's tendency to psychically disappear. Ellen Coates held her son out of kindergarten because she was afraid contact with the other children would make him sick. The next year, she swallowed her fears just long enough to enroll him in first grade at the local Catholic school, but when his teacher remarked on Louis's inattentiveness and disturbing tendency to stare vacantly straight ahead--and then suggested that he be tested for autism--she withdrew him and taught him at home until he was thirteen years old. Ellen Coates was right about one thing: Louis was not autistic. But his detachment from his surroundings was sometimes so complete that he appeared completely insensate. Between an obsessive mother and a daily regimen that provided no time for play or playmates, Louis learned to travel in his head, first to different places, then to different times. What began as a mechanism to escape the stultifying boredom and occasional terror of his home, gradually became a refuge from any dissonant contact with the world.

During the seven years that Louis was confined to his house, he spent eight hours a day at the piano, five hours studying his academic subjects, and the rest of the time helping tidy the house, eating, or taking a mandatory midday nap. He might never have escaped had his father not returned from England to take a job as first flutist for a prestigious symphony orchestra located several hours from his ex-wife and son. He was no warmer a person than Louis's mother and seemed pained by the effort it took to visit his son twice a year, but he insisted that Louis's isolation from the world end. Recluses were unlikely to develop into world-class pianists.

"You have no right to come here and tell me how to raise my son!" Louis heard his mother rage at his father. "You gave up that right when you left us and went back to England with Dennis."

"Dennis has nothing to do with this. You're the one who's turning him into a little freak in this prison camp you're running." *Dennis*? Louis was quite sure his parents had said *Dennis* and not *Denise*.

"A freak?" She tried to slap him across the face, but he stepped back, and she stumbled. He did not help her up. "It's you and your filthy little friend who are the freaks. If I tell the judge--"

"--darling, you already told the story to the judge, remember? You've got custody of your little boy. What you need to worry about is *me* telling stories to the judge, stories about sons who have never been to a restaurant or who have never played outside, stories about unfit mothers."

Ellen went white and slowly picked herself off the floor. She sat down on a bench in the entryway and squeezed her head between her hands. When she finally looked up, her eyes were wild. "I won't let you have him."

"But I don't want him, Ellen dear." He looked down on her with disdain. "I'm just insisting that he go to a proper school next year. Your little experiment in . . . gulag education," he smiled at his own cleverness, "needs to end before you ruin what could be a successful career on stage. I've heard him play, and he has potential."

As usual, talking about Louis's talent at the keyboard calmed down the horribly mismatched former spouses and a compromise was eventually reached: Louis would attend high school at Glenwood School for the Arts, an exclusive private school forty minutes from home. Although Jack Coates wanted him to board there, Ellen insisted that she take him and pick him up every day. By the time Jack left, some of the tension in the household had dissipated, but Louis did not know it. Within earshot at the top of the stairs, he was far away, in a land where parents had no place at all.

Before Louis started at Glenwood, Ellen Coates visited all of his teachers in order to apprise them of what a special student they would be privileged to have in their classes when the fall term began. Of course, she admitted, he has a tendency to daydream, but he's inherited his famous father's musicality and must be protected from the inevitable jealousy of the other children. Most of the teachers indulged the strange woman with a nod and a smile but some developed an instant dislike for her that was transferred unconsciously to her son. None of the faculty at Glenwood was prepared for the boy who arrived in late August. In a school famous for its freaks and nonconformists, Louis stood out.

He made eye contact with no one. He never spoke unless spoken to first, and even then his responses were inevitably monosyllabic. He thought of himself as an alien, and soon his classmates and teachers came to the same conclusion. He seemed impervious to ridicule, even to harshest lines of attack labeling him *faggot boy* and the *piano room pudpounder.* Had he responded violently or been a poor test-taker, the school would have been glad to get rid of him, but he managed to pass his classes with A's and B's, and he won several important junior piano competitions before he graduated. The school felt obliged to keep him, and the faculty even occasionally stepped in when the teasing went too far. Everyone breathed a sigh of relief when he was unable to attend graduation because of a stroke his mother had suffered during the last week of classes.

Louis did not begin to smell bad until after he went to college. His mother's plans to accompany him to Clarkeston were stymied by the lingering effects of the stroke, leaving Louis to fend for himself in a small off-campus apartment. He could not remember her instructions about how to work a washer and dryer, so doing the laundry consisted of occasionally dipping his socks and underwear in some soapy water in his bathroom sink.

The freedom he experienced was both liberating and disorienting. It was thrilling to be able to go to bed at any time he wanted or to practice or read past midnight, but he found that mornings met with only two or three hours sleep were hard to take. In one sense, his newfound freedom made him more normal. The control he exercised over his life made him less fearful and suspicious of the people that he met. He slowly grew more assertive, but his lack of social skills doomed most of his encounters with his fellow students. By the time he was asked to play with the Men's Glee Club, he was almost as much of a cipher as he had been in high school.

\* \* \*

"Professor Roberts?"

Evan looked up from the score he was studying. "You wouldn't be Louis Coates, would you?"

"Uh, huh," he replied, showing no sign of surprise that Roberts seemed to be expecting him.

"Professor Gabel just called to tell me that you might be coming. He said you're just the person I need to help out with Men's Glee." Roberts forced a smile as he inspected the doughy, expressionless face before him. In reality, Gabel had described Louis as a fine talent, but nuttier than a Viennese streusel. He asked Louis to sit down and play a difficult piece by Samuel Barber that he was hoping to introduce to the choir the next week.

"Good! Not quite how I want the choir to sing it, but if you pay attention during rehearsals to what I tell the group about how I want a piece interpreted, you'll catch on." Louis sat at the piano, staring at the score. It had been ridiculously easy to play, but something in the odd melodic line of the song appealed to him. He began to tune Roberts out as he tried to figure out what it was.

"Coates! Over here!" He jerked his head toward Roberts. "The toughest thing about being my accompanist will not be learning the notes of these pieces, but staying alert during rehearsal. I switch back and forth to various parts of a score very quickly, sometimes asking you to play all the parts, sometimes just a particular vocal line. If you're not paying attention to where we are, valuable rehearsal time will be wasted." By sheer force of will he held Louis's gaze. "You're probably not used to that, but for my purposes, it's a skill more important than being able to play all the notes right. Do you think you can do it?"

"I don't know . . . Herr Gabel wants me to try."

"Well, right now I'm desperate enough to let you have a chance. Rehearsal is tomorrow at four-thirty." He got up and retrieved several pieces of music and handed them to Louis. "Here, go over these tonight, and we'll see how you do tomorrow."

Louis spent much of the night virtually memorizing the music. The intense young professor had made a strong impression on him, and he did not want to be a disappointment. After four years of being barely tolerated and sometimes openly held in contempt by his high school teachers, meeting an adult who needed his services and offered the prospect of something like a partnership was a novel and disquieting experience. He got to the rehearsal room fifteen minutes early, and nervously ran through several of pieces while the choir wandered in and took their places.

Several of the young men asked him if he was going to be the group's accompanist. He nodded each time and was rewarded with expressions of favor that ran from *Cool* to *Dude*! No one seemed overtly offended by his appearance. Although he had not showered, he had pulled his greasy hair back in a short pony tail and put on a shirt that had aired out for a couple of days over a door knob. When Roberts entered, he quickly strode to the podium, asked Louis to give the group an E flat, and began to run the group through a series of vocal warm-ups. Louis had no trouble playing the ascending and descending scales Roberts demanded of him, but early in the warm-up he misunderstood what pattern of notes he was supposed to play and Roberts was forced to walk over to the piano to play it for him once before he caught on. Louis saw him wrinkle his nose when he bent over the keys, and wondered if the bad smell in his apartment had stuck to his clothes.

When the group started running through the songs, Louis felt a mixture of excitement and frustration. Although his teachers sometimes demanded he play a piano duet or a four-handed piece with them in practice, he had only seldom played the piano with other musicians. Once, as the first prize in a competition, he had been allowed to play the first movement of a Brahms piano concerto with a small chamber ensemble, but he had never been with so many people making music at the same time with him. Although being part of the larger sound was intriguing, he did not quite understand his relationship to it. Unlike playing the concerto, his part was not the focus of the music making. He was mostly a railing for the singers to lean against and sometimes an unsteady one, given that the breathing and phrasing Roberts demanded was not what he intuitively wanted to play. Several times he felt like he was beginning to be part of the flow, only to be cut off by Roberts as he demanded a section be sung again. Once, he continued to play, oblivious to the silence around him, until Roberts thanked him loudly for the solo and sent him back to the proper measure in the score amidst a buzz of friendly laughter.

He was completely unaccustomed to attending to the direction of another person for an extended period of time. Previously, it had been just he and a score, his focus inward as he wrestled with the notes. Now, he not only had to stay in touch with Roberts, but with the forty men also trying to follow their director. As hard as he tried to ignore the choir, their imperfections kept intruding on his playing. There was little he could do about the tendency of the group to drag behind the beat, but he did battle with various voices who went flat or sharp or were simply not singing what was on the page. Several times he banged out the left-hand part of songs especially loudly until the basses became aware of their communal pitch problem. The tenors were no better, and toward the end of the rehearsal he prepared them for the more difficult key changes by emphasizing their line. He enjoyed the small measure of control he had, but the effort left him frazzled and completely unsure of whether the music was in the piano, in the voices, behind the podium, or weirdly scattered in a way he had not thought of before. By the end of practice, he was exhausted

Roberts made a point of thanking him in front of the group after practice was over, and he was treated to a warm round of applause. "Louis, let me talk to you for a moment." Roberts waved him over to the far corner of the rehearsal room while the choristers filed out. "That was very good. You picked up quickly where some of the parts really needed to be led. Pounding out those lines is okay for now, but I'll want you to back off as we get closer to the concert. We'll have to get them standing on their own as soon as we can." Getting no immediate comment, he added, "Did you like it?"

"Uh, huh." Louis was caught off guard by the Roberts's use of *we*, as if they were somehow together in charge of the group. "I liked it. It was weird, but I liked it."

"One more thing . . ." Roberts frowned and looked straight at him. "Louis, I'm a very direct New Yorker, so please don't be offended by this, but you're really going to have to clean up a bit for this job. You're part of this group now, and you need to be bathing regularly and wearing clean clothes to rehearsals."

"Okay," Louis said quietly, "I guess I'm not used to living alone."

"Well, living on your own for the first time is hard. But you can't let things slip too much."

"No, sir."

Roberts nodded and dismissed him. "Alright, we'll see you on Wednesday."

Louis did not do as well on Wednesday, but over the course of the following weeks he became more comfortable with his role in the group and less forgetful of personal hygiene. He continued to lead a mostly reclusive life, but for the first time since the early days of his confinement at home, he began to long for some contact with his fellow creatures. His fear of rejection was paralyzing, and a profound struggle began within him. His old self, alienated and cut off from the world, yet self-contained, coherent, and safe from outside pressure, fought a pitched battle with his emerging self, an unsure and increasingly dissatisfied young man, stumbling dumbly toward a relationship with others. His two selves maintained an uneasy coexistence during the fall semester in Clarkeston, but gradually the camaraderie of the Glee Club subsumed him, and he spent less and less time imagining himself away from his real life.

One day in October, his fragile progress was threatened while waiting outside of Roberts's office to pick up some more music to learn. He overheard a conversation between two students.

"I just can't get away from that faggot! When I dropped Men's Glee, I figured I'd never see him again, but who shows up to teach the only section of music appreciation offered this semester? Professor Pole-Smoking Roberts himself."

"Is he really that bad?"

"Shit, I've heard he's sucking off half of the guys in the choir."
When the two boys noticed Louis staring at them, they lowered their
voices and he heard little more beyond their snorts of laughter.

Louis was not a homophobe, but between the taunts he had suffered
in high school and what he had guessed about his father and Dennis, he
was enormously distrustful of the whole notion of homosexuality. He was
deeply shaken by the conversation he had overheard, and he was no
longer sure he could trust the person he liked most on campus.

That same afternoon, after a satisfying practice during which
Roberts had encouraged him to improvise on the bland instrumental
introductions and codas to the pieces the choir was singing, he found the
music department secretary waiting for him in the hall outside the
rehearsal room.

"Louis Coates? Your mother's been calling the office all day. She
says it's urgent that you call her as soon as possible." Louis stared at her
as she stalked back down the hall, her body language communicating that
she did not consider delivering messages to students properly within her
job description. *Mother.* How long ago had he last talked to her? During
the first few weeks of class, she had called every day. He dreaded the
phone ringing because he knew it was either his mother trying her best to
direct his life from three hundred miles away or wrong numbers meant for
a popular campus pizza delivery place. In the first open act of rebellion
since he was a small child, he took the phone off the hook when he
realized that he could excuse his action by appealing to the need to sleep
through the night without taking someone's order for a large pepperoni
with extra cheese.

He rehearsed his explanation to his mother as he walked home,
hoping that the tongue-lashing he would receive for four weeks of silence
would not be too hysterical. If he called early enough, perhaps she would
not be drinking. He paused with his hand on the receiver a moment before
he collected the courage to call. The distance between them helped, and
the confidence he had gained in front of the chorus lingered, at least until
he heard her voice.

"Mother?"

"Louis! Where have you been? I've gotten nothing but a busy
signal for weeks and that horrible secretary at the music school refused to
give you my messages, even though she knew you were in rehearsal with
some professor every day."

"Sorry." Louis had learned that the fewer words he used with his
mother, the less potential to set her off on some wild tangent.

"And what are you doing with this Dr. Roberts anyway? I thought Herr Gabel was giving you lessons?"

"He still is, but he asked me to accompany the Men's Glee Club as part of my training." Louis braced himself.

"Training for what?" she croaked. "To be an elementary school music teacher? What kind of a college am I sending you to?" She paused for a moment, and Louis could hear her breathing heavily into the phone. "Well, it doesn't matter. You need to come home anyway. I'm still extremely weak, and we don't have the money to keep paying someone to take care of me."

Louis had a recurring nightmare that he was in the basement of his house, creeping toward the stairs, vaguely aware of an evil presence stalking him. As the presence approached, he tried to run up the stairs, but he always tripped, and as he scrambled to the top, he could feel a hand grip his ankle and pull him back down. When he understood what his mother wanted, he felt like two strong arms had grabbed him and dragged him through the floor, altogether out of this world and straight to the bottom of a dark frigid ocean. He swayed there slowly, like a stalk of kelp, far beneath the surface light and motion of the real world.

"Louis . . . Louis! Did you hear what I said?"

"Yes, ma'am." He could feel his lips move, but he had no sensation of actually directing the sounds coming out of his mouth.

"How soon can you come home?" Long silence.

"I don't know."

"You must come soon, because I've given Imelda her two weeks notice. I'll send you plane tickets as soon as I can." She sighed. "I can't wait to get you home again. It's been just horrible being here all by myself. I'm sure it's been terrible for you too."

"Yes . . . terrible." With great effort he pushed the phone away from his ear, "I've got to go now." He put down the receiver and unplugged the device from the wall.

He sat down on his sofa in between a half-eaten sandwich and an open pizza box and stared at the stereo on the other side of the small room wondering whether anyone in Clarkeston could help him. Herr Gabel would be happy to see him go; Professor Henderson would probably side with a sick woman her own age; and Professor Roberts could not be trusted with a problem so personal. As despair swallowed him, the stereo shimmered and bit by bit began to fade from view. Although he knew his head would soon be pounding, he was fascinated by how the periphery of his vision remained intact while the center held nothing at all. If he tried to focus on his amplifier, he could see the speakers, but if he turned his head to inspect the speakers more closely, they disappeared. He lay down when he felt the throbbing begin and barely managed to turn off the lamp at the head of the sofa as he collapsed into oblivion.

## 9

### Friends and Lovers

As autumn closed in, Dorothy appreciated more and more the evenings and Saturdays when Terri came over to help with the unending task of organizing her music collection.  Resting in quiet contemplation had been fine as long as her shoulder did not bother her, but when the deep throb of pain became more persistent, the distraction of conversation provided welcome relief.  And what an interesting distraction!  Terri arrived with fresh stories of her eccentric brother and his mysterious, widowed, earth-mother fiancée or common-law wife or whatever-she-was.  Dorothy also relished the sometimes shrewd, sometimes naive, observations of the newcomer on life in Clarkeston.  But most of all, Dorothy developed an obsession with Terri's love life as it unfolded in unexpected directions on the porch of Arthur and Suzanne's white clapboard house.

Dorothy was surprised by her own interest until she realized that Terri reminded her of herself as a young woman, and she instinctively wanted to help her avoid making the same mistakes she had.  On one of the first evenings they worked together, Dorothy set out a bottle of red wine to share while they were dealing with her chaotic collection of sheet music.

"Boy, that tastes good," Terri sighed.  "I haven't had any alcohol for over five months."

"This isn't going to start you bingeing, is it?"

"No," Terri laughed.  "I bought a beautiful size twelve wedding gown on clearance in Iowa City six months before the ceremony, and I really cut down on my calories so I could squeeze into it.  I don't think I've been this slim since high school.  A couple of the guys at my father's old coffee shop were even starting to flirt with me before I left."

"You do look lovely," Dorothy said, sensing her friend's insecurity about her appearance.  Cursed with a short waist and thick farmer-girl ankles, Terri would never cut a figure like the models on the covers of Vogue and Glamor, but from the shoulders up she was beautiful enough.

Her complexion was creamy and clear, and her thick flaxen hair set off startlingly green eyes.

"No," she said reflexively, "I don't." She paused for a moment. "I'm not even the prettiest one in my house. You should see Suzanne! Even though she's six months pregnant, she still looks like some beautiful gypsy woman."

"Tell me more about her," Dorothy asked as she poured Terri some more wine. "Not that I'm complaining about holding on to a good tenor, but I've wondered about what's kept Arthur in town."

"Well, the most amazing thing is that she won't marry him, at least not right now. When she got pregnant, he asked her but she wants to wait."

"For what? Your brother's a handsome, well-educated young man."

"Well, I think she was married to someone like that already and it didn't work out too well. She's extremely careful and wants to see if he's really serious about staying down here, because there's no way she would ever leave Clarkeston or that wonderful house." She took a sip of her wine. "She has this quiet sense of power about her, I can't really explain it, sort of magnetic and peaceful at the same time. When Arthur asked her to marry him, he wasn't doing her a favor, he was *asking* for one. A big one."

"I can't imagine saying that about someone asking for my hand," Dorothy laughed.

"Me neither."

"Why? Don't you think I'm special?"

"No," Terri giggled, "I mean I can't imagine anyone chasing after me like that either. I can't imagine anyone chasing me at all--except maybe some Iowa farmer who needs my nest egg for a new combine."

"Nonsense!" Dorothy said emphatically. "I can't stand self-pity. It's a very ugly thing." Terri looked surprised at the conviction in Dorothy's voice and the vigorous shaking of her head.

"Well," Terri said conspiratorially, "I did meet someone interesting in the coffee shop the other day, but I bet nothing comes of it."

\* \* \*

Every afternoon, Terri walked downtown to pick up a newspaper and spend a couple of hours sitting in one of the coffee shops in the historic section of Clarkeston just across the river from the college. As she sat reading in Café Cappuccino one lazy Friday afternoon, she overheard an energetic argument carried on by three Latino students at the table next to her. Although she could not make out much more than the repeated emphasis on the words *rubia* (blond) and *morena* (brunette), she gradually determined that they were discussing the color of the waitress's hair. She looked over and surveyed the tangled, dark brown cause of the argument and recalled her college Spanish professor's insistence that there were only two acknowledged Latin hair colors: blond and not blond. She called the waitress over with a sense of mischief that had lain dormant for years.

"Tish, what color is your hair?" The conversation beside her instantly stopped and one of the men looked nervously over at her with a quiet whisper to his companions. Tish, a painfully thin girl who had dropped out of Clarkeston College several years before, was more than happy to be asked a question she knew the answer to.

"This is my natural shade of brown." She flounced it with her left hand. "Why, do you think I should dye it?"

"No, it looks lovely just the way it is. I'm just doing an informal survey on . . . uh . . . comparative hair color designations by regional origin."

"Uh, okay, Terri. You want another cup?" Terri shook her head, and Tish dutifully went back to wiping down the counter where the cream and sugar were dispensed.

The three students looked at Terri surreptitiously while she searched for the right words with which to address them. "*Ella tiene pelo castaño. ¡Mira, acquí hay mas que dos colores de pelo!*" She spoke without stumbling too badly: *She has brown hair. Here, there are more than just two colors of hair!* All three took this interjection into their conversation with the good humor it was intended and soon they were talking to her in what Jorge later described as "Spanish lite." When Carmen and Emilio left the café together, Jorge moved over to Terri's table to continue their conversation.

"Your Spanish is very good," he said with a spectacular smile and an evident but pleasingly lyrical accent, "but let's speak English for now. Carmen and Emilio are from Costa Rica, but I'm from Miami."

"Sure," she replied as he gracefully slid over to her table. He was only slightly taller than her five foot, seven inches, but he had an athletic build and the disproportionately muscular legs of a soccer player or serious cyclist. His sensuous lips and piercing dark eyes were the most attractive features on his handsome face. It occurred to her that she had completely forgotten how to flirt.

"What do you do in Clarkeston?" he asked her.

"Well, I'm basically on vacation--visiting my brother who teaches history at the college."

"This is a strange place to come on vacation."

"I guess it sort of is," she replied, managing a smile in spite of her nervousness, unconsciously showing off her face at its prettiest, green eyes flashing and smooth alabaster skin momentarily creasing into an expression that lit up the whole café. "But this is a strange place to find someone from Miami, too." She wanted another cup of coffee to hide behind, but did not want to give him the opportunity to check her out on the way to the counter.

"Maybe so, but I'm hardly the only Latino in town. In fact, Carmen and Emilio and some other friends are having a party tonight. Would you like to come? It'll be at Monica's house, a girl from Colombia." Terri hesitated a moment. Her Midwestern core found suspect both the invitation from a stranger and the shiver it sent down her back. Before she could answer, Jorge scribbled down the address on a napkin and pushed it over to Terri's side of the table. Monica's "house" turned out to be an apartment on the edge of campus. "You have to speak Spanish when you come. At the end of the week, everyone's tired of speaking English, so we speak our own language."

"I don't know. I was never really fluent."

"No," he said with a grin as he got up from the table, "you are fine. I'll see you there." He turned and glided out of the café. She stared out the door for a long moment after he had gone, holding the napkin in her hand.

"Oooh, what a cutie." Terri turned and noticed Tish standing next to her. "Are you going out with him?"

"No, he just invited me to a party."

"Are you going to go?"

"Maybe."

"You should," Tish said with a wink. "You know how crazy those Mexicans are about blonds." Terri looked up at her with a frown and turned her attention back to the newspaper, but she could not keep her mind on the headlines. Why am I hesitating to accept the first invitation I've gotten in years? The more and more she wavered, the angrier she got at her indecisiveness. This is what I get for wasting so much time with Tommy and never busting out of Iowa. She remembered the last three years spent commuting between the small town where she grew up and her job, cleaning teeth during the day to earn money and sitting at home nights and weekends afraid to spend it. *I've forgotten how to have fun.*

"I'm going," she said firmly to herself.

"Good for you." She glanced up with a start to see Tish smiling at her.

When she arrived home, she went straight up to her room. Suzanne followed and soon pried from her the news of the invitation. From an objective standpoint, Terri knew that the party was no big deal, but she had set Suzanne's emotional antennae tingling from the moment she entered the house.

"I have nothing to wear," she complained to Suzanne for the third time as she slid her clothes one by one across the bar in the guest room closet. "I packed for a short visit to see my brother. I'm afraid I left my huge collection of Latin party clothes behind in Iowa."

"What about those slacks?" Suzanne asked from her perch on the bed, secure in the knowledge that her days of dating trauma were behind her.

"They make me look like an elephant." She picked out a long, lightweight fall skirt. "This one hides my derriere better, but I've got no top to go with it."

"We can solve that problem. Follow me." A brief trip to Suzanne's bedroom provided Terri with a dark knit blouse that accentuated her ample bosom and matched the skirt perfectly. She tried the outfit on and grimaced in approval at the mirror. "That's as good as it gets, girl."

"You look great, Terri. You're going to knock this guy's socks off."

"I doubt it, and I wouldn't know what to do even if I did." She looked at Suzanne and shook her head. "I haven't been asked anywhere by anybody except Tommy Grier for over seven years. I mean, this isn't even a date and I'm already freaking out. What if my Spanish totally disappears and I can't even make conversation at this party?"

"Don't worry about it. Just go and have fun."

"Fun?"

"Yes, you remember the concept, don't you?" she said with genuine affection to her friend. "You are beautiful and smart and you don't have to worry about anything except showing up and having a good time." Terri blushed and gave Suzanne an awkward hug around her swollen belly.

"You're the best sister-in-law . . . I mean live-in-lover-in-law a girl could ever want."

In spite of Suzanne's encouragement, Terri's anxiety remained high as she drove around the east side of town looking for the apartment complex Jorge had written on the napkin. A couple of wrong turns meant that she did not arrive until fifteen after seven, but she reminded herself that it would have been impolite to arrive exactly on time. As it was, the apartment seemed oddly silent as she knocked on the door. It was opened by an attractive woman wearing a stained green apron.

"*¡Hola! ¿Esta la casa de Monica?*" Terri asked, politely making sure she had the right address.

"*Si.*" The woman's face was not unfriendly, but she clearly was not expecting Terri.

"*Jorge me invito a una fiesta acquí esta noche, pero me parece que estoy un poquito temprano.*" At the mention of Jorge's name, the woman smiled and invited her in, explaining that she was in the middle of making a special salsa for the party. She took Terri back to the kitchen and offered her a beer before turning her attention back to her avocados. Monica was delightful and talkative, and best of all, as a native of Colombia she did not speak Spanish in the rapid-fire manner of the Spaniards Terri had met during her college semester abroad in Salamanca. After a few minutes, she asked Monica if she could help with the food, and she spent the next hour calming her nerves through the therapeutic chopping of onions and rolling of spicy little meatballs. At eight o'clock she looked at her watch.

"I'm sorry that I got the time wrong. I was sure that Jorge told me that the party started at seven."

"But it did, didn't it?" Monica laughed. "I told everyone to come at seven, but I know my friends, and I wouldn't be surprised to see the first group come around eight or eight-thirty." She was as unconcerned about the timing of her party as she was about a stranger showing up at her door with an invitation she did not know had been made. At that moment the doorbell rang.

"Could you get that, Terri, while I start setting the food out on the table?"

"Sure." She walked to the front door, relieved that the two beers she had consumed seemed to have improved her foreign language skills. She let in Carmen and Emilio with a smile and a huge shrug in response to the surprised look on their faces. "*Bienvenidos a la casa de Monica.*" An older couple entered behind Carmen and the party was on. It started in the kitchen with everyone admiring the food and progressed into the living room where Monica's stereo was playing, only to be pushed out onto the balcony as most of Clarkeston's small Latin population forced its way into the apartment. Terri had not had so much fun in years. Most of the guests wanted to meet the exotic, green-eyed blond who spoke Spanish so well for *una Americana*, and the music was turned up loud enough that Terri had a credible excuse for asking people to repeat what they said when she did not catch the gist of a question. Jorge did not arrive until nine o'clock, but Terri was so engrossed in a conversation about Salamanca with a girl who had also been a visiting student there, that she did not even notice.

"Monica told me that you came at seven. I'm sorry that I didn't remind you about Latin time." He handed her a bottle of beer with a playful smile.

"Don't worry about it," she said earnestly, "I haven't been to a party this fun since . . . since I was in Salamanca. To tell you the truth, the Iowa party scene is pretty pathetic. Sometimes I think that Americans just don't know how to have fun. Look at Diana and Roberto over there. They're almost as old as my parents, but they're having a great time. If they were fifty-year-old Americans, they'd be in bed already watching Johnny Carson. Thanks for inviting me."

"Monica says I should make you a standing invitation. We all get together somewhere every week. Now that you're an honorary Latina, you need to come every Friday." He looked directly in her eyes, admiring her without a shred of shyness or false modesty. "I also hope I'll see you again before next Friday, maybe at the coffee shop next week?"

"I'm there every afternoon catching up on my reading."

"Good, I will see you for sure." They talked for a while and eventually separated, spending the rest of the evening circulating around the apartment, occasionally acknowledging each other's presence with a smile or a nod. When Terri bade her new friends farewell to a cacophony of assurances that her presence would be welcomed and expected the following Friday, Jorge got up and escorted her to her car.

"Thanks so much again for inviting me! I can't remember when I've had so much fun. Your friends are wonderful." He gave her a knee-weakening smile and kissed her lightly on each cheek, hands lingering on her waist for a moment as he reminded her of their coffeehouse rendezvous. He remained standing on the sidewalk as she backed out, offering a brief wave as she drove away from the apartment.

Her mind spun as she drove home. Latins kissed everyone they know, she said to herself. Don't be an idiot and get all excited. That's what happens when you're twenty-five and have only dated one guy since high school. God that's pathetic! I'm twenty-five and I've only slept with Tommy, she thought. On the other hand, I'm rid of him, I've got some money, and I'm free to do whatever I want. Then why fantasize about the first man I've met? Am I scared to be free or is he really special? She shook her head as if to clear away the jumble of thoughts. I just don't want to do anything that I'll regret.

When she returned home, Arthur was in bed, but Suzanne was still awake, sipping a mug of tea in the living room downstairs, curled up on the couch in front of the television with an afghan pulled up over her legs.

"Your nephew is giving me horrible heartburn tonight. It feels like half the acid in my stomach is trying to work its way back up my throat." She stuck her tongue in disgust. "I'm trying to beat it back down with some green tea. So, tell me, how was your big date? You didn't let him past first base, did you?"

"It wasn't like that at all." She sat down on the sofa next to Suzanne. "It was a big party with a lot of really nice people. Jorge didn't even get there until nine o'clock, but by then I was having such a good time that I didn't even notice him come in. I talked with him for part of the time, though, and he walked me down to my car and asked me to have coffee with him next week." Her face glowed as she spoke about her Latin adventure in rural Georgia and the unexpected amount of attention Jorge was paying her.

"So, you're still interested in him?"

"Suzanne, he's so hot! I mean, he's way out of my league, but he's mysterious and really nice. I want to find out what he's really like."

"In my experience," Suzanne said with a laugh, "that may be setting your sights way higher than just trying to get into his pants."

\* \* \*

Dorothy listened to Terri's story with rapt attention. They had accomplished little cataloging work so far. "I hope she wasn't suggesting that getting into his pants was an unworthy goal."

"What!"

"Oh nothing. I just want you to have a good visit here in Clarkeston."

"Helping you out here is quite enough excitement for me."

"I doubt that." Dorothy picked up a pile of music and considered her own love life. "You need to go out and have a little excitement for the both of us."

59

## *10*

## A Chance Connection

Evan delayed telling John about the rocky start with the Men's Glee Club and his creative approach to dealing with the malefactors. His reaction would have been too much for Evan to deal with. John would likely project his own horror at being singled out for ridicule and bury Evan under a jumble of his own anxiety and resentment. What if a group of students complained to the college administration? Would the music department stand by him? How would he deal with further harassment from students? John's fearfulness about the future was his most trying trait. The ideal mate, Evan thought, would be as handsome and loyal, but would respond to the story with a laconic, "Fuck 'em if they can't take a joke."

Evan felt increasingly torn each day as he drove home. Compared to New York, Clarkeston was a musical backwater, and it was impossible to envision making a satisfying career there. I need to be in the middle of things, he thought, and this is about as far from the center of the musical universe as I can imagine. Unfortunately, John seems to like it more here every day. I'm not sure he'd come with me if I decided to leave. In some ways the contrast between Clarkeston and New York was like that between John and his former lovers. He longed for the hard edges of the city and his friends, but he longed for something else too. John's the key, he thought. How the hell did I let that happen?

"Tell me about week four of computerizing the federal courts," he yelled out to the backyard one Friday evening when he returned home from the rehearsal. Hearing no answer, he wandered out onto the patio and found John clipping the aggressive, redtip hedge that guarded the edges of their property like a huge security fence. He watched the progression of the work for a moment as the cold sweat from the beer bottle dripped off of his fingers.

"You must be the replacement for José Maria, our usual yard man. He trims more evenly than you, but you've got a nicer butt."

"Careful, Señor, or I will have to file a complaint for sexual harassment."

"A couple of weeks working for the federal courts and we're already getting litigious, are we?" Evan kicked the fallen branches into a pile. "You about done here? Should I get you a beer and wait on the patio?"

"Si, un momento, por favor."

Evan went back to the kitchen to fetch two more cold bottles and pulled two cheap plastic chairs into the shade next to the house. John pushed a wheelbarrow full of clippings next to the patio and sat down facing him.

"Well, how was rehearsal today? Are they making any progress at all?"

"They need to work on their vowels," he answered, "and they've still only got three dynamic levels--loud, stun, and kill--but I can see some potential. The problem is that all they're used to singing is the alma mater and barber-shoppy sorts of stuff. There really is some serious music written for men's choruses--especially some really nice Slavic stuff that they could probably do well--but I don't know if I can sell them on singing in Russian or Old Church Slavonic."

"What a great concert idea: Stephen Foster followed by Rachmaninoff."

"You see the problem. Henderson concentrated on the College Chorus and the Women's Glee Club and left the men to a series of student assistants who never developed any kind of sophistication in the group's repertory. I've got my work cut out for me . . . in more ways than you want to know." His voice trailed off and the two listened to the sounds that drifted into their back yard, power trimmers whining in the distance, a seesaw creaking back and forth, squirrels scratching in the desiccated brown leaves under the magnolia tree, a screen door slamming shut, the occasional swooshing of a car as it passed the gaps in between the houses lining the street. John was first to add a sigh to the sounds of the Indian summer afternoon.

"Do you think we're in the right place, Evan? Or would you be happier back in New York?"

"Well, we're sure not in Kansas anymore, Toto. And you're going to have to help me battle with the Wicked Witch."

"Fair enough," he replied, "just remember that I've got my own battles too."

* * *

"Why don't we come down in the middle of December, dear?" John's mother spoke to her son in a bright and cheerful voice. She and her husband had talked for years about spending one of the winter months in Florida, and now that he was about to retire, she could not stop thinking about how wonderful it was going to be to walk the beaches of St. Petersburg when it was snowing back home in Ohio. The chance to stop and see her favorite son on the drive down south made planning the trip even more delightful. "I checked on the map, and it's practically on our way to scoot over and see you."

"Great, Mom!" John was thankful she could not see the look of horror on his face. When he lived in New York, he could always plead the size of his studio apartment and the crime rate in his neighborhood as excuses to fend off parental visits. His biannual trips to Dayton also lessened their desire to travel to New York City to see him. Why had he told them that he now lived in a three-bedroom house? "Sounds good, Mom, we'd be happy to have you."

"We?"

*Oh shit.* "Uh, yeah, I'm sorry. Haven't I told you? I've got a roommate, to help out with the rent and stuff. He's a really nice guy . . . you'll enjoy meeting him."

"Are you sure he won't mind us staying with you for a couple of days?" John hated lying to his parents, but years of hiding his sexual identity from them had enhanced his skill in dissimulating. While he was considering the possibility of asking them to stay in a motel, a voice chimed loudly from across the room.

"I can't wait to meet your folks, roomie."

"Was that him, John?" He glared at Evan and repeatedly slashed his left index across his throat. Evan just grinned.

"Tell 'em we've got plenty of room!" Evan cried out, his voice easily carrying over the long miles from Clarkeston to Dayton.

"Sure, Mom, we've got plenty of room . . . stay as long as you want."

"Well, we won't stay too long, dear. I can't wait to see what our condo looks like in St. Pete. Do you want to talk to your father?"

"No, I've got to leave for a hair appointment in a couple of minutes." John hung up the phone and stood staring out the kitchen window into the small backyard. The pruning had done wonders and the space now looked tidy and inviting. A couple of sparrows flitted about the feeder he had put up the day before.

"You've got a hair appointment?" Evan snorted. "You might as well just shout, *I'm a limp-wristed pansy.* If you're going to keep hiding from them, at least make up a manly excuse like, *I must be off to reinforce my deer stand* or *My girlfriend and I have to go out shopping for hot tubs.*"

"You're not helping."

"Sure I am!  In two months, you're going to be outed to your parents.  You'd better start getting used to the idea.  In fact, you might want to get some practice before they come."

"I almost told someone yesterday," John said suddenly.

"Who?"

"I met one of the Judge's former clerks in his office, and we must have talked for a half an hour while I hooked up the secretary's computer to the new system.  He's from the Midwest too and seemed to be a super nice guy.  When he mentioned that he sings in the College Chorus, I had this incredible impulse to tell him about us and let him know what a great director you are."

"You should have," Evan said definitively.  "Like I said, you need the practice."

"Right there, in the Judge's chambers?"  He sat down at the kitchen table across from Evan.  "He would have punched me in the nose."

"Nah."  Evan picked at a bit of dried tomato sauce on the oak table and flicked it with his finger across the recently varnished surface.  "Just out of curiosity, how many guys have you told in your life?"

"You mean how many of my friends know?"

"No, I mean how many have you told.  And girls don't count--they just get all fascinated.  Telling a guy is like telling your parents.  He might flip out or he might not."

"Well, I told my college roommate, but he said he'd figured it out the year before."  He laughed at himself.  "I sweated telling him for about two months, and then it turned out to be nothing."

"Why do you think it will be any different with your parents?"

"Well, for one thing, I never heard my roommate scream *god-damn fucking faggots* at the television screen."

"Maybe your dad was just using a colorful metaphor.  Or was that your mom?"

"Dad . . . watching a news report on the San Francisco gay pride parade."

"Well, no one said it was going to be easy," Evan sighed.  "Maybe we should invite Oprah to mediate."

* * *

63

About a week later, John ran into his courthouse acquaintance unexpectedly in a campustown bar called the Wild Boar. John had arranged to meet Evan on Friday afternoon after work and claimed a prime seat for them where the bar opened onto the street. Although the table was inside, the feeling was delightfully spacious because the window along the sidewalk was custom-made to slide up to the ceiling whenever the manager wanted to let in the breeze. At five o'clock, Arthur, the former law clerk, drifted into the bar along with the warm fall air. He surveyed the room while his beer was being poured and saw John watching the students stroll past on the broad sidewalk. He brought his drink over and asked if he could sit down.

"For being new to town," he said, "it didn't take you long to discover the perfect place to have a beer." He put his elbow on the window sill and joined John in contemplating the steady stream of young people leaving campus. After a few minutes, Arthur spotted a curvaceous brunette gliding toward the bar. "Good Lord, Babe-O-Rama on the left."

John knew the game to play, and he turned, preparing to offer some compliment on her anatomy, but he suddenly felt profoundly tired of playing games in bars and at parties and at work . . .

"Actually, I sort of prefer the young guy walking behind her."

*That wasn't so hard.* Arthur gave John a look which was more amused than shocked. He had seen a lot during his prior year with the Judge, and being gently corrected for making assumptions about someone's sexual orientation was something he could easily deal with.

"Well, he does have nice shoulders," Arthur replied, "but I never liked that greasy hair look." John stared for a moment and then began to laugh so hard that he was still shaking when Evan walked through the door and approached the table.

"We've just been talking about you," he said when he caught his breath. "This is Arthur, the guy I met the other day in the Judge's chambers."

"Nice to meet you." Arthur extended his hand. "Come and join our discussion of the relative merits of hair gel."

"This is Evan." John gestured with his glass. "We live together over in Clarkeston Hills."

"What do you do here in town?" Arthur asked the stunned newcomer. Evan took a moment to recover and then sat down with a smile.

"I teach in the Choral Department at the College."

"So we're colleagues, then. I teach over in the History Department." Arthur poured a glass of beer. "You must know Dorothy Henderson pretty well then?"

"You might say that."

Arthur drank deeply from his glass and warmed to one of his favorite topics. "I think she's amazing! When she asked me to join the college chorus, she literally changed my life. If it weren't for her, I'd be alone and miserable in Washington, D.C., right now."

"She changed your life?" Evan could see now that Arthur had had one too many.

"Watch out, or she might change your life, too." He nodded knowingly and finished his glass.

"I've no doubt about that," Evan sighed, "no doubt about that at all." He went to the bar to get himself a glass and a fresh pitcher. When he sat back down, the subject had mercifully changed, and the three men spent the rest of the afternoon in quiet conversation as a living panorama of Clarkeston passed by their window.

## *11*

## A Dinner in Clarkeston

When she carried her newspaper into the café on Wednesday, Terri found Jorge sitting and studying at a small round table close to the front window. He looked up as the door creaked open and stood as she approached. He brushed her cheeks with two swift kisses and insisted that she let him buy her a cup of Cuban coffee.

"It's not on the menu, but I taught them how to make it by putting sugar into the espresso before they steam it. You'll love it."

"Jorge," she asked when he sat down, "have you spent any time in the Midwest?"

"No. I know Miami, and I know Clarkeston. That's about it." He sipped his coffee contentedly. "My family came over from Cuba to south Florida in 1963. My father could speak English quite well even before he escaped, and it didn't take him long to get a job as one of the first Cuban State Farm agents in Miami. He's been selling insurance to each wave of immigrants ever since . . . so busy doing business that we never traveled very much."

"How did you end up in Clarkeston then? I mean, I really love it here, but this must be a lot different from Miami."

"That's easy," he said with disgust, "my parents don't think Miami is safe anymore. So, they sent me deep into the heart of Anglo-America, far from the violent brand of Cubans that are taking over South Florida. I think my parents would be thrilled to see their grandchildren raised in some obscure place like Nebraska or South Dakota." He spoke with undisguised sarcasm, deliberately pronouncing the words with the thick accent of his parents.

"Or Iowa."

"Or Iowa," he replied. "Come on now, you must humor me and try the coffee." He watched her sip the mud-like fluid congealing in her cup.

"It's good," she lied, adding more sugar. "You know, Clarkeston seems just as foreign to me as it probably does to you. My hometown consists of a truck stop, grocery store, hardware store, a school, and a couple of churches built around a huge grain elevator. The place is so dead that people drive fifteen miles to the McDonald's on the interstate for a special meal. A couple of old farmers having coffee and pie at the truck stop is the town's idea of a major party. If I didn't drive into Iowa City regularly, I'd go completely crazy. You're going to laugh, because you feel like you've been banished to the sticks, but sitting here having coffee with you and walking home through town afterwards feels like a real vacation to me."

"So, I'm part of the exotic scenery then?"

"No," she blushed, "but meeting you and your friends is part of what's so nice about Clarkeston."

"So, when you go back to Iowa you'll always associate the Deep South with speaking Spanish instead of boiling peanuts or eating grits?"

"I'm not sure I'm going to go back," Terri said abruptly, considering for the first time the possibility that she would not return to her old job in her home state. "Why shouldn't I just stay here? I already have more friends than I do back home, and there's so much more to do here." Her eyes flashed with the excitement of unlimited possibilities, of making a complete break with the past just as her brother had done. She leaned forward over the table and tried to explain. "Suzanne, that's my brother's, uh, fiancée, is like this sister I never had. And you guys invite me to great parties without even knowing me. Wouldn't I be stupid to go back home?"

"You are a strange person, Terri." He looked like he was going to say more, but instead he stopped and scratched behind his left ear while he examined at her.

"What do you mean? Dental hygienists almost never get called anything worse than boring."

"I think that maybe you're not completely and irredeemably Protestant."

"What?"

"Well, you're still a Puritan. You went to college to get a degree to earn a living, probably not because you love other people's teeth, but because some counselor told you jobs were plentiful and well-paying. Then, you worked hard and saved for years, never taking time to enjoy your life." He was teasing, but the tone of his voice indicated that if Midwestern and Puritan were related concepts, then assimilating into Iowa society would be a terrible fate. "Although that is the most Protestant story I've ever heard, something inside you has snapped and the repressed Latina in you is beginning to express itself. People and places are becoming as important to you as putting money into your IRA."

"401(k)," she corrected him with a smile.

"Alright, 401(k)." He smiled back. "See, you're already growing a sense of humor."

"Hey, I've always had a sense of humor. My dentist used to call me the Laughing Hygienist."

"I rest my case. But I will make you an honorary Cuban as soon as you stop stiffening up when someone kisses your cheek."

"I do not!"

"Yes, you do," he insisted, "I don't know how the Puritans ever populated this country when they could barely bring themselves to shake hands."

"I am not a Puritan!" she protested. What Jorge did not realize was that she was truly tired of Iowa and coming over to his world sounded like a good idea. She slid her chair closer to him and put her arm over his shoulder. He's not the only one who can tease, she thought.

"Do you want me to prove that I'm not a Puritan?" She whispered in a throaty voice. "You could come back to my place and we could cook up something hot together." She moaned softly and saw him begin to squirm. ". . . in the kitchen with my brother's pregnant girlfriend and her four-year-old daughter." She backed off and giggled.

"That's just the problem with you Puritans," he attempted in vain to maintain a stoic expression, "you go straight from frigidity to nymphomania." He excused himself to go the men's room, leaving Terri to wonder whether she should really invite him to dinner. Why not? Suzanne and Arthur loved company. Dorothy would get a kick out of meeting him too.

"You know, Jorge," she asked when he returned, "being spontaneous is a sure sign that I'm losing my Anglo-Protestant values, so let me seriously invite you over for dinner tonight. I think you'd like my brother; he just gave up lawyering for teaching."

He thought about it for a moment and accepted with a gracious smile and a promise to arrive on time. With a glance at her watch, she excused herself and started the walk back home with the same sensation in her stomach she had felt before singing the national anthem at the homecoming football game her junior year in high school. God, she thought as tried to quell the butterflies, I hope dinner goes better than that.

* * *

68

"I'd love to come." Dorothy had not received an impromptu dinner invitation in a long time, and she was certainly not going to turn down a chance to meet the young man that Terri seemed so excited about. She hoped that inviting him to dinner with strangers was not a terrible mistake; it would be painful to see her friend fall just as she was trying to spread her wings.

Shortly before seven o'clock, she stood on the slightly sagging porch of Suzanne's house. She knocked lightly but failed to get the attention of anyone over the stereo she heard playing inside. As she started to knock again, she noticed a handsome young man with thick curly hair climbing up the steps toward her.

"You must be Jorge?"

"Yes."

"Hello. I'm Dorothy Henderson." She offered her hand. "Let's give knocking one more try and then I'm afraid we're just going to have to let ourselves in."

When no one responded, she glanced at Jorge and stepped tentatively into the foyer. Unlike some of the expensively refurbished mansions on the street, the house was not quite ready to host next year's debutantes coming out party. The furniture inside was old and worn, the walls needed painting, toys were stacked in the corner of every room, and the artwork on the walls consisted of finger paintings and pictures taken of various beach vacations. A stereo played loudly in a room off the long main hallway and a little girl slid fearlessly from room to room on the slick heart pine floors. They walked down the hall to the back of the house where they found a pregnant woman with a wild mane of thick dark hair sauteeing garlic and onions in a huge stainless steel pan. Dorothy knocked on the door frame and held out a bottle of wine.

"Hello! Professor Henderson, you probably don't remember me, but we met when you did a choral workshop at my high school years ago. And you must be Jorge," she pronounced his name perfectly and took the wine first from Dorothy's hands and then his. "Thank you both! Terri and Arthur went off to get some more wine about a half an hour ago and they should be back any minute. Why don't you sit down and open up what you brought?" She handed Jorge a corkscrew and went back to her pan.

After a few minutes of pleasant conversation, Terri and Arthur returned. Arthur and Dorothy were assigned to take Jorge out on the porch with a fresh glass of wine while the two young women put the finishing touches on dinner.

"Terri tells me that you just transferred to the college," Arthur said as he leaned against the porch railing and studied the handsome young man sitting defensively in the porch swing. Terri had warned him somewhat ambiguously that Jorge was not an "assimilationist."

"Yeah, my parents wanted me to finish school up north instead of in Miami."

"Up north in Clarkeston! I love it!" He flashed Jorge a broad smile. "Do you like it here? Terri might've mentioned I just moved down last year. This is such a great place. I came down dead set on practicing law in Washington, and now I'm teaching at the College."

"I like it here okay," Jorge conceded, "but there's not much to do compared to Miami. As soon as the *Matlock* reruns come on, this whole town goes to sleep. And to tell you the truth, I get sick of the looks my friends and I get when we speak Spanish in public." Dorothy checked Arthur's expression for any sign of annoyance with the critique, but she saw only a mixture of interest and sympathy. "Race relations are better here than in Miami, but people have troubling handling a Latino presence in town. They see us as invaders or something."

"I hadn't noticed that before," Arthur replied, "but now that I think about it, Blacks and Whites have lived together here for over two hundred years. People may have their racism under better control than their xenophobia."

"Well, wherever these people are coming from, I'm not going to start drinking ice tea and talking with a drawl in order to make them feel better."

"You're right," Arthur responded with no apparent thought of suggesting that removing the chip from his shoulder might not be too terrible a compromise to make, "just be yourself, and the hell with 'em."

Dorothy raised an eyebrow, but refrained from comment when she realized that Arthur had succinctly summed up her philosophy of living. The dull throbbing in her arm made her wonder whether it was a creed worth taking to the grave.

"Dinner is served!" Terri pried open the blinds right behind Jorge's head with her fingers and made her announcement through the living room window. Dorothy and Jorge followed Arthur and joined the rest of the household, including Suzanne's daughter Maria, around a large mahogany table.

"Maria, can you say grace, darling?" Suzanne took the hands of those next to her and the rest of the group followed suit. Dorothy watched Jorge brace himself for a blast of Baptist piety.

"Oh Lord, bless the food around this table and the people we eat. Amen." Dorothy felt Terri squeeze her hand in lieu of embarrassing Maria with a snort of laughter.

"Uh, Maria," Suzanne gently corrected her when the giggles died down, "it's the people around the table and the *food* we eat."

"Okay, momma."

"We'll save that one for the next time we're entertaining cannibals."

"Okay, momma."

To Dorothy's way of thinking, the dinner was a huge success. She was constantly reminded of the old Frank Capra movie *You Can't Take It With You*, which portrayed a motley group of eccentrics sheltered together in the same house during the Depression. One can almost forget George Bush is President, she thought as the conversation rollicked along. At first, Jorge had been reticent to join in, but once he determined that this was no stodgy suburban household, he felt free to add his acerbic wit to the mix of opinions blowing about the room. She decided that she liked Terri's handsome friend. And after a third glass of wine, she found herself hoping that he might get more serious about Terri, because despite his pretensions, Jorge was as middle class as Beaver Cleaver, and just as likely to fall in love with a green-eyed blond girl whose smile lit up the room.

"How hard do you think it would be for me to find a job with a good dentist here in Clarkeston?" She directed her question to Suzanne and Dorothy both.

"I don't think it would be too hard," Suzanne answered, "but I don't know if there's some sort of certification process that you need to go through."

"Actually, I could check on that tomorrow." Arthur pushed himself back from the table and patted his stomach appreciatively. "That was an excellent meal, ladies. Why don't you all retire to the porch for brandy and cigars while I clean up the dishes?"

"Here, let me help," Jorge offered as he stood up and gathered his plate and Suzanne's from the table.

"Thanks, Jorge, but let me get those," Arthur said. "You bring out a new bottle of wine and some glasses for the women, for, alas, we have neither brandy, nor cigars, to offer."

"Are you ever going to remember that I'm not drinking?" Suzanne admonished Arthur. "Give me those plates and come help me make some decaf."

Terri and Jorge left the dining room together and walked slowly down the hall to the front door as he admired the stately lines of the old

71

house. Although the paint was peeling in places, the wood floor was polished to a golden glow, and distinctive wainscoting and ornate crown molding framed the hallway and the four spacious rooms on the first floor. "The top floor is the mirror image of this one," Terri explained, "and there's an old summer kitchen off the porch out back."

"What a great old house," he replied with genuine appreciation. The charm of Suzanne's home seeped into the bones of everyone who walked through the front door. He turned and faced Terri with a questioning look in his eyes, "A great house for a party, *ojos verdes*."

"*Ojos verdes*? Green eyes? I suppose that's a better nickname than *culo grande*." She returned his smile with a flick of her hair and suddenly grasped his train of thought. "Are you suggesting having a Friday party here someday? Suzanne loves to have guests, and Arthur's Spanish is better than mine. Hey, Maria fits in on the basis of her name alone! You could be the official host . . . what do you think?"

"I think your idea has definite possibilities."

"Come on. Let's sit outside before Arthur changes his mind and makes us wash the dishes." She pushed the sticky door shut behind them and led him over to the porch swing. He sat down first and laid his arm over the back of the wide wooden swing, as if to dare her to sit next to him rather than on the rocking chair that also faced the street. She slid beside him without hesitation. As they settled in, Dorothy moved from the dining room into the front room to study the extensive collection of china cups and saucers displayed on an antique breakfront. With the blinds closed, she could hear everything the young couple said. She assuaged her sense of shame by promising herself to leave if she heard anything too embarrassing.

"Well, I hope we weren't too puritanical for you tonight," Terri said with an exaggerated sigh.

"No, not at all. In fact, if I hadn't seen your black frocks in the closet and that picture of Miles Standish in the bathroom, I never would have guessed how strict you all are."

"You know, for someone who's so judgmental, you sure have a good sense of humor."

"Me? Judgmental? I'm the most laid back guy you've ever met."

"Yeah, and the least sarcastic too! And you're about as laid back as Generalissimo Franco . . . or should I say Fidel Castro? But maybe it's too dangerous for a member of the colonizing class to bring up the subject of politics?" Dorothy wondered for a moment if Terri was going too far with her teasing, but Jorge sighed and surprised her by responding seriously to the question.

72

"It's always dangerous to ask a Cuban about politics, but maybe I'm an exception. As you can imagine, my parents are totally anti-Castro. They had to leave their whole lives behind in '63. But they were so fanatical about their politics when I was a kid that I naturally drifted over to the left when I was in high school." He laughed. "That was my rebellious phase. Instead of smoking dope or drinking, I pretended to be a Communist with some of my friends. It took me quite a while to figure out how naive we were and to see that we were just driven by the need to piss off our parents."

"And then you confessed to your folks and joined the Republican Party."

"No. In my pinko phase I learned about some of the good things Castro did, so I was still really turned off by my parents' crazy ideas."

"Aha! So, you've become a pragmatic Midwestern moderate."

He laughed. "My parents left Cuba with their education and not much else. They scraped around for the first few years in Miami, but they always thought of themselves as solid middle-class citizens. Once they had secured a good living and a nice house, they never looked back. They made sure my sister and I had the best education money could buy, and we always wore nice clothes and drove new cars. They could see that learning English was the key to getting ahead, so that's all they spoke at home when we were growing up.

"But there was one little flaw in their plan--they brought my grandfather and grandmother along with them. You see, *Abuelito* and *Abuelita* lived with us and never had any desire to learn English or to fit into the American world. They only ate at Cuban restaurants and only went to the Spanish services at church. They watched all the crazy Latin soap operas on the Spanish television channel and taught my sister and me to speak just like we'd been brought up on the island. Most of all, they never forgot where they were from and they never stopped dreaming about going back."

There was a pause; a breeze quietly rattled the window blinds. "To sort of answer your question, I'm probably more like my grandfather than my father."

"Have you ever written about all of this stuff?"

"Huh?"

"I mean, it sounds like Miami is filled with quite a cast of characters. Have you ever thought to write any stories about them?"

"I translated some of my grandfather's stories when I was in high school, but everybody thinks they're writers, don't they?" He deflected her question, putting his empty cup on the gray slats of the porch floor.

73

"What about you?  What are you going to do?  Are people's teeth dirtier down here, do you suppose?"

"I don't know where I want to be or what I want to do right now," she laughed, "but it's the most wonderful feeling I've had in a long time." Her laughter went right to Dorothy's heart; she wondered if it did the same to Jorge. "You're a bad influence, though.  If I hang around with you too much longer, I'm not sure I'll ever be able to go back to puritanism."

Silence followed Terri's admission, and Dorothy strained to hear something that might have been the sound of a kiss.

"Terri, telephone!  It's your mom."  Dorothy started as Suzanne yelled down the hallway of the house.  She took four quick steps into the dining room and began gathering plates to take into the kitchen.  Terri entered the house with a blush made all the worse by the fact that she knew she could not hide it.  She slipped into Suzanne's room to take the call.  It was a long talk, and when she emerged, she found everyone gathered on the porch except Jorge.

"Where'd Jorge go?"

"He said he had a lot of homework to do and asked us to remind you that the party on Friday is at Emilio's."  Suzanne glided back in the swing and gave her a knowing look.  "He seems to be a very nice boy.  I think he likes you."

Terri turned bright red.  "What makes you say that?"

"Oh I don't know, but sometimes I think that I can hear this old swing talk to me."

## 12

### Louis

When Ludwig opened his eyes, he did not recognize where he was. Instead of waking to the heavy brocade curtains and dark lacquered furniture of his apartment in Vienna, he found himself on a soft divan facing a strange black device backlit by the sun's glare on a closed window shade. He blinked hard and stared at the unfamiliar surroundings. Then he blinked again. Nothing changed. He slowly sat up and pushed the debris from his resting place. *Mein Gott*, this place is filthy, he thought. They say Mozart lived like this, in total squalor, moldy bread and manuscripts everywhere. No wonder he died so young.

At first, he assumed that a bout of heavy drinking had landed him in the unfamiliar room, but the closer he inspected the place, the more confused and suspicious he became. If he was drunk last night, why didn't he have a headache this morning? Everything about the room was odd. The carpet completely covered the floor from wall to wall, except where it met a dingy covering that looked like marble at first, but was scuffed and pitted in a way that marble could not be. The table in front of the sofa was covered with scratches that marred its shiny surface, but did not extend to the wood beneath it. Upon the table lay the thickest newspaper that he had ever seen, at least twenty-five pages of print. The headline--*New Student Council Elected*--meant nothing to him, but the date in the corner of the publication took his breath away: October 10, 1989. I'm dreaming, he decided, I've eaten too much spicy wurst and read too many of E.T.A Hoffman's fantasy tales. Dreaming and time-traveling--this is all Hoffman's fault!

Shaken, he got up from the sofa and walked across the room to the black device to inspect a red light flashing next to the edge of a dark, delicately grooved platter. The whole room was strange. The lamp by the divan had no visible source of oil and the furnishings were of a strange style, maybe Turkish or Persian, but it was the odd red light behind the tiny glass square that captivated him. Perhaps a tiny candle burned inside the box, for there was no other way to explain the light. Checking to see if the bit of glass was warm, he pushed it and took a startled step backward when the platter began to spin and a crooked rod swept down toward its top. What happened next drove him backward in wonder and fear.

Music, HIS MUSIC, streamed forth from the two boxes on either side of the device. His Fifth Symphony pounded him against the back of the divan with eyes wide as he recognized the familiar motives of the opening section and realized with a start that his hearing was somehow miraculously restored. The strings were clear, not muffled, every cut-off was crisp, and the horns sounded distinctly above the violins and cellos. *Gott im Himmel*, he thought, I must be dreaming! Or dead and condemned to listen to my own music for eternity. This is like some horrible story Hoffman might think up. His fascination got the better of him as the music continued. But this is wonderful, he decided. This is not hellish: Hell would be listening to Schubert for eternity. When I wake up, I'll write Hoffman about this. He won't believe it, not even in a dream.

The sound stopped after the first movement, and a piano concerto began. Amazing! The pianist plays well, he thought, although he's taking the adagio section too fast. No matter, his technique is wonderful. And the instrument is unlike any I've heard before; it's singing out each note with such fullness and clarity. He closed his eyes and listened until the record finished. When the slight hiss from the speakers ended abruptly and the tone arm moved back, he opened his eyes and approached the turntable. He carefully picked up the disk and noticed the writing on the center label. The music is somehow trapped on these disks, he thought.

"Classics of Western Music," he read aloud. Classic? That's an odd way to describe music. Then he noticed that the design on the label matched a box holding more disks lying on the floor. The box contained the same title in large letters and nine more disks numbered consecutively. The disk in his hand was #4 and was clearly labeled: *1. Beethoven, Fifth Symphony (First Movement) 2. Piano Concerto #5 in E flat (The Emperor)*. He flipped through the disks and saw his name again and young Schubert's on disk #6. Other vaguely familiar names appeared on disk #7, along with someone named Mendelssohn. The names Chopin, Liszt, Debussy, Dvorak, Mahler, Schoenberg, and Webern meant nothing to him. He read the back of the box carefully, guessing the collection was meant for educational purposes. For school children in the next century, if the dates on the box were to be believed! When I wake up, I'll make Hoffman pay me a year's wages for this story.

He examined the disk more closely, looking at the grooves as if to see whether the music was somehow visible on its face. When he turned it over, he noticed that there were more grooves and a different label. *Side Two: Beethoven, Ninth Symphony (Fourth Movement).* Ninth Symphony? I suppose I'm honored to be the subject of study by magicians who can make music play from boxes with no performers, he thought, but they could at least number my works properly. I've written eight symphonies, only eight . . . As his hands started to shake, he flipped the disk over and put it back on the device, struggling momentarily to match the hole in its center to the metal knob protruding from the top of the platter. He pushed the red flashing button and fell back down on the divan.

At first he was simply mesmerized by what he was hearing. Then, as he began to realize what would grow from a few measures of notes hastily scrawled on the back of an envelope lying on his desk in Vienna, he opened himself to the revelation that could only show itself in the hot tears streaming down his face. When the final triumphant chord sounded, he sat still for a long time, body still reverberating with the music. Hoffman, my friend, you shall not have this story. It's mine, and I shall write it in strings and horn and timpani in such a way that the world will remember it forever.

When he finally stood up, he realized he was thirsty but could find no water pitcher. He saw an opaque cup filled with a brown fluid on the table in front of the divan and picked it up with suspicion. The container was soft in his hands, as if it were made of paper coated with some sort of paraffin. "Burger King," he read aloud. How can a burgher, a staunch member of the bourgeoisie, be a king? He sniffed the cup. The odor was vaguely sweet. He took a sip and swished the fluid around in his mouth. Not too bad. He rapidly gulped down the rest of the large cup and felt his hunger subside as his toes began tapping restlessly in his shoes. He wanted to move, but he was afraid to go out, especially after a peek through the window blinds revealed a scene that resembled no place in Vienna that he knew.

I'll just stay here, he decided, and listen to some more music. One probably shouldn't travel in a dream anyway. I might sleepwalk right out my window. So he decided to give himself a musical education up through this fellow Webern, the last piece listed on the box, whose selected composition had been written almost one hundred years after Ludwig's last. He sat for hours, playing disk after disk, moving only to keep fresh music on the platter. When he finished, he was far more frightened than when he began.

The form and texture of the music had been familiar up through the end of the nineteenth century. Although the last composers of that era were bolder in their dissonances and more comfortable with tonal ambiguity than he, he understood the medium in which they were working. Mahler and Wagner were recognizable, and he envied them the tolerant audiences they must have been writing for. Bach did some outlandish things in his day too, he reminded himself. An audience can sometimes be bent to the will of a good composer, but it must be ready to hear the message. When he got past Mahler, however, to Schoenberg, Berg, and Webern, he realized something must have gone horribly wrong for the center of music to have crumbled so completely.

What had happened to the world that people needed to hear this kind of music? He was not judgmental of what he heard in an aesthetic sense. It was not that he found it ugly: He simply could not fathom what had happened in a society that expressed itself in this way. He could not imagine what had crumbled in the center of Germany to prompt the creation of these pieces. If mankind had lost its soul, then he truly dreaded setting foot outside his fetid hiding place. Nevertheless, he was curious to know more, and he searched through other disks lying side by side on a shelf underneath the black music machine. The disks would have to serve as a history book if he wanted to understand what went wrong with the world as humans began to mark their years with the number nineteen. He looked for pieces composed around the turn of century and was soon captivated by the colorful abstract painting on the cover of a recording of Stravinsky's *Rite of Spring*. If this is twentieth century art, he thought, then the painters have gone as mad as the musicians.

He put the disk on the platter and pushed the button to learn what was going on in 1913. Stravinsky's music was more tonal than Webern's and Berg's, but its violent undertow was radically more pronounced and he found he could not sit still as the primitive drumbeat and cascading strings followed the oboes and bassoons down a path he could not believe mankind had been willing to travel. It was beautiful, but the savagery with which it laid bare the human soul left him shaken and sweating profusely. He had trouble getting along with the world. People had never understood him, and he had never understood them. But even in his most pessimistic moments he had never felt so lost and alone. *What could have happened? There is darkness in me; I see it in others too. Did mankind's dark side swallow the rest?* He stood up in a daze and prepared to leave the apartment, ready to die, ready to walk into the dark heart of modern man.

He grabbed a long, tan coat that lay over the arm of the divan and wrapped it tightly around himself. Seeing nothing resembling a weapon that he could take with him, he opened the door, trudged down the narrow stairs and stood in the vestibule looking out into the street. Metal carriages lined both sides of the broad avenue. While he was puzzling over how a horse could be hitched to such a contraption, two carriages traveling far faster than any horse passed each other in the street. He turned quickly to go back up the stairs, but as he spun, he bumped into a young woman who excused herself with a smile and pushed past him. He stared at her as she walked down the sidewalk, utterly unafraid, and utterly shameless in a skirt that revealed all of her ankle and even some of her calf! Curiosity finally triumphed over terror, and he left the building, following her down the sidewalk.

He walked slowly for a couple of blocks, unwilling to keep pace with the girl, lest he be accused of accosting her. When she crossed a busy intersection ahead, he turned down a side street in order to avoid a confrontation with the endless stream of carriages she miraculously passed through. He walked a long time, in an ever twisting pattern to avoid the main arteries of traffic. He finally found himself in a neighborhood of huge wooden houses standing in neat rows on quiet, tree-lined avenues.

It was early afternoon, and the streets were quiet, except for music playing faintly in a large white house a dozen paces away. When he walked to the front of the house and investigated the broad shaded porch wrapped around three of its sides, the music faded to silence. But before he turned to go, the low tolling of a bell echoed out of the house and then a storm of sound swept out of the open windows like a wind whipping through the headstones of a country graveyard. Just as he was about to run for his life, the wind faded and an organ began playing mournfully, slowly making its way through and finally dispelling the elemental forces of the beginning of the song. Then, the tempo changed and the organ was replaced by a piano, developing the original melody and building on it. He recognized the familiar contours of sonata form and the predictable, but nonetheless pleasing, key changes the composer ran through.

Fascinated, and curious as to the source of the music, he walked up to the porch and sat down on the top step, facing the street and ready to leap down if the owner of the house were to object to his perching there. He listened until the music thrust before him a life that he could hardly recognize. Sadness and terror overwhelmed him as he stood outside himself, within himself, surrounded by all the contingencies that had brought him to this shady stoop. He stared panic-stricken and paralyzed, memories of people and the violence of their words all flickering in the theater of his mind.

As the strange sonata wound down toward what might have been a logical endpoint, a voice began singing passionately:

79

*The roses in the window box*
*Have tilted to one side*
*Everything about this house*
*Was born to grow and die*

*Oh it doesn't seem a year ago*
*To this very day*
*You said I'm sorry honey*
*If I don't change the pace*
*I can't face another day*

*And love lies bleeding in my hand ...*

As the song continued, a lifetime of memories poured back in. A life that made no sense from the inside made terrifying viewing from the outside. For the first time he caught a true glimpse of his parents, the vastness of their neglect and cruelty, the years of isolation, the possibility of escape . . . then the song ended and he heard the door open behind him.

"Excuse me, may I help you." It was a woman's voice, worried and hesitant, but kind.

The gentleness in her tone kept him from bolting. He turned and looked over his shoulder. A tall, dark-haired woman stood just outside the entrance to the house. A little girl stood behind the oaken door, peering through the pane of glass in its center. "I'm sorry," he managed to blurt out with superhuman effort, "I was just listening to the music."

He was a pathetic sight, wrapped in his filthy trench coat, hunched on the top step and clearly disoriented. Calling the police would have been a reasonable thing to do, especially with her daughter home, but the woman sensed little danger in the figure before her.

"Do you live in the neighborhood?"

"No."

"Where do you live?"

"I'm not sure." She had expected him to tell her the name of the homeless shelter, or maybe the Salvation Army, but she did not expect him to be completely lost. He was obviously disturbed, but she stayed on the porch and talked to him. It was a gift of love like none bestowed on him before. "Do you listen to a lot of Elton John?"

"Who is he?"

"He wrote and played and sang the song you were listening to. It's called *Funeral for a Friend*."

He thought about the modern music he had heard earlier in the day. "It's not new music, is it?"

"No, it's an oldy," she replied, still standing behind him and to the side.

He was pleased to guess that the sonata and song he liked must have been written before Schoenberg and Stravinsky. The instrumentation was strange, but it was more traditionally tonal than the excerpts he had heard from that Wagner fellow who had worked at the end of his own century. "When was it written?"

She waved her daughter back inside the house and motioned for her to lock the door. Then she sat down on the step next to him. "Oh, I don't know, about ten years ago, I guess."

That can't be, Ludwig thought to himself, but suddenly Louis knew better. The music had taught him that much; playing for the choir had brought him at least that far. And Louis sensed deep in his own heart that admitting his fantasy was not enough, so he did something that he had learned as a small child never to do--he turned to the woman and looked in her eyes. Perhaps in that instant he was saved, but he had no words to express himself. He searched her face for clues and then followed the thick cascade of her hair down to the huge expanse of her belly.

"What's your name?" She drew his eyes back to hers.

A breeze rustled the leaves over their heads and he turned away, his forehead leaning onto his arm-encircled knees. "Sometimes I'm not really sure."

She waited for more, but he was silent. "Do you want me to call someone who can help you?"

Maybe that's why I'm here, he thought. Maybe that's why I'm hearing old music with new ears and new music with old. He closed his eyes and nodded gently to her.

## 13

**Regrets (Part II)**

"Evan, do you have a moment?" Gordon Samuels phoned Evan at home on a late Friday afternoon. He looked over the streets of New York City as he spoke to his former student. Although it was late September, a warm spell left Manhattan a sticky smudge on his window.

"Professor Samuels? Sure, what can I do for you?"

"Nothing. But I might be in the position to do something for you, if you want me to. I just got a call from the search committee up at Syracuse School of Music asking me to recommend someone for an opening they have coming up. You'd be perfect for the job, but I hesitated to push you without knowing whether you'd consider moving." He paused. "You mentioned the last time we talked that you were less than happy in Georgia, so I thought I'd touch base with you."

"Georgia's less the problem than your old friend Dorothy Henderson. Without her, it wouldn't be that bad down here and John really likes it, but when your only real colleague is barely speaking to you . . . it's kinda tough."

"What happened?"

"Let's just say I think she's interfering with one of my choirs. When I confronted her, we had sort of a blowout."

"Evan," Gordon said patiently, "do I have to remind you that one day she will be voting on your tenure?"

"Not if you get me a job at Syracuse."

"I see." Gordon tried to imagine Dorothy and Evan on the same faculty. In many ways they were a lot alike: brilliant, intimidating, impatient, pig-headed, and passionate. Most of all, passionate. He wondered how Dorothy found any outlet for her passion in a small town like Clarkeston. Maybe by bullying younger colleagues? "I'll certainly put you on Syracuse's radar screen then."

"Thanks. I'd appreciate that."

"Would you like me to call her?" Gordon asked impulsively, realizing immediately after he spoke that it would only make things worse.

"No, that's okay. Let's let sleeping dragons lie for now." Evan thanked him for the help and rang off, leaving Gordon to ponder his motivations for offering to talk to Dorothy.

He wondered why thinking about her was so difficult, why it left him feeling hollow and incomplete. Professionally, he could not rise any higher. He taught brilliant students at the finest music school in the country and directed world-class choirs in New York's most famous venues. His personal life was satisfying too. Although he had been divorced for ten years, he was involved with a beautiful graduate student in the violin department. He maintained a close relationship with his daughters who were accomplished musicians in their own rights.

The simple answer, he supposed, was that he was still in love with her, but the feeling of emptiness went further than romance-denied. It called into question every important choice he had made since they parted. It cast into bold relief the boredom he sometimes felt at the podium and in the bedroom.

He stared out at the city's swelter and wandered back thirty years into the chill of a winter storm.

* * *

A week before Christmas, leaden flakes of snow began to plummet onto the slick, black streets of Urbana. Having handed in his paper minutes before the University closed for the holidays, Gordon trudged back across campus to his apartment. By the time he turned onto his street, he was wondering whether he would be able to drive safely back to his parents' house in Chicago. The wind was pushing the precipitation against the cars in waist-high slopes, and even areas that showed no sign of drifting were covered with eight to ten inches of new snow. Resolving to call the state highway patrol before he left, he stamped his feet on the steps of his apartment building and entered its tiny vestibule with eyes cast downward to check how much slush he was tracking in.

"Hello!" A voice sounded cheerfully above him. "I was beginning to wonder if you were ever going to get back." Gordon jerked his head up and was met by the sight of Dorothy peering over the top of a paperback book, seated comfortably near the top of the stairs that emptied into the vestibule.

"What are you doing here?"

83

"Waiting for you to give me a ride to Chicago, of course." She smiled and offered no further explanation, content to enjoy the look of confusion on Gordon's face. He took out his keys and checked his mail while he regained his composure.

"Come on upstairs and tell me what's going on," he finally said. She popped to her feet, revealing a heavy, leather suitcase behind her. "Lemme grab that . . . I'm on the third floor, on the right."

She explained her predicament as they climbed. "My bus got canceled because of this wretched weather, and there's no train, unless you want to go down to New Orleans and then back over and up to Atlanta. Since the grad dorms just closed for the holidays, I'm stuck in this godforsaken place with no means of escape."

He expressed his sympathy as he struggled with the lock of his apartment door. "Don't be grossed out by the mess in here, I was gonna clean up all my crap before I left today." He entered first and grimaced as he saw the place through the fresh eyes of his visitor. "Try not to trip over anything."

In the middle of the apartment stood a chipped formica table covered with the remnants of his all-nighter, a typewriter, crumpled papers, empty coffee cups, a crumb-covered plate, pencils, and his toothbrush. Other furniture seemed to be used primarily for hanging dirty laundry, but the number of shirts and underwear strewn on the floor, the sofa, and other chairs proved they were not very effective clothes racks. He asked Dorothy to make them some coffee while he spent three minutes throwing the rankest of his clothes into his bedroom and opening up the window shades in the hope that the snow-refracted light would penetrate the gloom of his abode.

"Where's the coffee?" She made a face at the sticky paper lining the cabinets of his kitchenette.

"In the freezer."

"Where's the pot?" She cast a fearful glance at the heap of moldering dishes piled in the sink.

"In the stove."

"Why is it in the stove?"

"That's where I keep it warm." He emerged from his bedroom and pulled out a battered, ceramic-coated coffee pot from the stove. "When I turn my burners low, they go out, so I keep the coffee nice and toasty in the oven . . . here, let me do this. Sit down and explain why you need me to take you to Chicago."

She removed a bowl of mashed potatoes from the cleanest chair, brushed the seat off with her mitten and sat down. "When I found out that

84

no buses are leaving town, I called up Midway Airport in Chicago to see if it was still open. The snow's drier up there, and the guy I talked to thought they could keep it plowed long enough for the evening flight to Atlanta to take off. I remembered you saying that you were going home today, so I didn't think it would be too huge a favor to ask you to give me a lift." He nodded.

When the coffee pot was loaded up and put on the stove, Gordon turned around and took a long look at his guest. Her hat and mittens were off, but she still wore her coat, and its felt collar framed her winter blush. Her dark eyes shone and her hair glistened with melted snow. She was calm about her plight and regarded him with at least as much curiosity as he did her. If Audrey and Katherine Hepburn had been sisters, she would have made an intriguing third sibling.

"I'd love to give you a ride." He felt some of his nervousness subside when he realized he was in a position to do her a good turn, "but let's call the state police first. We don't want to get out on the highway and find that the roads to Chicago are all closed." He handed her a cup and pushed the sugar bowl toward her. Apologizing for the lack of uncurdled milk, he went back down to the apartment entryway to use the pay phone. When he got back a few minutes later, he thanked her for cleaning off the table and delivered bad news about the weather. "The state police told me to stay home. Chicago itself is not in too bad shape, but they say that the winds whipping around in between here and there have drifted the snow so high that cars can't get through."

"Shit."

"Miss Dorothy, I'm shocked!"

"Expressing myself forcefully is a trait I picked up in New Jersey," she explained and then paused for a moment. "No, I learned forcefulness from my father--it's just the profanity that I learned up north."

He sat down across the table from her and warmed his fingers around his mug. "The good news is that the Illinois Central train to downtown Chicago leaves here in an hour and should get you there in time to catch a cab to Midway." He basked for a moment in the look of appreciation with which she rewarded his initiative. "Let's finish our coffee and get over to the station before the streets get even worse."

Gordon put on his coat and carried Dorothy's heavy suitcase down to his car. Lacking any implement to dig with, they scuffled around the vehicle and kicked away as much snow as they could from the tires. The passenger's side door could not be opened until the drift leaning against it had been knocked down. The motor rewarded their work by turning over on the first crank. By gently rocking the car backward and forward,

Gordon was able to jerk out into the street and slowly crunch his way toward the main road that led to the train station. As he approached the turn, he noticed that a city plow had created a barrier ridge of snow at the end of his street.

"Any cars coming down Green Street in either direction?" He accelerated slightly.

"No. All clear."

"Then hang on." As they thumped into the fender-high wall of snow the car rose up slightly and the chassis scraped in protest over the pile before it slipped down onto the street. The Rambler fishtailed dramatically, but he resisted the temptation to brake and was soon guiding the car along a relatively straight line.

"Nice driving, Gordon!" She slapped him excitedly on the shoulder. He shrugged off the compliment and concentrated on piloting the car through downtown Urbana, scanning the roadway for the next obstacle that might cross his path. He noted with relief that the streets were nearly deserted.

"It's still a good bit to the station, but if the street's been plowed all the way, we should make it." As he spoke, he saw the light a block ahead turn green and watched a large Ford struggle to accelerate through the slippery intersection. Gordon braked slightly as he started rolling downhill toward the car and discovered that his balding tires gained no traction in the slippery snow.

"Get moving," he urged the Ford as he quickly weighed his options. An oncoming snowplow prevented him from passing the stalled sedan on the left, so when it became clear that the Ford would not make it through the intersection without an unwelcome boost from Gordon's Rambler, he took his foot off the useless brake pedal and veered over the curb around the right side of the car. He managed to miss the last parking meter, but when he bounced over the edge of the far curb, he lost the ability to steer the car and watched helplessly as it slid sideways across the street and toward a drug store parking lot. It entered the lot and the car suddenly straightened as the left rear tire bounced against another curb and was kicked toward a huge pile of snow plowed up against the store. When all attempts to steer or brake failed, Gordon and Dorothy desperately braced their arms against the wheel and dashboard. The car entered the pile with a sick scrunch, completely covering the windshield with dirty clods of snow and ice crystals, but sparing its occupants of any injury worse than Gordon's split lip.

"Gordon, that was fabulous!" Dorothy's eyes were bright with excitement. "That's the most fun I've had since I got here!" Her exuberance momentarily turned to concern as she saw the trickle of blood on his lip, but the questioning look on his face told her that he was not seriously hurt. "Good driving, darling," she said, giving him an impulsive peck on the right cheek. "How's your lip?"

"Uh . . . it's okay . . . Are you sure you're alright?"

"Absolutely," she exclaimed. "Never better!"

He let out a long sigh that fogged up his side of the windshield and tried to crank the car, but the engine would not turn over. Suddenly bone-tired and at a loss for ideas on how to proceed, he turned to ask Dorothy if she had any suggestions. When he saw the improbable smile still pasted to her face, he reluctantly volunteered to help her attempt the railway station on foot. "Let's get your suitcase out and see if we can hoof it to the station on time. It's only about ten blocks from here."

"Do you really think we can make it?"

"Not if we keep sitting here." He got out of the car, pausing for a moment to evaluate the damage done to its front end before pulling her bulging suitcase from the trunk. The wind stung his face as he trudged ahead of her through snow that in places drifted across the sidewalk at knee level. When she saw how he was struggling, she jumped in front and shuffled ahead to break the worst of the accumulation for him. Even so, he was exhausted by the time they were halfway there, forced by the weight of her suitcase and his lack of gloves to switch hands three of four times every block. Their conversation was reduced to an increasingly emphatic series of *thank you*'s on her part and an increasingly weary series of responsive grunts on his.

Although it was still early afternoon, the streetlights could not dispel the low-ceilinged gloom cast by the storm front that was dumping snow over the entire Midwest. The eerie, not-quite-day, not-quite-night glow complemented Gordon's mood as he slogged head down, eyes squinting against the wind. He drove himself on through sheer bloody-mindedness, a modern Sisyphus hopelessly toting luggage instead of rolling a boulder. With half a block to go, hands chafed, back and shoulders aching, shoes and socks soaked with melted snow, he sent Dorothy on ahead to purchase her ticket while he finished the last torturous stretch alone. When he arrived at last to the top of the station steps, he learned that his fate was, in fact, much the same as his Greek forbearer's.

"I'm really sorry, Gordon," she said sympathetically. "The train's just left." Too tired to curse their luck, he dragged the suitcase into the waiting room and sat down. She plopped down next to him, leaning against him and emitting a long sigh.

"Looks like you're stuck here for a while."

"Well, maybe the buses will start running again tomorrow or the next day," she responded optimistically. They looked out the window at the snow cascading against the yellow backdrop of the parking lot lamps. "But then again, maybe not."

"If you need somewhere to stay, you could camp out at my place tonight." The innocence of his suggestion was evident from the fatigue in his voice. "You can take the bed, and I'll sleep on the couch."

"That's awfully sweet of you, but maybe I should check out the Sagamore Hotel on the way back to see if they've got a room."

"Good idea, I just thought I'd offer, in case you're short of money or they're full up or something."

"Well, it's nice to know that I've got options . . . now, let's go back outside and try out a new method of lugging that suitcase." Before he could reply or convince his cramped muscles to lift him off the bench, she grabbed the suitcase and disappeared out the door. By the time he forced himself back out into the storm, she was standing at the edge of the steps with the suitcase tilted up under her right hand.

"Behold the suitcase toboggan," she cried as she pushed the slippery piece of luggage down the steps at a speed that took it a good fifteen feet onto the sidewalk. "Now, take your belt off." She bounded down to her parcel and as he went to meet her, she tied her scarf around the handle. Guessing her intention, he passed his belt through the grip so that they could pull the suitcase in tandem like a sled.

"Much easier than toting it, don't you think?"

"It sure is, but aren't you afraid we'll ruin it?"

"Probably, but Daddy'll buy me a new one."

Pulling half of the suitcase was far easier than carrying all of it, and Gordon eventually began to see the humor in the ridiculous spectacle they presented. They had the sidewalk to themselves as they blazed a broad trail over the hummocks and valleys of the snowswept avenue. An occasional car crept carefully past, but mostly they were alone in a white-speckled, gray-yellow, acoustically dampened world of their own. The unreal tableau appealed to something deep inside him.

"*I'm singing in the snow, just singing in the snow.*" His mellifluent baritone did not carry far, bouncing dead off the sound-eating precipitation, but the lightness of his voice and his soggy dance steps elicited a string of giggles from Dorothy. Exhaustion and absurdity converted the awkward boy who had been such a painful date three months before into someone quite attractive. He continued, holding the belt over his head and pirouetting underneath it. "*What a glorious feeling, my car will be towed . . ."* He improvised a few more lines to the accompaniment of her laughter and then paused dramatically at the top of the gentle incline that led down to the intersection where Gordon's car still lay embedded in a drift.

"Would you care to rest your feet, Milady?"

"What are you talking about?"

"Seat thyself on yon chariot, and I'll pull you down yonder valley."

"You're crazy," she replied, but she sat down cross-legged on top of the suitcase and rocked forward to help budge the makeshift sled. When he finally got them going down the slope, he pulled harder and harder until the suitcase was sliding swiftly along beside him."Don't pull me into the street!" she shrieked, and in response he jerked back on the belt and scarf and sent her spinning off of the suitcase, sliding on her back down the sidewalk until she came to rest against a small drift. "Daddy, Daddy, can we do that again?" she squealed as he strode over to help her up.

"I'd love to, but that's the only hill in the whole town, and I'm not climbing back up it." He brushed the snow off the back of her coat before they resumed their march through town.

"Look, Gordon!" she pointed down the street, "the dining room at the Sagamore is still open! Let me treat you to some dinner for everything you've done today." This was such an unexpected and sensible request that he did not protest her offer to pay until his soggy feet and empty stomach had already propelled him into the brightly lit restaurant.

Although it was early, business was brisk with salesmen and travelers who found themselves stranded in town for the night. The hostess found them a table for two tucked back in a corner and handed them menus with a warning that none of the seafood items were available that evening. Before Gordon opened his, he leaned back with a long sigh and drank in the oak and black leather ambience of the city's most popular restaurant. After a semester intensely focused on his studies, the serendipity of finding himself in a cozy spot with a pretty girl while the worst storm of the decade roared outside put a grin on his face that he could not wipe off.

"What are you smirking at?" Dorothy asked with a smile of her own, but the waitress arrived and demanded their orders before he could respond.

"White wine?" She nodded and scanned the menu while he tried to find out something about the house wine from the unhelpful server.

"I'll have the fettuccine Alfredo," she said after a moment.

"Me too." Gordon handed the unopened menu back to the waitress who turned smartly, and moments later returned with the wine.

"Here's to snow," Dorothy said as she raised her glass.

"To snow!"

"Are your parents going to be horribly disappointed not to see you tonight, Gordon?"

"I doubt it," he answered matter-of-factly. "I've got two older brothers and an older sister, and with all my nieces and nephews running around the house, they probably won't even notice I'm not there. As long as I can make it home by Christmas morning, they'll be okay . . . What about you?"

"Although you'd never guess it from my selfless demeanor, I'm an only child. So yes, Mummy and Daddy will be very upset not to see their little girl step off the Greyhound bus tomorrow." She was suddenly serious. "Which reminds me that I should call tonight to let them know I've been delayed . . . You know, you really were very sweet to take me to the station."

"Well, how else was I going to spend my afternoon? Cleaning my apartment? You saved me from a horrible fate. And to tell you the truth, the less time I spend with my parents the better. You're a lot better company than they are."

"That's not a very respectful thing to say. They don't beat you, do they?" Every time Dorothy smiled, Gordon felt a rush of the same feelings she had stirred in him the first time they had lunch together. She pulled him deeply into her eyes, and he inched his chair toward the table to be closer to her. Fortunately for him, the wine bottle was also close by, and he used it strategically to erase the self-consciousness he felt when he wanted desperately to impress someone.

"Nothing like that." He poured them both another glass. "My father just doesn't understand why I want to get another worthless music degree. He grew up in the city and was a tool-and-die maker until he started up his own shop in the north suburbs about twenty years ago. He's been really successful and thinks education is great, but he doesn't understand why anyone would want to go to college to learn something other than business or engineering. To give you an idea of his opinion of musicians," he lowered his voice, "I once overheard him tell my mother that he thought I might be a homo."

"Well," she laughed at Gordon's conspiratorial tone, "I'll just have to call him up and tell him that you're one of the manliest men in the Music School."

"Is that like being the most feminine shot putter on the women's track team? Seriously, I'd much rather be here eating with you than be under the microscope back home."

"Well, I do miss my parents, but I haven't had an adventure like this in a long time." She topped off their glasses. "To snow!"

"To snow!" He took a sip and when the waitress delivered the steaming plates of pasta to the table, he asked her to bring them another bottle. They were both surprised by their hunger and ate ravenously for several minutes before pausing to wash down their food with the first glasses from the second bottle.

"I never asked you what your father does in Clarkeston."

"He's a lawyer with a general practice. I spent a lot of time at the courthouse when I was a kid." She looked pensively at him. "Someday I'm going to write an opera that takes place in a courtroom. You wouldn't believe the amount of acting and role-playing that goes on during a trial. There are all the elements of opera: anger, tears, laughter. There's jilted lovers, murder, judgment, and retribution all in one room. Finding a plot would be easy . . . all I've got to do is write the libretto and the music."

"But other than that, you're just about done with it," he interjected enthusiastically, prompting another incongruous stream of giggles. When she stopped laughing, he changed the subject. "How did you end up studying in New Jersey? I don't guess that most of your high school friends left the South to go to school."

"You're right, but my father went up to Columbia to get his law degree, and he actually encouraged me to go away if I wanted, which I did." She wiped a drop of wine from the corner of her mouth with her napkin. He nodded and they continued to compare their disparate childhoods as a pleasant, viniferous fog slowly tinged Gordon's world a rosy color.

"I think I'll check with the front desk to see if they have a room tonight," she said during a pause in the conversation.

"Great idea!"

She rolled her eyes at him and walked out of the dining room into the hotel lobby. He finished off the wine, toasting his good fortune and imagining a reprise of their meal, perhaps after a concert when they returned to town. He had barely set down his wineglass when she walked back into the room with a sphinx-like expression on her face.

"I'm afraid I'll have to take you up on your offer to put me up; this place is jammed full of folks stuck in town tonight." She sat down and watched him for signs that he regretted making the offer.

"No problem, but let's get going before the snow gets any deeper."

When they got back to the apartment, senses sharpened after their walk in the cold air, Dorothy excused herself and Gordon furiously picked up the clothes and trash that still littered the place, and unceremoniously tossed them into his bedroom closet. By the time she returned, he was scraping the crust off the dishes filling both basins of the kitchen sink. She turned on the large radio he kept next to the sofa and began helping with the kitchen chores, drying the dishes for him and wiping down the counters while he put away a pile of mismatched glasses, plates, silverware, and bowls. Singing together the familiar Christmas songs played by the local station, they made quick work of the kitchen mess, and when they were finished, stood admiring the sparkling room under the bright fluorescent light.

"Thank you! I haven't seen that counter for a month. I'd forgotten it was such a wonderful shade of puce." He stuck his head momentarily in the fridge. "I'd offer you a soda as a reward, but it looks like I'm totally out."

"That's okay, I'm not much of a soda drinker . . . but I could handle one more glass of wine, if you've got any."

He looked at her curiously, wondering if she was still as fuzzy as he was from the two bottles they had consumed at dinner. "Unfortunately, I don't have any, but the previous tenant did leave this in the cupboard for me." He pulled out a squarish bottle of wine and cradled it in his arms like a rare, nineteenth-century Bordeaux. He read from the label: "Manneschevitz Cherry Wine: Specially Sweetened for Passover." He examined it more closely. "No year of production." He unscrewed the metal cap and waved it under his nose. "Ahhh, but it smells like a very good month indeed. Would you like a mug?"

"Only if you're going to have one," she laughed.

"Ahhhh, it's a saucy little wine, petulant, yet nauseating. A fragrant nose that hints of skunk cabbage, and with a finish like a fine varnish." He swallowed the syrupy nectar with relish and waited for her to try her glass. She studied it for a moment and then took a sip.

"Lord almighty, it tastes like cough syrup!" She gave it another try. "But in a cozy, Christmassy sort of way . . . and speaking of Christmas," she asked, looking over her shoulder into the farthest recesses of his apartment, "you haven't exactly overdone it on the decorations this year."

"Nah, it's sort of a holiday tradition."

"Christmas with no decorations--that's a new tradition."

"Hey, you're the one drinking Passover wine while listening to Christmas carols," he protested good-naturedly. "To make a long story short, my mother is Jewish and my father is a lapsed Catholic. One of the few concessions my father makes is to not put up any decorations during the holidays. I mean, we still exchange gifts and stuff on Christmas morning, but my mom can't tolerate the sight of Christmas stuff around the house."

"How were you raised then?"

"Well, my Dad's mom whisked me off and had me baptized when I was a baby, but my parents never took us to any kind of church. We were mostly raised with a lot of yelling followed by nerve-racking silence." He was still smiling but his tone grew more serious. "I think my parents really do love each other, but I've sure sat through a bunch of dinners where the tension was so thick you could cut it with a knife.."

"Is that why you went into music?"

"What do you mean?"

"To search for universal truths that transcend petty human conflict?" He could not tell whether she was serious or not.

"I never thought about it that way, but it sure sounds more noble than: 'I thought it would be a good way to meet girls.'"

Her smile at him turned into a yawn and she curled her legs up, lay down on the sofa, and put the side of her head in his lap. When his hand brushed the hair away from her face, she smiled again, and he gently stroked the strands that fell from her temple to the nape of her neck. Instead of falling asleep, she listened to him talk about his passion for music and his plans for finding a way to make some of his own. After a long while, he paused to simply enjoy the sensation of her hair between his fingers. "You're really wonderful to listen to me babble like this." She shifted her weight and sat back up, looking deeply into his eyes.

"You've been pretty sweet yourself."

They would argue later over who initiated their first kiss, but it's most likely that they leaned forward at about the same time and gave in to the curiosity that had grown in them both over the course of the day. In any event, once they started, they found it hard to stop and they broke off only to move into the bedroom where Gordon eventually slowed down their foreplay with a firm and somewhat desperate embrace.

"Uh, Dorothy . . . don't get your hopes up too much, 'cause this would be, uh, my first time." He addressed his speech to a spot on the wall over her left shoulder.

"Well, lucky for you, it's not mine." She pushed him slightly away from her so she could read any disappointment on his face. Seeing only relief, she smiled, "Another bad habit I picked up in New Jersey." They fell into the bed with a laugh and seldom left it during the long, snowy weekend that followed.

REHEARSAL

## 14

### A Beginning

Whenever Dorothy felt the massive and invisible vise begin to clamp down on her shoulder, she sank into the nearest chair to avoid being forced to her knees. As the pain faded, she would look around, always surprised to discover that no one had noticed the agony etched on her face. Late afternoons were the hardest. She was tired even before the four-thirty rehearsal began, and even though she had never been a Leonard Bernstein-style arm flapper, the strain of merely holding her right hand above her elbow made her shoulder throb. To make matters worse, on days when she had a morning radiation treatment, she experienced an overwhelming lethargy in addition to the pain.

At the beginning of October, she still felt much like her old self when she took the podium. Adrenalin surged through her as she walked into the chorus room, and her intense focus on the task at hand blocked out much of the pain. On the first day of rehearsal for the Beethoven *Missa Solemnis*, she stood confidently in front of the podium and surveyed her choir. They had performed well in a short concert the last week in September, but she needed to refocus them before they tackled the Beethoven. She waited until the room was completely silent before she spoke.

"I don't care how many wrong notes you sing in practice this October and November."

It had been several years since she had given a variant of this particular opening speech, and she scrutinized the group for their reaction. A couple of the newer girls looked horrified. Arthur Hughes, back with the tenors in the last row, let out a quick laugh, but most of the group seemed intrigued. When they were quiet again, she continued.

"I'm not joking. When I auditioned you all, I had in mind a particular sound that I wanted to hear at our concert in December. I did not choose the best sight readers nor the most gymnastic voices I heard. In fact, several very upset divas are singing with the glee club this fall. What I'm aiming for is a blend of voices that will, if they sing perfectly on pitch, cause me to shiver and melt into a small puddle at the bottom of the podium." She smiled and walked down to stand directly in front of the first row of risers.

"So, in practice, let's pay attention to the sound first and the notes later. The pitches will come, I assure you. And if you're not sure of a note coming up in your score, sing it loud enough so you can hear whether you're wrong or not. Take a chance, and we'll all learn what we need to correct." Several of the new members who had never seen her eyes search the choir for wrong notes nodded enthusiastically. "One bit of advice. Although the world will not end if you sing a B flat instead of a B in practice, it's important that you sing one or the other, not something nasty in between."

To make her point, she did not let them open their scores during the first rehearsal. The group spent the entire ninety minutes warming up their bodies through a variety of stretches, and then their voices by running through an increasingly difficult series of scales and vocal exercises.

When she came home afterward, she poured herself a glass of wine and sank down in the sofa to receive a furry welcome from Beverly, Placido, Kathleen, and Luciano.

"It's going to be good, you guys," she told them, setting her glass down and scratching two cat heads at the same time. "I can already tell. I've never seen a group so focused right at the start."

She realized this was her cue to start sobbing, but she did not feel like giving in. She had always known deep down that the cancer would come back.. She felt lucky to get five more years, lucky to have one more concert left in her. She struggled to push her doubts aside. As long as she could make music, she had the courage to spit in death's eye. But she feared that there would be a time at the end when she would lose it, when she would need help for the first time since she moved back to Clarkeston.

Pouring herself a glass of water, she sat down at the kitchen table and stared at the pill bottles sitting on the window sash over her sink. Three more Tylenol; or do I finally break open the Percodan that Doc Burton gave me? I'm not going to be a hero when things get really bad, she promised herself, but I've got too much to do right now to dope myself with the strong stuff. She swallowed down the acetaminophen and fought back the tears that had been welling in her eyes all evening. It's the good days that get to me, she thought. Fighting with Evan Roberts leaves me feeling fat and sassy, but working with young people who have their whole lives ahead of them sucks the energy right out of me.

Terri was an exception. The spark and resilience of the young woman reminded Dorothy of herself at the time she had snapped the picture of Gordon now sitting on the mantle. She wished Terri more luck with men. She wondered how an old picture could engender such strong feelings of protectiveness for her new friend, but the mewling of cats demanding their dinner interrupted her reverie. She stood up from the table with an unladylike grunt. "Yes, yes, I'll feed you, you furry little nuisances. You could at least yowl on pitch."

## 15

### Mr. Nice

Well, Evan thought as he got off the phone with his old professor, at least there's one other person in the world who doesn't think Dorothy Henderson hangs the moon. He wondered whether to tell John about the Syracuse possibility.

"Who was that?" John emerged from the kitchen with two beers in his hand.

"Gordon Samuels."

"What did he want?"

"To commiserate with someone about Dorothy Henderson. It seems her reputation precedes her." He decided John did not need to know about Syracuse and felt no need to determine whether he kept silent out of selfishness or kindness. Sometimes he let the competing sides of himself just lie together. "Damn! It's been a hell of a semester so far."

"Maybe for you, but I'm having a great time at the courthouse." John settled next to Evan on the sofa. "They're so grateful for someone who knows how to keep the computers running that they might just make me a judge. Plus, I get to hang out with the local legal celebrities. What I could tell you about the federal prosecutor!"

"Well, let's have the poop," demanded Evan, more than willing to be distracted from his own work situation.

"Sorry, sworn to secrecy."

"Tease."

"Yes?"

"No." Evan got up and paced across the thick wool rug in their living room. The home improvement projects had been a success, and the room was aglow in the late afternoon sun. They had lovingly stripped and waxed the oak floor, replaced the smoked-stained curtains, and filled the room with inexpensive but compatible furniture found at rural auctions and estate sales. "You really like it here don't you?"

"Yeah, I really do."

"And you'd like to stay?" He scowled out the window. "Then you better hope next semester is better than this one."

The next day Evan arrived at his office just in time to receive a visit from his department head. As the newest faculty member, he was stuck on the top floor of the building in an interior office with no windows. A fresh coat of paint had done little to cheer up his cinder block walls, and were it not for the piano wedged into the corner, the office, with its ancient desk and rusted file cabinet, would have looked more like a janitor's closet than a professor's lair.

"You should start looking for a new accompanist," Saunders informed him, his attempt at a concerned tone unable to conceal his glee at being the bearer of bad news. He sat down on the piano bench and explained that Louis Coates was in the psychiatric ward of the county hospital. "They found him on some lady's porch, delusional and probably drooling. They called me because his student i.d. said he was a music major, so I ended up having to call up his mother." He chuckled. "That ended the mystery of his problems--she's whacko as hell. When she comes to get him, they'll probably lock her up too."

If Saunders expected laughter in response to his cruel humor, he was disappointed. Evan liked the strange young man who had begun to blossom over the course of the semester. Unlike many newcomers to accompanying, Coates adapted very quickly to his role, his tempos nearly always perfect, his ear so good that Evan made it a habit to talk with him after every rehearsal about what problems he was hearing in the choir. Evan had never seen him smile, but he now made eye contact on occasion and (thank goodness) had taken Evan's advice about personal hygiene to heart. Because he loathed tip-toeing around people, Evan generally did not see himself as a nurturer of students. He preferred to steamroll along and let others adapt to him. But Coates was so fragile, and so responsive to a kind word, that he found himself taking a real interest in the kid's welfare.

"Anyway, just thought you'd like a head's up." Saunders got up to leave, but he stopped and turned as he reached the door. "I've heard you've had some trouble with the Men's Glee Club?"

"Not since the first day."

"Do you know what caused it?"

"No, but I have my suspicions." Saunders eyes narrowed to slits, but he said nothing more before he left.

Evan decided to visit his accompanist after he finished teaching his 1:30 class. When he arrived at the facility, a candy striper directed him to the sixth floor where he found his way to a nurse's station next to a pair of locked metal doors labeled, "Residential Recovery Program." A row of colorful fabric chairs along the wall functioned as a waiting room. They were empty, except for a florid woman in a plaid wool suit scribbling furiously on a small pad of yellow paper. He approached the nurse and asked whether he could visit Louis. Before answering, she cast a glance over at the woman.

"I'll have to check with the Doctor. Mr. Coates is here under a 48-hour observation order, so the normal rules on visitation don't apply. Unless he okays it, you'll have to come back between 2:00 to 4:00 on Saturday afternoon." He turned to take a seat, but before he could take a step, the woman stood up and confronted him.

"Why do you want to see Louis?"

"I'm Evan Roberts," he said as he held out his hand with a warm smile designed to relax the aggressive woman. "Louis is my accompanist. I'm a professor in the music department."

"So you're the one responsible for him being here." Her eyes flashed and she moved closer to him. He took a step backward.

"Uh, ma'am, I'm not sure I know what you're talking about. I only just got word that Louis was . . . uh . . . ill, and I came straight here."

"I'll tell you what I'm talking about, and believe me, the president of the University is going to know too when I'm done writing this letter." She shook the notepad in his face. "When you destroy somebody's dreams, what do you expect is going to happen? The only thing Louis has ever wanted is to be a concert pianist. He's worked his whole life to achieve that one goal, and then you decide all he's fit for is accompanying a bunch of amateur singers at a second-rate school." She pointed in the direction of the metal doors and accused him, "You drove him to this." Evan took a deep breath and suppressed his impulse to match or exceed the vehemence of her rhetoric. Instead, he looked straight into her wild and desperate eyes and spoke as calmly as he could.

"Mrs. Coates?" He extended his hand again, but she looked at him like he was offering her a cobra. "I think you would be less upset if you knew more about Louis's situation at the music school. He is still studying with our best piano professor, and he remains on the performance degree track. His professor suggested that he get some experience as an accompanist, not with switching careers in mind, but rather to improve his phrasing and his sense of musicianship. Believe it or not, even a great pianist can learn something from a singer. And, from what I understand, it seems to be working. I've been hearing very good things from Professor Gabel about Louis." This last statement was a lie although he suspected there was some truth behind it. Gabel was reclusive with his colleagues, and Evan had only met him once.

"So you've already started a cover-up! Well, let me tell you something. I called Louis's old teacher, and he said that once you start accompanying, you're stuck in that role, and it's impossible to get out. It's crystal clear to me what's going on here. All you frustrated musicians in this hick town are jealous of his talent and you're out to destroy him. I never should have let him come down here."

Before Evan could respond, the supervising psychiatrist on the ward called him over to the nurse's station. Mrs. Coates followed, but the doctor waved her back. "I would like to speak with Mr. Roberts alone for a moment, please." He motioned Evan away from the steel doors, and down the hall to his office.

"We can get into the ward this way without her seeing us," he said with a cryptic smile when Louis's mother was out of earshot. The doctor stepped into his office, introduced himself, and asked Evan to sit down. "That was excellent anger management out there, by the way."

"Well, it was all I could do not to smack her," Evan replied. "It must be convenient to have the source of a patient's mental problems show up in your waiting room."

"To tell you the truth," he replied, "it may be helpful diagnostically, but it's a royal pain in the ass as far as treatment goes." Doctor Peterson was about sixty, tall and basically slender except for a paunchy beer belly that rode low on his hips. His hair was thinning and his beard was almost totally gray. Kind eyes sparkled behind a small pair of silver wire-rimmed glasses, and Evan wondered how he had maintained his enthusiasm over the years. "Professor Roberts," he asked, "Louis tells me that you supervise his work at the music school?"

"At least some of the time. He's my accompanist, and a very good one, too," he emphasized as he leaned forward. "What's wrong with him? Are you going to be able to let him out?"

"In answer to your first question, it's difficult to say after such a short period of time. When he arrived, he was disoriented and seemed to be recovering from some sort of delusional episode. But the more I talk to him, the more control I believe he has over his fantasy life. In other words, any apparent delusions he experiences are probably responses to extreme stress, a rational coping mechanism that helps him escape a difficult situation. That's not to say I'm not very concerned. I've seen patients completely retreat into their fantasies, and I would not like to see that happen here. It would help me if you told me what you've observed."

103

"When he first started working with me, he would kinda zone out on occasion, but that's been happening less and less as the school year goes on."

"That's consistent with what I've observed," the doctor said, careful not to repeat anything that Louis had told him, but implying with a nod that the main source of the boy's stress was sitting in the waiting room at that moment. "School does not seem to be his biggest problem."

"As far as your second question goes, we can only hold him against his will for forty-eight hours unless he poses a danger to himself or others. Sometimes people like him become suicidal, but he did not try to kill himself and hasn't done or said anything self-destructive since he got here. And quite frankly, I think it might be a good thing for him to get back into his routine at school and continue to struggle with being a young adult. With some help, I think he's got a good chance."

"Is there anything I can do?" Evan asked the question with some reluctance, but the doctor's concern was contagious and he felt a combative impulse to protect his student from the lady in the plaid suit.

"You could start by talking to him today and then by keeping an eye on him when you can. Mostly, I suspect that he needs regular doses of kindness and positive human contact and," he added with a smile, "a couple of sessions a week with me."

"Let me mention one more thing. Louis thinks very highly of you but, for reasons I can't disclose, he does not entirely trust you." Evan gave him a puzzled look. "Don't be offended. It's nothing that you've done, but I would like to see him learn to rely on at least some of the adults around him. If you could do something simple, like drive him home from the hospital tomorrow, it would be a good start for him."

"That's all I have to do?"

"That's all. He needs safe places right now where he can do some of the growing up that he's never had a chance to do." He stood up, but told one more story before they went to see Louis. "In one of my favorite books, a psychiatrist who's tried everything to help a severely disturbed lady finally tries a radical therapy: he invites his wife and four children to have tea with the woman in his office. Of course, she's not instantly cured, but that teatime is the turning point and beginning of her recovery. Whenever I get too fancy with my psychoanalysis, I remember that book."

They walked down a brightly lit hall, past a television room where three patients in street clothes were watching a soap opera and through the open door of the last room on the right side of the corridor. Louis was reading a book in a chair in the corner of the room. His bare feet rubbed slowly back and forth on a braided wool rug laid to break the monotony of the cream-colored tile and the cream-colored walls. He looked up as soon as they entered.

"Louis, you have a visitor."

"Hello, Professor Roberts," he said in a quiet voice.

"Hello, Louis." He thought something looked different about the boy, like some of his anxiety had been replaced with sadness. "What are you reading?"

"*The Guns of August.*"

"What's it about?" The title sounded familiar, but he could not remember anything about it.

"It's about the first month of World War I. Professor Henderson made up a list of history books for me to read. She says I'll play better if I understand history." He leafed slowly through the book, looking for something. Evan thought he was more intense than before, more focused, but also more depressed. His movements seemed heavy. He stopped at a page and reread part of it to himself before he spoke. "St. Cyr is the West Point of France, and they have a plaque there that lists the names of the graduates of each class that have been killed in action. For the year 1914, there is no list of names. It just says *Class of 1914.* None of them from that year survived the war." He shut the book. "Professor Henderson told me that I'll play twentieth century music better if I remember the Class of 1914."

"I think Professor Henderson is right," he replied. "If you want, I could lend you a recording I have of Benjamin Britten's *War Requiem*. He was a British composer who wrote a requiem mass for World War One using poetry written by an English soldier. You might like it."

"Thanks." He reached down into a bag sitting on the floor next to him. Looking a little embarrassed, he held up a handful of compact disks. "The lady who brought me to Doctor Peterson gave me these. I haven't heard of any of them." Evan took them and to his surprise saw a collection albums by various rock and new-wave artists, from R.E.M. to the B 52's.

"This is good stuff, Louis! It was really nice of her to lend these to you." Evan saw his face light up with the memory of his encounter with her.

"She's the nicest lady I've ever met."

"Louis," Dr. Peterson interrupted, "if you have another good night's rest, I'm going to release you tomorrow." He cast a conspiratorial look at Evan. "We do have one other problem we haven't discussed yet . . . your mother. She's still here, and she still demands that you go home with her." With the mention of her name, the small spark that Evan had seen in Louis was extinguished. His head sagged, and he no longer made eye contact with the two men in the room. "With your permission," the doctor continued, "I will try to make her my problem. In my clinical judgment, your treatment will proceed more effectively if you stay here in Clarkeston and stay enrolled in your classes. You could have a session with me every Thursday and Saturday afternoon, and Professor Roberts," he said as he glanced at Evan, "can help you with any problems you might have in school. What do you think about that?"

Evan thought that the decision would be an easy one, but Louis agonized over it for several moments, a struggle raging within him that the two older men could only watch. Louis looked at the records and the books and his teacher, and finally spoke. "I want to stay."

"Excellent. Let me deal with your mother, and I'll see you tomorrow morning." He turned to Evan. "Do you think you could drive Louis back to his apartment tomorrow around 9:30 a.m.?"

"I'd be happy to." The two left the room and went back through Peterson's office to avoid Mrs. Coates. Before he left, Evan turned to the doctor. "How are you going to convince Louis's mother to leave?"

"Well, I'm going to calmly explain to her why her son is much better off staying here rather than going home with her."

"What if she won't listen to you?" Evan looked doubtful.

"In that case," the doctor said with a smile as he took several folded yellow sheets of paper from his pocket, "I'll have to remind her of this incredible note that she wrote me yesterday and suggest to her that if I wanted to make an issue of it, no judge in town who read it would refuse my request to lock her up in here along with her son."

# *16*

## A Change in Style

As Dorothy was searching for a box of Spanish renaissance sheet music in the closet of her guest bedroom, she found an unopened videotape entitled *Great Directors of the Twentieth Century*. It had been a present from the college choir two or three years earlier, but she had not owned a VCR at the time so it had lain forgotten and unviewed ever since. Wondering whom the producers might have included on their list, she popped the tape into her new VCR and discovered wholly by chance the key to directing the choir as she grew weaker and weaker throughout the semester.

She sat on her sofa and watched impassively the excerpts of Solti, Szell, Klemperer, Reiner, and Bernstein, but after two minutes of von Schlieffen she made an important discovery. An imperious German, he eschewed the traditional, graceful arm motions of his fellow orchestral conductors and adopted a minimalist style in which he kept the beat by tapping his pointing finger down onto the thumb of his right hand, and made volume adjustments by opening or closing his left hand. His eyes, surveying the orchestra and registering his approval or disapproval, performed the remainder of the conductor's job. Even in the brief film clips, she could see that his control over the orchestra was absolute.

"I can do that," she said to Jesse, an enormous Calico snoozing on her lap, "and I can do that sitting down." She spent the next three hours practicing his technique to recordings of the her recent performances. By the end of the evening, she was convinced that she had found a way to work even in the face of pain and overwhelming fatigue.

She came to rehearsal early the next day and asked the first two men who arrived to move the podium from the small platform that stood fifteen feet in front of the choir risers. She replaced it with a chair and sat down to study the Beethoven score while the rest of the singers filed in. When they were all seated on the risers, she made her announcement.

"We have lived with this piece for a couple of weeks now, and you are beginning to figure out that one of the keys is our dynamic level." She spoke so seriously that half of the chorus thought she was mad at them; the other half shook their heads knowingly, already directed by her voice, even though they had not yet begun to sing. "If we are not able to sing *pianissimo* with one voice, if we are not able to sing *fortissimo* with one voice, then we cannot convey the incredible emotion demanded from us by Beethoven." She remained seated and accompanied her lecture with a steady beat from her right index finger.

"The title of the work is *Missa Solemnis.* We haven't talked much about its history, but some of you may know that unlike virtually all of his contemporaries--and his predecessors for that matter--Beethoven did not write anything labeled a requiem mass. When asked why, he said Mozart had already beaten him to it with his great *Requiem in C minor.*" She would have gotten a better response to her apocryphal story had the group not been staring at her finger and wondering what was coming next. "But even though he did not formally title the *Missa Solemnis* as a mass for the dead, that is precisely what it is." She paused, but kept her finger tapping the top of her thumb.

"It's all about death, young people. And if you are to communicate everything Beethoven thought about the subject, you're going to have to get your eyes out of your scores and onto me. For the rest of our rehearsals, I'm going to be borrowing a technique from the German conductor von Schlieffen to force your eyes up and your voices together." She stopped her finger. "Just keep your eyes on me and think about death."

After the usual, extended warm-up, she ran the group straight through several sections of the mass without pausing to correct their errors. Normally, she started on trouble spots or focused on particularly difficult measures before letting the group sing anything through, but she wanted to see how they were going to cope with the minimal direction she provided. Although she heard them sing numerous wrong words and notes, she was encouraged by the intensity of the sound they produced.

"Get your heads up! I don't care if you sing *la la la* instead of the words. I want your focus up here," she lectured them with a frown after catching several malefactors moments by closing her left hand for *pianissimo* unexpectedly in a section marked *forte.* "Ignore the dynamics written in your score! Given his hearing problems, Beethoven's choice of the proper dynamic levels for this piece is questionable most of the time. We are going to experiment and see in each section what is most convincing." Looking up at the clock, she dismissed them with a curt nod.

The choristers filed out of the room, she could not suppress a smile when she overheard two of the altos promising each other to go over their parts on the piano before the next rehearsal in order to avoid the wrath of their director.

"Dr. Henderson, I see you've gotten lazy in your old age! I wasn't able to find you in your office this morning and now I catch you sitting down on the job." Stan Saunders leaned against the doorway, smirking at his ancient antagonist. He was shorter than Dorothy, barely five foot four inches tall and with all of the charm of teapot Napoleon in a plaid sports coat. *At least Napoleon conquered Europe*, Dorothy had once told a colleague, *I've never even seen Saunders play an instrument.*

"What are you doing?" he demanded.

"Just trying a little experiment. What did you want to talk to me about?" Saunders had always made her skin crawl. Although she had no belief in Eastern religion, she could only describe him to people as having bad karma, the aura of his negativity occupying conversational space the way stench of a cat's leavings befouls a room. The sense of unease he generated was exacerbated by his habit of keeping constant eye contact and his refusal to treat any question he asked as rhetorical. He would repeat, "Don't you think so?" or "See what I mean?" until his interlocutor finally broke down and responded with inanities only slightly less vapid than his own. Worst of all, no matter how rudely she treated him, he would show up in her office at least once a week, sit down without asking permission, look her straight in the eye with a meaningful nod, and inevitably introduce his passion for musicology with the same line: "Listen to this. I've had a new idea that no one has ever had before ..." No matter what subject he broached, she had never heard an original thought pass his lips. His election as department head was a testament to how undesirable the job was and how little discretion the Dean of the College of Arts and Sciences allowed the music faculty head.

"We need to talk about Dr. Roberts," he said ominously.

"He's not a doctor yet as far as I know."

"And from what I've heard, he never will be if you can help it."

"That's absurd." Dorothy controlled her temper; the only time Saunders ever got the better of her was when she lost it.

"Who have you been talking to anyway? The little twerp himself?"

"As a matter of fact, no. But you know how the music school is: rumors fly." He looked at her as if she were the subject of more than one rumor herself and abruptly adopted a conspiratorial tone. "How do you think he's doing? Is he going to make it?" She got the distinct impression that Saunders was perhaps hoping that he would not. Regardless of her feelings about Evan, she was hardly going to give Saunders any satisfaction.

"I have no idea how he is doing, but I intend to let him direct the College Chorus next spring so he can satisfy the performance requirement for his degree. And if he ever bothers to ask me advice about teaching or directing, I'll be happy to help him out, but I haven't been partying with him, if that's what you mean."

"That's good, because if he doesn't make it here, I don't want him to be able to blame us. You know how litigious people are these days."

She peered at him over her glasses, wondering what he was trying to get at. "I sure do," she finally said when she realized he expected a response. Still seated, she shook her head slowly as he left, feeling vaguely as if she had just bumped up against something slimy.

# 17

## The Call of the North

When Evan arrived at the hospital, Louis was alone in the waiting room reading his book. He looked a little less worried than he had the day before, although he still moved like someone recovering from a serious injury. He got up when he saw Evan, but did not offer a smile or any other sort of greeting.

"Good morning, Louis."

"Thanks for giving me a ride." They walked out of the room together in uneasy silence. Evan wished he had planned some sort of conversational gambit beforehand. *What do you say to a kid who's just gotten out of a mental ward? I should leave the good deeds to the freakin' Good Samaritans,* he decided as their footsteps echoed down the hospital halls. He asked Louis directions to his apartment, but was unable to think of anything more to say until they reached the car.

"Sorry about the mess. I'm famous for keeping a nasty car." He turned the ignition and looked over at Louis. "I think I wash it about once a year."

"I don't even know how to drive. My mother told me it was too dangerous." Louis looked out the passenger window as they drove out of the parking garage and Evan could barely hear him. "She told me that she had a stroke."

"Pardon me?" Louis turned to Evan and some of the focus that he had seen in the boy's eyes the previous day returned.

"She told me she had a stroke and that I needed to come home."

"She looked pretty healthy to me yesterday," Evan commented skeptically. Louis was watching him intently as he drove.

"I think she was lying . . . I think she was trying to trick me to come home." Something more than pain was evident in his voice. "I think she has some problems. She needs to talk to Dr. Peterson."

"Well, lying is not a good thing, and talking to Dr. Peterson has got to be a good policy." Evan tried to tread carefully, but he did not know

111

how to respond. "Maybe she was just worried about you or something. Maybe she just didn't know how good you're doing down here on your own."

"Maybe." Louis looked like he wanted to say more, but he clutched his book bag in silence as they rode the next few blocks. When he finally spoke, his voice was barely above a whisper. "You and Dr. Peterson and Ms. Suzanne have been really nice to me . . . I'm not used to people being so nice." Evan could think of no appropriate response beyond nodding his head. They drove in silence the rest of the way.

"Do you think that you'll be able to play this afternoon?" Evan asked as they pulled in front of his building. "Dr. Peterson told me to let you have as many days off as you wanted."

He thought for a moment before he answered. "No. I want to play." He got out of the car without elaborating. Evan watched him walk away and thought he saw something like a wave just before Louis entered the building.

On the way back to the college, Evan wondered whether it was a mistake to get involved with someone who obviously had serious problems. Why do I feel responsible for this kid? Back in New York we just put the crazy people on the street and tell them to live in cardboard boxes.

Having chosen the cheapest parking option when he first came to campus, Evan had a long walk from the car to his office, but in October he did not mind. The gingko trees on campus had turned a brilliant banana yellow tinged with gold, and a cool breeze scattered them before him as he walked. As the leaves fell, the deep red brick of the nineteenth-century buildings on the main campus quadrangle was revealed, contrasting gloriously with the yellows, golds, and lighter reds scattered all over the campus. The anxiety he felt at the beginning of the semester before his classes or rehearsals had faded, and he was able to appreciate the beauty of the college for the first time.

When he finally arrived at his office, he found a note from the departmental secretary asking him to return the call of a Professor Carlson from the Syracuse School of Music in Syracuse, New York. He remembered Carlson as the head of the search committee that had ultimately decided not to hire him when he was on the teaching market the prior year. He immediately picked up the phone and dialed the number.

"Evan! Thanks for getting back to me so quickly. We have a bit of an interesting situation here, and our appointments committee asked me to get in touch with you. The fellow we hired two years ago has just tendered his resignation. So, we're going to crank up the search process again and wondered whether you wanted to throw your hat in the ring? You don't have to let me know right now, but think about it and get back to me before the first of the year. We'll probably be bringing people in to interview beginning in January."

Evan remembered how unenthusiastic John had been about Syracuse when he had interviewed there before, and hesitated before giving Carlson an answer. It was one thing to let Gordon Samuels throw his name in the ring, but quite another to commit to the hiring process. "Let me think about it," he finally said, figuring John could not complain if he kept his options open. Whatever came of the invitation, Evan was flattered that someone outside Clarkeston was interested in his skills as a director and a teacher.

He was more manic than usual during his afternoon lecture, and he took his good mood straight from the classroom to Dorothy's office to see if her offer of letting him direct the College Chorus in the spring was still open.

Her door was shut, but the glow of light through its glazed glass suggested she might still be in. Before he knocked, he peeked into her office through a sliver of unglazed glass exposed by the imperfect fit of the panel on the door. He was shocked at how tired she looked. She sat stiffly, in obvious pain, slowly massaging her right shoulder with her left hand. He saw her rise with an effort and stare out the window onto the idyllic, autumnal scene he had traversed earlier in the day. When she turned away from the window and reached for her purse, Evan thought she might be leaving, and rather than be discovered a voyeur, he knocked lightly on the door.

"Come in!" When she saw him, she waved him in. She popped a pill in her mouth and took a sip from a can of soda on her desk before she spoke. "Just the man I wanted to see."

Evan still suspected Dorothy of outing him on the first day of rehearsal, but in the absence of any direct proof, he was willing to be civil to her. And, it occurred to him, if she wanted something from him, it would give him some leverage when he asked for assurance that he could still have the college chorus in the spring.

"I know that we have not exactly become good buddies this semester," she grimaced and her hand strayed to her shoulder, "but I've got a favor to ask you. After three years of using Debbie Collingwood as my accompanist, I've just discovered that she is a terrific soprano, as good as any that I've got singing for me right now. As you know, the *Missa Solemnis* is very demanding for the women, and right now my soprano section could use all the help it can get. If your accompanist is as good as

113

I hear he is, I was wondering if he might be able to work with us so that I can integrate Sally's voice into the choir and give the sopranos some of the help they need."

Not even a *please*, he thought, just a request to take my accompanist. His first impulse was to say no. After all, why should he help her with the group that she denied him? But the call from Carlson had put him in a good mood, and the combination of her physical distress and obvious discomfort at having to ask him a favor mitigated his response.

"I would be happy to share him," he offered. "He reads extremely well, and I'm sure he could learn the Beethoven pretty quickly, but he hasn't been feeling good lately, and I don't know whether he'd be able to handle both groups." Concern for Louis's privacy prevented him from providing any details of his illness.

"I see." She spoke in a hard tone that indicated to Evan she really did not see, that she suspected him of making excuses in order to hold on to Louis for himself.

"Let me see how he does this week and then let me talk to him about working with you," he continued in the most encouraging voice he could muster. "He talks about you a lot, and I'm sure he would be thrilled to do it, but can we just wait a little while to see if he's gotten well enough to do it?"

"Of course, he's your accompanist." A stern lecture on sharing lurked behind her terse concession. "Now, why did you come to see me?"

Although he realized that he had picked a bad time to talk about her, he had no excuse for his visit on the tip of tongue, and *I just stopped by to chat* was simply too incredible a claim. He decided to plow ahead. "I was wondering if you would still be willing to let me direct the college chorus next semester? I know it's a lot to ask, considering that I need them next fall too, but I thought it would be nice to get to know the group and have the chance to make some serious music this spring."

"What were you planning to do?" A glitter of interest flashed in her eyes.

"What do you think about a performance of Bach's *St. John's Passion* during holy week?"

"I think the crowd choruses are great, but the chorales get boring by the end and some of the arias are total snoozers." She criticized Bach in the same way she would a first-year composition student.

"Well, I was planning on cutting a couple of the more tedious arias."

"What else did you have in mind?"

114

"What about *Haydn's Creation*?"

"We did it two years ago."

"*The Messiah*?"

"Unfortunately, we don't have a decent enough organ on campus. I lobbied for one in the Watkins Center, but it wasn't in the budget." Evan concluded that she was simply unwilling to share the college chorus with him in the spring. Fair enough, he supposed, given that she thinks I'm holding Louis back on her.

"Well, I'll just see what I can do with Men's Glee in the spring." He got up to leave.

"Mr. Roberts," she looked up at him with extreme weariness and perhaps some disappointment that they could not have a more prolonged argument over the sort of music that might best be made on the campus, "I have no doubt at all that you will be directing the group in both the spring and the fall."

"You're serious?"

"Deadly serious, Mr. Roberts." The regret in her voice robbed him of any feeling of victory, and he realized that he preferred the combative Dorothy to the tired and defeated woman before him. God, I just don't understand faculty politics, he thought.

Halfway out the door, he remembered his promise. "I'll get back to you about Louis Coates as soon as I can." She nodded, and he slipped out. On his way back to his office, he decided to call Carlson and tell him that he would be interested in being a candidate for the Syracuse job. Surely, he sighed, not every academic position comes with such a collection of hassles.

## 18

### A View from the Piano

Louis jumped at the chance to work with Dorothy Henderson, and playing for her was unlike anything he had done before. Not only was the music far more interesting than the Men's Glee Club repertoire, the collection of mixed voices was more expressive, and the fanatical devotion she inspired resulted in a cohesiveness and unity of sound that would take Evan Roberts years to replicate. Best of all, after only a half-rehearsal's worth of suspicion, the group had accepted him, especially the chubby, former accompanist who led the soprano section in a standing ovation at the end of the first rehearsal. She hurried down to talk to him afterward.

"You did great! Thank you so much for doing this! You can't imagine how much fun it is just to sing and not have to think about twenty-seven different things at once. I've seen you around," she continued with genuine enthusiasm, "but I've never heard you play before. Are you going to have a recital in the spring? I'd love to come."

"This is easier than singing," he replied, still a couple of beats behind her.

"Huh?"

"I can't sing at all. I'd much rather play." If she noticed how uncomfortable he was or how he avoided eye contact with her, she did not let on.

"Well, you know, I never thought I could sing either, but Mrs. Henderson recruited me anyway. It will be so nice to actually be in the concert! Unless we're doing something that calls for a piano part, I always have to sit in the audience when it's time for the show. I feel a little left out, you know, sitting there and watching everyone on stage, even if they do give you a bunch of roses afterward." She looked at him compassionately, "I hope you won't mind."

He finally met her eyes and saw that they were pale, with the faintest hint of violet. "No," he said seriously, "I like roses." She laughed and her joy went right through him and flipped over his stomach en route.

116

While he was deciding whether to flee, she departed with a brisk "see ya," and he gathered his music in a daze of unfamiliar emotions..

Throughout the course of the semester, Louis noticed Dorothy looking more and more lethargic. She was already directing from her chair when he first arrived to play, but by the end of rehearsal she seemed to tire even in that position. Sometimes, as she kept a perfect beat in her right hand, elbow propped on the back of her chair, left hand fine-tuning the other elements of the music, he could see her back stiffen as if she were suddenly in pain. From his position on the side of the room, only he could see the muscles along her spine spasm and her shoulder blades slowly curl backward until she could not take a breath. Having read once that Brahms had horrible sciatica, he assumed that she must be having a similar sort of back problem. Why else would she be sitting down to direct?

Whatever her problem, she was getting a glorious sound out of the chorus. As a funeral mass written for orchestra, chorus, and soloists, the *Missa Solemnis* was not in the repertoire of the concert pianist. But Louis kept hearing things that Beethoven did in the vocal and instrumental lines that helped him understand some of the piano pieces that Louis had been working on for years. He sometimes went straight from rehearsal to the practice room and played through pieces that he knew by heart but had never understood as more than a challenging series of notes printed on a page. Even Professor Gabel noticed that his playing was losing its mechanistic aspect, and for the first time Louis heard genuine praise in his teacher's voice.

A few days after his debut with the chorus, he heard a knock on the door of the small, third-floor piano room when he paused in the middle of a marathon practice session. It was Debbie Collingwood, the soprano with the violet eyes.

"Can I come in?" Debbie poked her head into the room. "Would you like something to drink? I've got a Coke and a Sprite." She held them out with an uncertain smile. He looked at her for a moment, unsure what he should do. Then he saw the condensation beading off of the cold, red can and remembered that he had not had a drink in over two hours.

"A Coke would be nice." She handed it to him and popped the remaining can. The soda fizzed past her pop-top and she slurped the excess off before it fell to the carpet.

"I heard you playing," she said after taking a proper sip. "I hope you don't mind me eavesdropping, but it was very beautiful."

"Thanks." He looked down and occupied himself with the popping of his can, methodically wiping the lip with the front of his shirt before slowing piercing the top. He took a sip and peeked over the can at her. She was a year or two older than him, short and hopelessly overweight, but her face was animated by a beautiful smile and dark mysterious eyes. Her hair was curly, and Louis was reminded of a fresh-faced milkmaid in one of his childhood Mother Goose readers.

"I wish I could play like that," she continued, perfectly happy to keep up more than her share of the conversation. "My fingers just don't move fast enough. They're a little short, and my teacher says that all I can ever hope to be is a good accompanist. *Which is a very rare thing*," she added in a husky voice. "He always throws that in to make me feel better." She smiled again, having dealt with the limitations of her musical destiny long before. "You're awfully sweet to play for Professor Henderson, especially when it's obvious you're going to be a soloist."

"I'm not sure what I want," he surprised himself a little by admitting what had gone unspoken for so long, "but I'd do anything for Ms. Henderson. She understands music better than anyone I ever met." If Debbie guessed that this was one of the longest sentences he had ever spoken to a girl, she did not let on.

"You're right, but it's more than that. She *cares* more about the music than anyone, too. She knows exactly what she wants to hear, and when the choir gives it to her, it's just the best feeling in the world. Sometimes the singers just look at each other and go, 'Did we just do that?'"

"Like the other day," he said, "at the end of the first section, when she just sat back and closed her eyes like she could still hear the notes . . ."

"Exactly," she jumped in before the pause dragged on too long, "she really knows how to get people to perform together . . . which reminds me of something I wanted to ask you." She blushed and looked down at her drink. "Every year the music school sponsors a four-hand piano competition, and I was wondering if you'd like to work up a piece to play together?"

"Four-hands?"

"I don't know if you've ever done it before, but two people playing the same piano can be a lot of fun. It's the only formal competition of the year, which I thought was really strange until Professor Henderson explained to me that musicians' egos are less of a problem when people have to play with partners, and there really aren't enough great players here to justify a solo prize anyway. All sorts of people come out of the woodwork. I finished third last year with a guy who graduated, so we really would have a chance."

"I don't know." He never liked it when his piano teachers sat down next to him in practice to demonstrate or to play a short piece with him. Sharing the bench did not seem like such a good idea, but she was really nice. "Let me think about it, okay?"

"Okay." She seemed delighted not have been turned down outright and quickly waved good-bye, telling him she had already taken up too much of his practice time. He worked for two more hours but found it difficult to concentrate with the soft scent of her perfume lingering in the air.

* * *

Louis went to Dr. Peterson on Thursday and Saturday afternoons in the small office that he maintained downtown. At first, Louis had been reluctant to talk in his sessions. Even though the psychiatrist seemed to be friendly and understanding, he was afraid that if he revealed the full extent of his fantasy life, the doctor would have no choice but to send him back to the hospital or, worse yet, back to his mother. But the doctor did not insist that Louis talk and in their first sessions seemed content to tell Louis about his other patients (without mentioning them by name) and to ask him occasionally what he would do if he were the doctor. Peterson's other patients seemed so much worse off than him that he eventually felt free to share some of his own experiences and fears, none of which seemed to shock or surprise the psychiatrist. By the fifth session, he no longer needed to be prompted to talk about what had happened in his life (and dreams) since their last meeting.

"Tell me more about this girl," Peterson asked one Saturday, ignoring other revelations by Louis of a frighteningly realistic dream and a panic attack he had experienced before school the previous morning.

"The girl?"

"Yes, the girl you mentioned who wants to play this competition with you. What did you tell her?"

"Uh, I told her I'd think about it." Louis was uncomfortable; he had thought for sure that the doctor would want to talk about the dream where he gave birth to himself in the middle of the local supermarket.

"Have you?"

"What?

"Thought about it." Unwilling to let his patient off the hook, he got up and watered the plants he had placed about the room. In spite of homey touches like a large oriental rug and comfortable overstuffed chairs, the old-fashioned office still looked like the set of a 1930's

119

detective movie. Both the room where he saw his patients and the small anteroom connected to it opened onto a dark hallway shielded from view by venetian blinds hung from the half-glass doors. There were no windows and few distractions.

"She's very nice," Louis finally said after the doctor sat back down. "She always talks to me after rehearsal."

"How do you feel about playing with her?" Louis thought the doctor was smiling in an especially queer way.

"I don't know. I mean, I like her--" he interrupted himself in a rush of words "--I don't mean I *like* her, but she's one of the only people who doesn't think I'm a freak, but I don't like other people sitting at my instrument. That's where I spend all my time. I spend it by myself, you know, and I can make it do just about anything." He calmed down a little and looked up at the doctor. "I don't really have anything else."

"You may have more than you think. You've got two professors, Ms. Henderson and Mr. Roberts, who think quite a lot of you. You've got two groups of students who are grateful for the work you do for them. You've got this girl who thinks you're cute--"

"--I didn't say that!"

"I know," he said with a broad smile, "I'm just teasing you, but you know something, I couldn't even tease you three weeks ago! And I left out the most important thing that you've got now: A life of your own. Your own apartment, your own decisions to make, your own mistakes to make, even." He got up and set the watering can back in the corner and sat on the edge of his desk. "You know, you should think hard about playing with this girl. You told me that when you were little your mother didn't let you play with the other kids in the neighborhood, that all you could do was watch them and pretend you were out there too. Think of it as jumping into the sandbox with her." He laughed suddenly. "You might make a nice castle or you might get sand in your eyes, but you should consider the opportunity. And remember, whatever happens, I'll be here for you talk to."

The thought of playing with Debbie was frightening, but deep down he knew that Dr. Peterson was right, and in a perverse way his memories of being excluded as a young boy made it easier for him to imagine taking his advice. How could he despise his childhood if he turned down the chance to make a friend now? How could he curse his loneliness if he rejected the chance to spend time with someone else? Isolation could only be regretted if it were forced upon him; the implications of choosing to be alone were deeply troubling. "I'll think about it," he said gravely, nodding his head and absorbing a dense pause. "But don't you think it's strange to dream about giving birth to yourself in a grocery store?"

## *19*

## **A Friend in Need**

Although Terri's presence that glorious October eased Dorothy's loneliness at home, teaching her classes and preparing the choir became increasingly difficult. She was able to stand during the first weeks of rehearsal, but she was often so tired that she could not go directly to her car after she dismissed the group. Instead, she slipped down the hall into the music library to slump bone-weary on a sofa, pretending to peruse back issues of choral magazines. When she finally gathered enough energy to make the drive home, she pushed herself up and rotated her shoulder slightly to measure the pain suppressed while she directed. It was always worse after rehearsal, and the dozen extra-strength Tylenol she was taking each day were doing less and less to help. She arrived home with little appetite and no desire to cook. Sometimes in the evening she did nothing but sit and imagine the dark rot throbbing and eating away her collar bone, and after a bad rehearsal, she imagined it nibbling on the edges of her soul.

Nights were the worst. Lying down made the pulse of the blood forcing its way through the tumor more noticeable, and she had trouble finding a position that remained comfortable for more than a couple of minutes. In the middle of the night, she would get out of bed and sit back in the huge sofa she had bought herself the previous Christmas. The pain seemed to ease when her shoulder was slightly above her heart, and sometimes the inanities of late-night and early morning television succeeded in boring her to sleep. On the most frustrating nights, she would put on a jacket and hold open the screen door to let the outdoor cats in and the indoor cats out, and then go out for a walk. Followed by Beverly, the small green-eyed black, she would make a slow circuit around her block, haunting the neighborhood in the quiet hours just before newspapers began hurtling through the early morning sky.

Finally, she broke down and started taking the strong painkillers that Doc Burton had given her. The pain did not disappear but it diminished enough in intensity that she could get through the day. She even found that taking a double dose before bedtime knocked her out for four to six hours, not quality sleep, but far preferable to tossing and turning all night long.

"I'm a drug addict now, Beverly," she admitted to her favorite as she popped a pill after her morning shower. "But I'm not going to be like the old lady in *To Kill A Mockingbird*, sweating it out cold turkey so I can die clean. No way. I'm croaking anyway, so I may as well just be another in a long line of drugged-up musicians. It's actually rather an impressive club." She stroked the kitty from ears to tail. "Hey, how would you like me to get you some catnip on the way home this afternoon?"

Terri was a painkiller of a different sort. After she noticed that Dorothy was consistently under the weather during their work and coffee sessions, she began stopping by at other times to check on her friend. During one afternoon visit, she discovered that Dorothy was barely eating and stopped by a couple of hours later with a casserole in hand, claiming that she had taken over the cooking duties from a morning-sick Suzanne and had made too much. Two days later she came over with a lasagne and a different excuse. By the time Dorothy realized that Terri's suppertime appearances were not coincidental, she was too appreciative to care. The pain had taken a toll on her pride, and Terri's positive attitude about everything proved irresistible.

One evening, Terri popped in with a pizza that she had been unable to finish. She carried it out to the back porch while Dorothy opened a bottle of wine. The back porch was a small, screened-in structure furnished with cheap plastic chairs and a round table with dark stains that showed to its usual status as a potting shelf. The porch got little use as living space except for the six weeks in the spring when the flowers were blooming and the shorter period in the fall when the leaves were at their height. As October drew to a close, the air temperature was still mild and the ornamental plum tree planted in the middle of the back yard cast a purple glow around Dorothy and Terri as they sat and listened to the breeze rustling its leaves.

"If you look carefully," Dorothy explained, "you can see that huge gingko tree is starting to turn. In a couple of weeks, it'll be a yellow-gold you can hardly imagine. Years ago, the school kids in town named gingko leaves the official town flower! Each school got to choose the official town something--you know like each state has a state bird or insect or whatever--and the kids in the elementary school down the street picked gingko leaves as the official flower," she laughed. "That's what they get for asking the kids in November." Dorothy reached for her wine, but before her hand touched the glass, she felt a burning sensation in her right shoulder that caused her to gasp.

"Are you okay?" Terri asked with alarm. She had seen her friend grimace before and wondered about the cause, but this was the first time she had seen Dorothy seriously distressed.

"Damn." She tried to pull her arm back to her side, but any attempt to use it resulted in more burning agony in her shoulder. Eventually, she reached her left hand over and slowly moved her right hand to her lap. She clutched her right wrist as she tried to stand, but the chair caught on one of the table legs. "Could you pull the table back?"

"Are you sure you should be getting up?" Terri quickly pulled it toward her as Dorothy stood up with another sharp intake of air.

"Let's go back inside." As she walked gingerly into the house, she started to feel faint and made a beeline for the sofa in the living room. "Oh shit, damn, pardon my French, but this really hurts." Terri stood over her helplessly. "Could you be a good friend and get me a glass of water and a couple of pills from the bottle on my night stand?"

"Sure." Terri raced to the bedroom and grabbed the pills. She showed them to Dorothy on her way to get a glass from the kitchen. "Are these the right pills? They're just pain killers."

"Trust me, pain killers are exactly what I need right now." She tossed the pills into her mouth with her left hand and then took the glass from Terri with the same hand. She closed her eyes as she waited for the pills to take effect.

"Are you sure there's nothing else I can get for you? Don't you have some nitroglycerine pills or something?"

"Nitroglycerine?" She managed a weak smile at the assumption she was having an attack of angina. "No, darling, I've got the heart of an ox. They don't make pills for what I've got. At least not ones that'll do any good."

"Well, if you've got bursitis or tendinitis, there's all sorts of exercises you can do." Dorothy's position in the chair took the pressure off her shoulder and the pills started to dull the edge of the pain; another curious smile crept onto her face.

"You know why I like you, Terri? Because everything you say is positive. You see me hurting, and the only thing you can think of is how to make it better. When you broke up with what's-his-name in Iowa, your first instinct was to turn it into a vacation."

"Are you calling me naive?"

"No, no," Dorothy protested, "you have a wonderful attitude. I think both of us are optimists, don't you?" She squeezed her eyes shut again, as she felt the pain surge and then subside. "I'm just sorry you have to run into something where optimism is useless."

"What do you mean?"

"I mean," Dorothy finally admitted, surprised by the sense of relief she felt, "that my shoulder hurts because a malignant tumor is growing and rearranging my nerves and muscles and bone and blood vessels. Every once in a while, something rips, and it really hurts. And there isn't a damned thing anyone can do about it." She looked at Terri with an expression that fell short of a frown but still managed to convey the message that pity was not what she wanted. "I didn't plan on telling you, but I figured if anyone can see the good in this, you could be able to."

Terri was stunned, and Dorothy could see her struggle with the news, uncertain how to respond and unsure of how to show she cared. "Well, I can see one positive thing . . . I've got a great excuse for coming over to visit you tomorrow."

The next day, Terri and Dorothy broke early from their cataloging and sat down in the living room. The windows were open and a mild breeze filled the room. Terri had noticed earlier that the picture Arthur retrieved from behind the piano had found its way onto the mantel over the small fireplace. She got up to study it and then looked back at Dorothy.

"Were you wondering how I ended up as an old maid?"

"Actually, I was just noticing what a handsome guy he was."

"You're going to laugh," replied Dorothy, offering up the improbable image of herself as a wild co-ed, "but we really had a hot thing going in graduate school. He was the most handsome man that I ever dated--or could ever hope to--but when I met him he had absolutely no clue how gorgeous he was. He was such a--" she searched for the right word, "--you know, not suave . . ."

"You mean a geek?" Terri laughed.

"Yes! That's it! He was such a *geek* that when we first met, I could hardly stand to be around him. When we finally got together, it was like one long roller coaster ride. We fought about everything. That's probably why our landlady was convinced we were married! We spent more time arguing than we did making . . . up."

"What happened?"

"We had a big blow-up over what to do after we got our degrees. Should we get married? When? Where should we live? Who should follow whose career?" She paused as she tried to come up with a moral for her selectively edited story. "When we broke up, I realized I should never get married. If I couldn't get along with a kind, incredibly

125

handsome, very talented man, who just happened to share virtually all of my interests, then I didn't dare inflict myself on some poor, less-qualified fellow."

"Is it possible to have *too* much in common?" She got no answer to her question and looked again at the picture. "He looks like quite the lady's man."

"He wasn't then, but from what I hear through the choral director grapevine, he still does alright." She brushed away any trace of self-pity with a mischievous smile. "At least I taught him something."

When Terri finished laughing, the two got back to work in Dorothy's study, but having breached the subject of love, they continued to pursue it. "Do you wish things had gone differently?"

"What do you mean?" Dorothy asked. "Do I wish I had a dozen grandchildren? No. I don't wish for anything that would have kept me from making music. Maybe nowadays women can juggle careers and families, but that wasn't an option when I was starting. And I'm not sure I could have pulled it off anyway." She leaned against an old, roll-top desk she had inherited from her father and watched Terri pull wads of sheet music out of a filing cabinet. She could not remember the last time she had talked about such things. "What about you?"

"Me?"

"Yes, you're what, twenty-six or twenty-seven? Do you ever think about the future?"

"I only just turned twenty-five for heaven's sake."

"When I was twenty-five I was having the affair of my life!" Her eyes twinkled. "I highly recommend it, in fact. You need to spend a little more time with that Jorge."

"We hang out a lot at the coffee shop and walk around campus. And you know that we've been to some concerts too."

"Yeah, with all his friends. You need more time alone with him."

"I'm not sure he wants to spend time alone with me."

"You're wrong. I remember how he looked at you over the table that night we had dinner at Suzanne's. You do like him, don't you?" Dorothy had never asked Terri directly about her feelings before. She hesitated before answering.

"You know I do."

"Well, then, you need to put the moves on him."

"What moves?" She laughed and stacked a pile of music next to Dorothy on the desk. "I don't have any moves."

"All women have moves, darlin'. Don't think I haven't noticed that you're a huge tease."

126

"Huge is right."

Dorothy laughed and started leafing through the music sitting between them. She was quiet for a moment and then looked up and smiled into young woman's dark green eyes. "You asked me before if I would do anything different. I can think of one thing--I'd have more friends like you."

Terri reached out and as Dorothy embraced her, she wondered if she could have kept Gordon somehow, for he was the prime example of something she had let slip away.

## 20

### Letters from the Past

By the time the last patches of snow melted late in March of their first year in Champaign-Urbana, Dorothy was spending almost every night at Gordon's small apartment. His landlord discovered her visits about the same time but was too embarrassed to confront them. He did little more than inform Gordon in writing that his lease would not be renewed at the end of the semester. Planning to spend the summer apart and to live together the following year, the couple immediately embarked on a tour of rooms on the west side of the campus, hoping that landlords' eyes were less sharp in the predominantly student neighborhood between the university and downtown Champaign.

Although both might have been characterized as free thinkers, at least by 1950's standards, their decision to live together was prompted as much by convenience, frugality, and an instinctive fear of marriage than by a philosophical commitment to experimental living. And as is frequently the case with important life decisions, pure chance played a major role. One morning, while listening to Dorothy lament the inconvenience of having to go back to her apartment to get clothes before going to school, he remarked casually, "Wouldn't things be much easier if we just lived together?"

Two possibilities did not materialize that day: Gordon did not ask the question: "Wouldn't it be easier if we just got married?" and Dorothy did not respond, "Well, we could live together, if we got married." Perhaps the following thirty-five years would have been very different if they had, but instead, as with most things, she met Gordon's statement head-on.

"You're right. It would. Do you really mean it?" He nodded while she thought some more. "No one who cared would ever know--people do it in Paris all the time."

Gordon never gave their decision a second thought. He was wildly in love with Dorothy and the thought of having her around all the time blotted out any contemplation of the downside of sharing an apartment with someone he had only known for seven months. So, they girded their loins for a summer to be spent apart out of financial necessity, and promised to write each other at least once a week.

\* \* \*

June 15, 1954

Dear Dee-Dee,

It's hotter than hell here in the beautiful suburbs!! I can't imagine it's any worse in Clarkeston, even if the south is famous for nasty summers. I can't wait until the fall when the breezes are cool and I can take you in my arms again . . . better edit my thoughts, in case one of your parents gets curious as to why you're getting four letters a week from some guy in Illinois and starts snooping around, but what I'd really like to do is tell you exactly how wonderful you make me feel when we're together. I NEVER imagined it could be like this. NEVER.

Forget about editing–I cannot wait until we're together this fall!! Once we put on a coat of paint (and buy some furniture), our little duplex will be just perfect. Sometimes I have horribly romantic thoughts about our future, but you're right, we're wise not to decide anything important until next year. In the meantime, I can't think of a more wonderful way to spend a year in boring, old Champaign!

Love,

Gordon

~ ~ ~

June 24, 1954

Darling G.,

You needn't worry about my parents reading my mail, but our maid is incredibly nosy (especially since she wrote me off as a professional spinster long ago!) and you might give her a heart attack if you went into too much detail about our love life. I'm just as excited about the fall as you are. I never thought of myself as the racy type, but when you think about it, we're just being sensible. I don't know why living together should not be the preferred thing to do. The mere mention of it drives the Baptists down here crazy (another reason to do it!). Of course, they're the worst for carrying on behind each other's backs once they get married, so I'm not so sure what the point really is. Anyway, I love you, I can't wait to be with you again, and I better not think about it too much or I'll find myself hopping on the next train to Chicago.

Love,

D.

~ ~ ~

July 1, 1954

D.,

Why not come to Chicago? Can't you make an excuse that you're visiting a friend you met in school? I never got the chance to show you around the city last year. I'm making enough in my Dad's shop to afford a couple of nights in the Palmer House downtown, and I could ask for a Monday off, so we'd have three days together to visit the museums and to hear (and make!)

music at night. I'd even be willing to spend some time shopping--the ultimate sacrifice!

Love,

G-Man

~ ~ ~

July 7, 1954

G-Man,

Shall I submit to your jurisdiction at the Palmer House so you can detain me for crossing state lines in order to perform lewd and notorious acts? Why not? Or rather, yes, please! How about the third weekend in July? Most of my piano students are gone that week-- time for the rich folk to start heading to the coast--so it would not be hard for me to rearrange my schedule. I'm tingling already.

Love and kisses,

Dorothy

\* \* \*

If Gordon's ex-wife had ever found and read the whole of his correspondence with Dorothy, she would not have recognized her husband's voice in his letters. Through a dry courtship and a drier marriage, she never saw the romantic enthusiasm of his youth. The box of letters that Gordon opened after his conversations with Evan contained all the passion that his ex-wife had missed. As he read them for the first time in years, he realized that he had never stopped loving Dorothy, but that anger and rejection had contorted his affection so completely that he could not find a word for the ancient lump left inside him.

* * *

He watched Dorothy get off the train at the Randolph Street station, he could not stop smiling. Even after they embraced, he could not wipe the ridiculous expression off his face.

"What no running to meet me in slow motion?" She began teasing him immediately, and he rewarded her with another kiss. "Are you at least going to pick up my suitcase?"

"Most certainly, Mrs. Berlioz."

"Mrs. Berlioz?"

"Of course, I made reservations under a pseudonym. You must call me Hector," he said with a small bow. She laughed and swung her floppy summer hat at him.

"Why did I ever get involved with another musician?"

"Because of the quality of my instrument, of course." This time her hat made solid contact.

"You're bad!"

"What do you expect after six weeks of celibacy?"

Dorothy's bag was not too heavy, so they walked from the station to the hotel, admiring the Chicago skyline and enjoying the bustle of the workers heading home on Friday afternoon. The summer heat wave seemed to have broken just for Dorothy, and a steady breeze off the waters of Lake Michigan acted like a huge air conditioner, dropping temperatures twenty degrees in less than six hours. It was one of those perfect weekends with which Chicago graces its residents each summer, while the landlocked portions of the Midwest still breathe the humid sweat of corn and soybeans. It was late afternoon by the time they checked into the hotel. Gordon opened the window to air out the stuffy room and to his delight, by the time he turned around, Dorothy had made it clear that they should delay the evening's sightseeing until they finished saying hello.

After dinner at the Berghoff, Gordon hailed a cab and told the driver to head north to the Wrigley Building and then cut east to Lake Shore Drive and then south all the way to Hyde Park. He made sure Dorothy was in the right-hand seat of the vehicle so she had a clear view of the skyline all the way past the Loop and down to the South Side. She was entranced by the sparkling lights of the city center, but as he stared at her profile, he knew he had the better view. Her smooth auburn hair was tucked behind her left ear, so he could see the lights reflected in her eyes, and a mixture of contentment and longing came over him as the skyscrapers leveled to less impressive storefronts and warehouses and finally to the vast residential neighborhoods south of Roosevelt Road. As the cab darkened, he pointed at a cluster of bright lights along the lake, several miles ahead.

"The Gold Coast."

"Is that where we're headed?"

"Not quite."

"You want to tell me where to go?" The cabbie was approaching the 47th Street exit.

"Why don't you just drop us off on 55th Street, near Woodlawn. We're going to hear some nigger music tonight." Dorothy cast a disapproving glance at Gordon but was quiet until they were dropped off in front of a lively strip of clubs just north of the University of Chicago. Although they were close to the school, the area was clearly no typical campustown. Many of those popping in and out of the bars were Negroes and most were dressed for a night out on the town.

"You know," she said as soon as he had paid the fare, "one way to tell the ignorant from the educated in Clarkeston is by counting how many times they use the word *nigger*." He looked momentarily confused that she could be offended by his language.

"That's just what the music's called."

"Well, since we're sophisticated musicians, maybe we could call it jazz or blues or ragtime or whatever it is we're going to hear."

"Whatever you want, sweetheart." He scanned the street. "Let's go down to the Top Hat Lounge." Gordon was unaware that Dorothy remained troubled by his comment. He honestly thought that since his hometown lacked the formal legal constraints against racial mixing found in the south, his own attitudes were not worthy of question. He knew he had more progressive views than the average Chicagoan, and his appreciation of the jazz and blues culture of the South Side showed he was considerably less racist than the gang of Bridgeport Irishmen who ran the city. He would eventually learn that Dorothy demanded a Socrates who rose above the crowd, a man constantly examining his motives and values.

"You know," she said in between sets in the smoky room, trying hard to find a volume for her voice that could be heard over the lively conversation around them, but not reach the ears of their neighbors, "my father's law office is probably the only place in Clarkeston that doesn't have separate seating arrangements for Negroes and whites."

"You see, that's what I'm talking about," he replied, "rules about where you can sit. Rules about where you can work. That's the real problem with race in this country--change the laws down south and the whole country would start to look like Illinois."

133

"Is that what you really want?" she asked. "I know we've got all those terrible laws back home, but Negroes and white people still mix together way more than up here."

"You can't make people want to be together, darling." Fortunately, the music was good enough to prevent the evening from being spoiled. As they drove back to the hotel, however, he could sense that all was not perfect. He decided to up the ante for the next day and chance an extended test of compatibility.

* * *

"You're going to see the real Chicago today," he told her as she cast a dubious eye over the blue collar diner he brought her to for breakfast. "Load up on the calories, we're taking a long hike and having a late lunch." After the greasy but tasty meal, they walked east to the Art Institute. He seemed to know the name of every architect of the skyscrapers they passed, details about the dates of construction and the history of each style they encountered. The buildings in New York City were taller on average, he explained, and there were more of them, but no city in the world displayed more diversity of twentieth century architecture. He stopped her outside the Art Institute.

"You're going to want to stay here all day, but we've got to swear to be out in two hours." The museum was overwhelming, and it was her turn to show off what she remembered from her courses in art history. "I didn't know that was here!" she exclaimed a dozen times as she rushed over to another painting. They missed making their deadline by a half an hour.

"Not to worry," Gordon improvised, "we'll get a cup of coffee and a sweet roll at Marshall Field's that'll hold us 'til lunch." They headed over to State Street and wandered through the store that catered to shoppers as graciously as the Art Institute did to art lovers. After they found her a conservative floral bathing suit and some souvenirs for her parents, they rested in a quiet corner of the coffee shop on the fifth floor.

"This is so different from New York!" Dorothy exclaimed. "When we used to go up from New Jersey, I always felt like I was jumping into a tornado. It was always so hectic and dirty, and the people were so rude. This is wonderful, Gordon."

"I'm glad you like it." Then a trace of hesitation entered his voice. "You know, I do have an ulterior motive. I was hoping you'd think about . . . that we could both apply for jobs here?" He studied his coffee as he swished it around in his mug. She thought about his proposal for a minute and then lifted his chin with her hand.

"Alright, I'll think about it," she said seriously. He responded with a smile as he took her hand and led her back out to Michigan Avenue. They spent the next two hours slowly making their way north, stopping in front of Symphony Hall, speculating whether they would ever direct there, but settling for buying tickets to that night's performance. They window shopped along the Miracle Mile, and by one-thirty, they had crossed the river and were strolling hand-in-hand through the residential neighborhoods north of the Loop, wondering aloud what life would be like living there together amid the apartment houses and brownstones.

"You weren't kidding about this being a hike," Dorothy observed. "How much farther?"

"Not too much, another half-hour if we stop gawking." Hunger increased their pace, and they arrived at the Drake Hotel in time for a very late lunch. Ordering a sumptuous repast, topped off with a bottle of champagne, they talked more concretely of their future together, how they might coordinate their job searches and where they might want to live after graduation. Whatever Gordon's other failings, he was not a knee-jerk chauvinist, and he never entertained the thought that Dorothy would give up her career for him. He recognized her talent and understood her commitment to making music. Was she working so hard just to find a husband? Very doubtful, and he was not interested in having children soon anyway.

"Okay. Now, sneak off to the Ladies Room and put your swim suit on underneath your dress. Then, we'll walk across to Oak Street beach, have a nice swim, lounge about in the sun, take a cab back to the hotel and still have plenty of time to make the symphony."

"What are you going to wear? Or is this just an ogling expedition for you?"

"Well, it most certainly *is* an ogling expedition for me, but I'll test the waters with you. I put on my suit instead of underwear this morning."

"Gross!"

"What's gross about that? It's perfectly natural," he gave a little squirm in his chair, "although I am bunching up a bit. Go on and change! Nobody will know, and you can just slip your dress off at the beach. That's what everybody else does." She looked dubious but took the bag from Field's with her to the bathroom as he took care of the bill.

The crowded beach was just a short walk across Michigan Avenue from the Drake, and soon they were wading in the cool lake water.

"Gordon, this is freezing! It's like the Gulf of Mexico in January, except it's July!" She wrapped her arms around herself and shivered hard, to which he responded by making a shallow dive into the surf, popping up twenty feet farther out into the water like a seal. "No, it's great, you'll see. It's warmer out here."

"Like hell it's warmer. I'm staying right here."

"Suit yourself." Gordon swam out even farther and then treaded water until Dorothy could stand it no longer. She pinched her nose and ducked under the water, emitting a muffled scream and sending a school of minnows darting toward Indiana. When her head emerged, she was out of breath, the cold water squeezing her chest like an iron band. She paddled out to him, kicking furiously to generate some body heat until she was close enough to grab him.

"Warm me up, you creep!" She grabbed his waist and maintained a brisk frog kick when she realized the water was over their heads.

"You want to go back to the hotel already?" he asked when her hands inadvertently slipped onto his trunks.

"No! I'll have pneumonia before we get back there. Give some of your body heat to me, Mr. Polar Bear."

"Okay, but let's get in a little shallower water before you drown me." They moved in until his feet could touch bottom and stood hugging each other tightly in the clear water. As their bodies slowly adjusted to the chill, they admired a view of the city only someone in the lake can have. Looking to their left, they could hardly believe they had walked all the way from the center of the city out to the beautiful little beach on the near North Side. A breeze was blowing in from the east, pushing any pollution onto the western suburbs and etching the edges of the downtown buildings into sharp relief against the deep blue sky. They stood without speaking for several minutes until Dorothy began shivering again and they headed into shore. "Uh, Gordon, I don't remember buying towels at Field's."

"Hmmm . . . damn . . . why don't we just sit on the rocks until we dry off?" She responded with a sigh, but soon they were sunning themselves on the warm rocks like lazy sea lions, luxuriating in the sweet exhaustion swimming in cold water brings. After the imperfections of the previous night, Gordon had planned their wanderings carefully. He had learned that she liked having breakfast on a worn formica counter, that she could walk in endless fascination through the concrete and stone canyons of his favorite city, that she was flexible and daring and open. As they sat on the rocks, he hoped that her doubts might be fading, and she could imagine her life with him extending far into the future. He suddenly knew for certain that they would be married, but he could find no reason to propose, no reason to upset their plans and risk disrupting the perfect day unfolding before them.

Before rush hour could start in earnest, they took a cab back to the Palmer House and immediately fell in bed together, emerging just in time to shower and dress for the symphony. A guest conductor led the orchestra through several questionable interpretations in an all-Richard Strauss program that provided them with plenty to talk about over a late dinner of ribs at Miller's Pub. Eventually, the conversation turned from the music to the practicalities of their own careers.

"How's this for a plan," she suggested, having heard Gordon's thoughts on the matter, "we both apply to all the openings in Chicago--"

"--but not the suburbs."

"Definitely no suburbs, and then as a back-up we remain open to any really good-looking opportunities in New York."

"Sounds good, but what if we don't find anything? We're being pretty picky for rookies," he replied.

"Well, I was hoping you'd keep Atlanta open as an option. I know you don't really want to move down south, but it would be a less competitive market," she said hopefully. "And it's only fair to leave open a chance of being closer to Clarkeston."

"It would have to be a perfect job to drag me away from Chicago or New York," he replied after a moment, "but I don't see what it would hurt to take a look at what's down there." They clanged their beer steins to seal the deal, and their discussion turned to more fanciful thoughts about where and how they might eventually show the world their talents.

Sunday brought with it the melancholy knowledge that their brief weekend was drawing to a close, and the lethargic couple found it difficult to get out of bed even as they heard the distant bells of a church chime 10:00 a.m.. When they finally got up and checked out, he suggested leaving her bags at the train station and strolling south to see Buckingham Fountain and Grant Park. They could then have a nice lunch and still make her train by three o'clock.

They were less animated than the day before, and if they could have snapped their fingers and advanced the calendar to August 28, the first day of the semester, they would have done it. Instead, they walked slowly down the empty Sunday morning sidewalks holding hands, unable to savor fully the other's touch with a month-long separation looming. When they got to the station, she insisted they reduce the desperation of their parting by saying good-bye on the platform rather than in the train compartment. They held on to each other there until the last boarding call was made. "I love you," he whispered as she bent to pick up her bag. "A month's not too long."

"I love you, too." A quick kiss, bag in hand, and she was gone.

He hung around the station until the train pulled away, wondering how he was going to while away the rest of the day. Thinking that twenty-five-year-olds should not ache like school boys, he hesitated to unburden himself on any of the casual summer friends he had made working in his dad's shop. Dorothy had rapidly become the person he shared his feelings with, but she was unavailable. Then he had an idea, something that would let her know something of his loneliness. He walked to the newsstand and bought a pre-stamped postcard that bore a picture of the train station. Knowing he could not be more explicit because Dorothy's parents thought she was visiting with a girlfriend, he drew a sad face on it and dropped the card in the mailbox before he made his way back to the suburbs.

* * *

You were such a *schlemiel*! Gordon thought as he held several of the old letters in his lap. He knew that he had been naive as a young man, but the letters to Dorothy made embarrassingly vivid how little he had known about the world. It had not even been a case of believing "love will conquer all"; he had assumed that whatever love faced would just lay down its arms and meekly slink away. He picked up the last letter he had written before the fall semester started and counted six "I love you's," eight other assorted references to the word "love," and eleven exclamation points. *That's more than my ex-wife heard during the last ten years we were married. Exclamation point!*

He had friends who laughed when they related the tales of their first amorous misadventures. They were amused by the valuable lessons learned during ancient romances, but at sixty and alone in New York City, Gordon felt neither gleeful nor wise. I still don't know if I was right to leave, he thought, but I do know that dwelling on the past is foolish. Taking his own advice, he pitched the letters in the trash can.

## 21

### The Party

Wrapping herself in the afghan draped over the back of the porch swing, Terri rocked gently to the faint sounds of the autumn night and pondered the cruelty of the death sentence handed to her friend. Although Dorothy appeared unafraid, Terri was filled with enough trepidation for both of them. She had never dealt well with the concept of mortality and had switched her major in college from general nursing to dental hygiene after her first rotation through the university hospital's intensive care unit. Her father's recent death had done nothing to improve her opinion of the design defect that eventually stilled every human body.

Terri admired but did not understand the stoicism with which Dorothy bore herself. Dorothy was neither fearful nor bitter, maintaining her interest in even the most mundane matters like organizing her music or prying into Terri's relationship with Jorge Ortega. Dorothy's interest in Jorge was especially surprising. I can't believe, she thought with amazement, that a woman my mother's age would tell me to sleep with someone I hardly know!

"Oh, just drag him into bed, for heaven's sake," Dorothy had said when Terri described the frustration of never getting beyond the occasional kiss on a park bench or the porch swing. "That's the only way you're going to find out what he's made of."

"But he never invites me up to his apartment."

"Then invite him up to your room."

"I'm uncomfortable doing that in my brother's house."

"You mean," Dorothy chided, "you're uncomfortable with the possibility of being turned down." Terri tried to strike a pose of righteous indignation in response to the jibe but only managed a scarlet blush.

"Maybe you're right."

"Are you sure he's not gay? There's no shame if that's the case. I've been fooled at music conferences several times over the years."

"Yes, I'm sure," Terri insisted. "He's a good kisser, and I am pretty sure . . . um, that he's getting excited."

"Maybe he's just thinking of Robert Redford."

"You are the most outrageous," she searched a moment for the right epithet and gave up, "dirty old lady that I've ever met! In fact, you're the only dirty old lady I've ever met."

"I resent the *old*," Dorothy said with a smile, "but I must confess to entertaining the occasional impure thought."

The two companions saw each other almost every day as October drew to a close. On days when Terri did not stop by Dorothy's house, they met downtown for lunch or a cup of coffee. When the walk across campus and over the College Avenue bridge to downtown Clarkeston became too much for Dorothy, they met in the college cafeteria, a surprisingly distinguished place, serving undistinguished food, housed in the former reading room of the school's first library building. The vaulted ceiling, stone walls and stained glass windows of the cafeteria gave it the air of a Gothic cathedral, rather than a place usually ringing with the clatter of cheap plates and glasses and the conversations of hundreds of students.

In a far corner of the room, surrounded by a dozen small tables and shielded from the clamor of the serving line, a large wooden counter salvaged from the old library provided serving space for the cafeteria's attempt at a coffee house. The chairs were hard and occasionally unstable but in the afternoon the sun streamed through the yellow and rose of the windows, bathing Terri and Dorothy's usual corner in a warm and sustaining light. It was here she confided her anxiety over the party she had committed to give for her Latin friends.

"The last party I gave," she explained, "was for my ex-fiancee's twenty-fifth birthday. Half of the people I invited didn't show up, and he got mad at me for spending too much of our money on the party."

"You spent his money?"

"No. He just thought of any money I spent as money that couldn't be put toward his dream farm."

"What a bore!"

"My sentiments exactly," Terri sighed, "but I still don't know what to do for next Friday. I gave Jorge a map to the house, and he's taking care of inviting everyone. The women will bring some food, but who knows how much or when they'll arrive. I'm turning into a basket case."

"Look," Dorothy explained, "this is all very simple, if you can spend some money."

"Believe me, money is no object."

"Good, I've done this a dozen times for student parties. First, buy a keg of good beer. It tastes better than anything out of a can, and you can be sure you won't run out. Set it out on the porch, where everyone will want to hang out anyway, and you'll prevent a constant line of people from barging into the kitchen. Then, set out a table with a couple of economy-sized bottles of decent white wine and some Coke for those who don't drink beer." She paused for a moment. "Food's a bit of a problem since you don't know what you'll get or when it will arrive, so I'd make massive amounts of some kind of appetizer to lay out and hold people 'til the rest gets there. Any ideas?"

"I don't think the traditional nut-covered Wisconsin cheese ball would be appropriate."

"No, but what about traditional southern cheese straws? My mother's recipe is foolproof and you could easily make several batches the afternoon before the party. Treat your Latin friends to some authentic southern cuisine."

"Great idea! I could put out the food and wine in this wonderful hallway that runs the whole length of the house. And if I open the door to the stereo room and crack the window to the porch, we'll have plenty of music no matter where people are."

"That's good, but have you thought about what to play?" Dorothy asked. Terri shook her head in response. "Professor Thomas has an incredible collection of Latin and Caribbean music in his office. I'll ask him if I can borrow a stack for your party." Terri nodded her head in agreement, but her attention had wandered to a distant point over Dorothy's left shoulder.

"It's him," Terri said.

"Who?"

"Jorge," she said as she smiled and waved. "He's coming over." Since his visit to the big white house, Terri had seen him about twice a week. They went to concerts, drank beer at the Wild Boar and coffee at the Café Cappuccino, talked at length at the inevitable Friday night parties at the apartments of Jorge's friends, and spent one spectacular fall afternoon feeding the ducks that congregated by the main bridge crossing the river. Even so, she still had no idea where she stood with him. He seemed to enjoy the time they spent together, and he struck her as a person who would have no patience with someone, especially *una americana puritana*, whom he considered a bore. He seemed to enjoy their occasional kissing as much as she did, but it never escalated into anything more dangerous. He was no prude, so she attributed his reserve to something more complex, something that she could not quite figure out. Sometimes he could be as frustrating as Tommy back in Iowa, but he was always more exciting.

"Jorge, you remember Dorothy Henderson from Suzanne and Arthur's dinner a couple of weeks ago." He smiled at Terri and then turned all of his attention to Dorothy.

"Very nice to see you again! You know, I forgot to tell you that one of my friends, Monica, sings in your chorus. May I sit down?" He took a chair and Terri watched in fascination as he and Dorothy fell into an earnest conversation about music and the odd mix of foreign students attracted to Clarkeston. They talked like old friends who had known each other for years. After fifteen minutes, Terri took both of their cups and refilled them rather than interrupt their conversation. As the next class period approached, Jorge excused himself with a regretful glance at his watch to go take an English literature exam. Dorothy turned to Terri with eyebrows raised.

"Good lord in heaven! What a charming young man! If I were thirty years younger, I'd have to steal him away from you." She looked backwards, but he had already left the room.

"Well, I'm not sure he's mine to steal."

"Then you've got nothing to lose." She gave Terri a conspiratorial grin. "Final party tip. Ask him to help you clean up after everyone leaves. You never know what might happen in a dark old house."

"That's one bit of advice I might take you up on." She and Dorothy got up to leave. "Oh, you never told me whether you could come."

"I promised Evan Roberts that I would attend the Men's Glee Club concert that night," she said after consulting her pocket calendar, "but I'll promise to stop by for a bit afterward."

* * *

When the big night finally arrived, Terri donned the black skirt and floral blouse combination that she considered to be her most slimming, cued up the top record from the stack provided by Dorothy's friend, fortified herself with a Dos Equis draft from the keg that Arthur had eagerly tapped, and began laying out her cheese straws on two narrow tables in the hall. Taking Suzanne's advice, she hid her bizarrely twisted first batch underneath her more professional efforts and arranged them neatly on two large silver serving trays. She posted wine and soft drinks sentries on either side of the spread and retired with a sigh to rock with her brother on the front porch swing.

"You know, as long as we're out here waiting, no one's going to come," she said.

"Like watching for water to boil?" He gazed with satisfaction out over the street. He was so different in Clarkeston than he was in Iowa, content in a way she could not have imagined her hard-driving, law student brother could ever be. He was still sharp and witty, but he seemed to be a better listener than before, more observant and considerate. She

142

wondered if her time in Clarkeston would transform her too. "I hope you don't mind me inviting Evan and John," he asked, "I don't know if they speak any Spanish, but they can hang out with me and Suzanne."

"No problem. They can talk with Dorothy too. She said she'd probably come by."

The first carload of guests pulled slowly up the street just as Terri got up to put on a new album. Arthur volunteered to take over stereo duties while she directed Mari Carmen to pull her car around to the alley behind Suzanne's house. In order to maintain the aesthetic appeal of the neighborhood, a local ordinance prevented cars from parking on the street, so she had told Jorge to direct people to park in the back. The next wave of guests paid more attention to his instructions, and soon a steady stream of Jorge's friends were entering the back of the house and filing past the cheese straws and onto the front porch. By nine o'clock, the house was buzzing with conversation, and she had been complimented many times on the beauty of the venue and the quality of the music. The cheese straws were less of a hit, perhaps because her translation of the dish made them sound like "cheese hay," but they slowly began to disappear as the volume of the keg and the wine bottles lowered.

At nine-thirty, Dorothy arrived with a bottle of wine, and Terri pulled a kitchen chair out on the porch for her. "How was the Men's Glee Club?"

"I don't know."

"Well, I'm flattered that you came to our little soiree instead."

"I didn't mean to miss the concert," she was clearly disgusted with herself, "but my shoulder was really giving me trouble this afternoon, so I took an extra pain killer and lay down. The next thing I know, it's seven-thirty and the concert's half over. By the time I got cleaned up, there was nothing to do but come over here."

"The music's probably better here anyway."

"No doubt, but I really needed to be there. It is very important to support the young faculty by going to their programs, not to mention I have some fences to mend with him." She took a sip of wine and sighed, "Well, it's not like I've never made any mistakes in my life. The party is just lovely, by the way. Is Jorge here yet?"

"No, but he's always late," she scanned the street to see if he might be pulling up as she spoke. "You might get a chance to apologize to your colleague tonight. He's a friend of Arthur's, and he might come over after the concert."

"Oh shit, that's all I need." She looked for a moment like she was considering bolting. "I'll just have to take my medicine, I guess. I hate the thought of having to tell that arrogant little bastard I'm sorry." A moment later, Arthur came over and swapped places with Terri when she was asked to get some utensils to serve a batch of tamales that Monica had just brought.

"Have you seen Jorge?" Terri asked Monica in Spanish as she took the plate of food and set it on the table in the hall with the other dishes her guests had brought.

"Yes," the slim brunette answered, pouring herself a glass of wine, "he came with me—I think he went looking for the bathroom." Terri's heart skipped a beat even though she did not suspect Monica and Jorge were anything more than close friends. "I just wanted to thank him for getting the word out to everybody. I'm so happy you all were able to come." She liked Monica and kissed her Spanish-style on the cheek. "Now, let me change the record. Do you prefer *salsa* or *meringue*?"

"*Salsa*!"

Things are going pretty well, Terri thought, but as she walked to the stereo room, she noticed some commotion on the porch and looked out the window just in time to see a young man storming away to his car, leaving another leaning sheepishly against one of the white porch columns. She quickly picked an album at random, put it on, and went outside to investigate. As Arthur talked to a paper-white Dorothy, she walked over to John who looked self-conscious, alone in a sea of Spanish speakers.

"What happened?" Terri asked. She had met him only once before in the Wild Boar with her brother, but he had struck her as very approachable. "Was that Evan taking off?"

"Yeah," he said with an embarrassed frown. Terri reached over and poured him a beer while he gathered his thoughts. "Professor Henderson didn't show up at Evan's concert tonight like she promised. I'm afraid he lost his temper with her, and they exchanged some words before he left." John cleared his throat, indicating that he had understated their disagreement. "I think he was surprised to see her here at a party when she had missed his performance. On the bright side," he added with a brittle smile, "everyone here on the porch seemed far more amused than distressed by the scene."

"Oh dear, what a horrible misunderstanding! Please tell Evan when he calms down that it wasn't her fault. She's been sick and her medicine made her sleep right through the concert. I know for a fact that she feels horrible about missing it. She told me so before you all got here." He nodded his head as if he suspected there must have been a reasonable explanation all along.

"I'll do that, but I'll need a ride home first."

"Why don't you come with me?" Arthur interrupted the twosome. "Dorothy's not feeling well and wants me to drive her home. I could take her in her own car, and John could follow in mine so I can get back here after I drop her off." Everyone agreed this was a good suggestion, and soon the porch was once again devoid of English speakers.

When Terri went back inside the house, she found Jorge at the stereo. She felt a shiver run through her as she watched his muscular shoulders and arms flex slightly as he flipped through the loose pile of records, and she wondered what his reaction would be if she crept up behind him and looped her arms around his waist. Three beers and the relief of seeing her party reach critical mass put her in the mood to take some risks, but she held back. Her instincts told her, as they often did with Jorge, to substitute the impulse to be affectionate with humor. "Do you like my collection? That's only about a tenth of it. I keep the best Cuban stuff locked away in the closet of my room." He turned around and kissed her cheeks.

"Why?"

"It's too incendiary. The people would go absolutely crazy."

"A disco inferno, eh?" His *deeeesco* parodying a bad Spanish accent

"Precisely," she giggled. He turned and took the top record off of the stack.

"Do you like this one?"

"It's one of my favorites."

"Me too. I love Victor Avila." A mischievous grin spread over his face as he hid the album behind his back. "Where is he from?"

"Colombia."

"Guess again."

"Now, I remember, it must be Puerto Rico."

"He would kill you for saying that--he's from Cuba. And I'll bet you didn't know he was a saxophone player in Desi Arnez's band."

"Of course, I did."

"Except he played marimba for Jose Martinez."

"Okay, I give up," she laughed. "I borrowed the records from a friend of Dorothy's. My Latin collection consists of one album of Pablo Casals's cello concertos, but you've got to admit there's some good stuff in there."

"Absolutely," he said emphatically. "You are very wonderful to host this party. I'm sorry I'm so late. Is there anything I can do?"

"Yes," she said without hesitation, "you could go say hello to Suzanne and Maria. Now that Arthur and Dorothy are gone, they don't know anybody here at all." Full speed ahead, she thought to herself. "And, if you really wanted to be useful, you could stay after the party and help me clean up."

"No problem. Now, I will go find your brother's beautiful companion and her impish daughter." He turned with a flourish and left the room. If he weren't so damn perfect, she thought, I might have a chance.

Many people stayed until well past midnight, as late an ending to a Friday party as Terri could remember. Jorge had cruised the party with Maria in tow, introducing her to everyone in Spanish and prompting her to respond to their simple questions. She was a startlingly accurate mimic and fearlessly repeated everything he told her. The two of them working in tandem were the hit of the party. When Suzanne finally put the tired little girl to bed, the remaining guests moved out onto the porch so she would not be disturbed. An hour later, as Jorge and Terri began to clean up, only a few stragglers were left leaning against the porch railing. They volunteered to help, but Terri politely refused their offer and shortly thereafter she and Jorge had the house to themselves.

Cleaning up consisted mostly of tracking down the myriad of plastic cups and paper plates left scattered around the house. There was little dishwashing to do, and Jorge quietly swept out the hall and the porch while Terri dealt with the handful of crumb-covered serving plates. When they were clean, she appeared on the porch with two cups of decaffeinated coffee and told Jorge any remaining chores could wait until the next day. "Here you go," she said handing him the steaming cup, "unless you want another beer. You certainly earned it for helping me out." She sat down on the porch swing and let out a long sigh. He took the cup and joined her. She spread the afghan over their laps.

"What are you thinking about Jorge?" As she spoke, she laid her head on his shoulder. The stress accumulated during the long hours of work had dissipated, replaced by sweet exhaustion and the lingering buzz of the Dos Equis. The sense of hesitancy she normally felt around Jorge had faded too, and she wondered if she dare take Dorothy's advice and try to seduce him.

"I was just thinking how nice it will be to sleep in tomorrow."

"You sleep in every morning," she teased him and ran her hand over his hard stomach and muscular chest, "that's why you only take afternoon classes." She started to nibble on his ear.

"Are you drunk, my little puritana?" He turned to face her, and she rested her forehead squarely on his.

"I like it better when I'm your little *ojos verdes*, your little green-eyed girl." She stared straight into his eyes, for once confident and unafraid, daring him to take her up on the invitation to kiss her. He pushed her hair back from her face but hesitated.

"You do have the most beautiful eyes that I've ever seen. God help the men of America if you ever learned how to use them." He brushed his mouth lightly against hers. "And God help me too." The kiss he gave her then was like nothing she had ever experienced before. Only their lips touched, but she felt the warmth of him deep inside her, kindling a heat that spread throughout her whole body, sending her tingling as if she had just escaped from the icy clutches of winter into a warm farmhouse kitchen. They had kissed before, but the sense of timidity and curiosity present in their earlier embraces was replaced with a sense of urgency that drove her hands through his hair and over his cheeks, across his shoulders and down over his body. Soon, his hands were exploring her too, touching her with a need she did not know she could arouse in a man.

"Let's go inside," she whispered in his ear, pulling on his earlobe gently with her teeth as she spoke. He responded with another kiss, but she took his hands and pulled him up, leading with the slow sway of her hips to the front door and into the hallway where they locked again in a furious embrace. She found herself pushed against the wall, his hands wandering into previously unexplored territory, eliciting moans that threatened to wake up Suzanne and Maria. They stumbled into the dark of the stereo room and onto the sofa where Arthur and Suzanne had first made love a year and a half before. Belts were undone and zippers frantically searched for. Terri's blouse was almost completely unbuttoned when they heard heavy footsteps make their way slowly up the front porch steps.

"Did you lock the front door?" Jorge asked, recovering his composure first.

"I think so," she whispered as they heard someone try the front door and struggle with its ancient and finicky lock. They both hurried to tuck in their shirts and refasten various buckles and buttons. She tried to make out Jorge's face in the dark as she spoke, "Who the hell could that be?"

"Your brother," he said, slapping his forehead with his palm. "He never came back from dropping off Professor Henderson."

"But that was hours ago!" She could not imagine why it would have taken Arthur so long, especially when he was so eager to get back to the party.

"Maybe they got bit by the love bug too," he said. She briefly entertained an absurd vision of her brother and Dorothy, and clasped her hand over her mouth in an unsuccessful effort to stifle a giggle.

"Terri? Is that you?" he whispered down the hallway as loudly as he dared. "Terri?"

"What is it?" She walked into the hallway, hoping she could deal with Arthur briefly and return to Jorge. "What took you so long?"

"It's Dorothy," he said. "I had to take her to the hospital. She fell and hurt her shoulder, but I think maybe she really had a heart attack."

"Is she okay?"

"I don't know. They moved her into intensive care and wouldn't let me see her since I'm not a relative." Terri stood motionless in the hall for a moment, her desire for Jorge replaced by a desperate concern for her friend. She felt an instinctive need to see her as quickly as she could.

"Where are you going?" Arthur asked as she walked past him into the kitchen.

"To get my keys. I'm going to the hospital right now. She doesn't have anyone else, Arthur."

"But they won't let a non-relative in."

"No, but they'll let her niece Terri in for a visit." She kissed him on the cheek. "Go to sleep. I can take over from here."

"If you see her, tell her we're all worried about her."

"I will." She watched Arthur disappear into Suzanne's room and walked back to talk to Jorge. She turned the small corner light on. "Did you hear all that?" Jorge was completely dressed, hair brushed, looking as fresh as if he had just arrived at the party.

"I caught most of it. Professor Henderson is sick and you're going to the hospital." He stood up and went to her. "You're a good friend." He took both of her hands and looked like he wanted to say more, but instead he kissed her cheek, turned down her offer of a ride, and glided quietly past her out of the house.

Terri drove to the hospital with her windows down, hoping the rush of fresh air would clear her head and cool her body. As she suspected, no one at the ICU demanded proof when she told them that she was Dorothy's closest living relative. Notwithstanding her status, she was not immediately allowed access to her friend. She was told to sit in the waiting room until the doctor on call had evaluated the patient's condition.

"Can you at least tell me how she is?"

"No ma'am, just that her condition is stable." Terri sat down and noticed it was past 2:30 in the morning. She flipped through magazines until her eyes would no longer focus and eventually gave in to the desire to curl up and sleep on the waiting room sofa. When she awoke, the early morning sun was streaming through the window next to the nurses' station. She immediately got up and asked about Dorothy but was informed that Dr. Burton was with her. After a long drink from the water fountain and a trip to the cafeteria for a cup of overboiled coffee, she returned to the waiting room in time to see a scruffy looking doctor in a worn, white jacket talking to the nurse. When the nurse noticed Terri, she pointed her out to Burton who strode over a moment later.

148

"Dorothy never told me about you," he commented suspiciously without introducing himself.

"I don't know why she would have. We only just met last month. My mother moved out to California before I was born and never brought me back here for a visit. When she passed away last year, I thought I'd come back and introduce myself to the family." Terri found that lying for a good cause came naturally.

"Did she die of cancer too?"

"Yes, in fact she did. She had ovarian cancer--the doctors caught it way too late." Terri looked at the floor, ostensibly overcome by the traumatic memory of her mother's passing.

"Doesn't surprise me," he nodded knowingly, "and you should get a Pap smear." With this abrupt bit of advice, he turned and left.

"Boy, he's a slick one," she remarked to the nurse as he disappeared into the elevator. "Can I see her now?"

"Yes, but just for a few minutes. She's very tired." The nurse led her down the hall to a surprisingly cheerful room overlooking a church next to the hospital. Dorothy was propped up by three pillows, sipping from a water bottle held in her left hand. She gave Terri a weak smile.

"I hear my niece has been waiting around here all night long." She lay the water bottle against her chest and extended her hand to Terri.

"Yes, auntie, we've been very worried about you." She squeezed Dorothy's hand and tried to hold back her tears.

"Well," Dorothy sighed and tilted her head to the right, "the arm's totally useless now. When I got out of your brother's car, I slipped and reached out to break my fall. When my right hand hit the pavement, my shoulder gave out completely. The doctor last night said the tumor has weakened and rearranged all the ligaments and tendons. The force of the fall just ripped everything." She let go of Terri's hand and took a sip of water. "I thought I was going to die. I have never hurt so much in my life. I figured that the mass had finally ruptured and I was going to bleed to death right there on the ground, but your brother picked me up and took me to the emergency room."

"What did they do when you got here?"

"They shot me full of dope for the pain and immobilized the arm. I pretty much have to keep it in this sling permanently. It still hurts, but now that all the anti-inflammatories are kicking in, I feel better." She took another sip of water. "You know what's funny? When I was lying there on the ground getting ready to meet my maker, the only thing I could think about was not being able to conduct the Beethoven. No life flashing before my eyes, no visions of a shining light, just thinking about one final concert. Do you think that's pathetic?"

149

"No, not at all," Terri said emphatically, "and besides you weren't really dying, were you? And it's not just a concert, is it?"

"No, I guess it's not," she sighed again. "Doc Burton says he'll let me out Monday, but I'll have to conduct left-handed." She flapped her left hand spastically back and forth. "The kids are going to love this."

"What else did the doctor say when he got here?"

"Nothing much, other than moaning about losing his favorite patient. The old crackpot's always been sweet on me--I thought he was going to cry there for a minute." She rolled her eyes. "The emergency room Doc last night said that I'm a time bomb. He said I've probably got bits of cancer everywhere by now, but he thinks I could hemorrhage to death before it concentrates anywhere else. He was just guessing, because I won't let him take a CAT scan, but he said someday I might look down and find myself bleeding to death, and there won't be a damn thing anyone can do about it."

## 22

### John Takes A Walk

"How'd you get home?" Evan asked with a generous portion of repentance in his voice.

"I met this cute Chilean guy at the party, and he brought me here after hours of passionate lovemaking at the Holiday Inn."

"Well, that's pretty impressive, since it's only been thirty minutes." Evan was sitting deep in an armchair in the living room, obviously relieved that John was still talking to him after having been abandoned. "I'm sorry I stormed out of there. When you didn't follow right away, I just said *fuck it* and took off without looking back."

"I drove Arthur's car over to Dorothy's and walked home." John sat down on the sofa and put his feet up on the coffee table. "He's going to pick it up after he drops her off."

"Why couldn't the old pterodactyl fly herself home?"

"She was pretty shaken by your little tirade and didn't feel like she could do it herself." John was tolerant of Evan's private temper tantrums, but his public outbursts were a different story. He was embarrassed by the scene at the house, even more so after learning that Dorothy had a perfectly good excuse for missing the concert. "She's been ill recently and has to take the kind of painkillers that can knock you on your butt. Apparently, she was very distressed that she passed out for your concert and planned to make a heartfelt apology, but you didn't really give her much of a chance."

"That's got to be bullshit," Evan replied vehemently. John knew that like many people with bad tempers, Evan got a perverse pleasure out of blowing up on the rare occasions when it was justified. Being told that he had made a mistake would leave an especially sour taste in his mouth. "Is that what she told you?"

"No, I didn't talk to her at all. Arthur's sister told me. She talked with Dorothy before we got there." He saw Evan slump deeper into the chair and waited patiently for him to respond.

"So, she misses a damn good concert--way better than it had any right to be--and I'm going to end up apologizing to her." He made a fist and pounded the top of his thigh. "I hate this town. I can't take a step without my foot landing in a pile of shit." John said nothing; he had learned long ago it was better to let Evan vent and then supply the voice of reason when he ran out of things to complain about. His anger usually turned against him, but this time he lashed out in a different direction. "You know I got a call from Peter Carlson up at Syracuse yesterday. They want me to be a candidate there again." He paused in the face of John's patient silence. "They lost the guy they made the offer to last year. Apparently, I was their second choice."

"What did you tell him?"

"I told him I'd send him my vita," he replied, as if it were the only rational thing to do. They sat for several more minutes without speaking. Evan closed his eyes in agitated meditation. John stared a hole through the blank television screen and waited to send up a trial balloon to test the seriousness of Evan's intentions.

"The Weather Channel reported heavy snow in Syracuse this morning,"

"I've got to get out of here, John." In other circumstances, the statement might have been a plea for sympathy or understanding, but Evan seemed hungry for more confrontation. The suggestion to move when they had just arrived, the hard work on the house done, and John satisfied with his new job, was deliberately provocative. I don't need this kind of bullshit right now, John thought, and I refuse to argue with him when he's like this. "You know, getting out sounds like a good idea right now." Without another word, he got up and slipped outside into the cool night air.

As a boy in Ohio, he had been a night walker, a habit he had lost in New York City. When things were too tense in his childhood home, he would walk around his neighborhood and out onto the country club grounds that lay alongside the nicest part of the subdivision. Sometimes he kicked his shoes off and walked the length of the manicured fairways, the comforting massage of the soft turf helping him to put his clueless family into perspective. Clarkeston at night provided a different sort of refuge. The city lights dimmed the stars that had swirled so brightly above him on the golf course, but they also provided a warmth and sense of belonging that slowly enveloped him as he strolled down the tree-lined avenue.

He walked carefully through College Hills as his eyes adjusted to the night. Much of the neighborhood was still awake, watching television, he guessed, or making love, washing dishes, arguing, folding clothes, talking on the phone, petting their cats, reading in bed. He was walking down the corridor of a beehive, honey-gathering done for the day, but the creatures not quite dormant for the night. After a couple of blocks, John emerged from his neighborhood into the campus town, a place that was never silent and motionless. Even when the bars and restaurants were closed in the wee hours of the morning, the neon and sodium phosphorescence of the storefronts and lamps moved the whole street in their shimmer, attracting a constant flutter of bugs, birds and bats. John hurried across the street, to avoid the crowd of students who loitered in front of the Wild Boar and Sal's Pizza Palazzo.

As he walked onto the campus, the sky darkened and a cool breeze brought down a flurry of leaves flickering past the old-fashioned gas lamps that lit the sidewalk, adding to the brittle carpet already laid beneath his feet. The old south quadrangle was like another world whose firmament comprised the rustling canopy of branches glowing softly in the faint lamplight. John half-expected a hobbit or an elf to stroll out from behind the trunks of the ancient oak trees, but he stumbled upon nothing more exotic than pairs of students escaping from their crowded dorm rooms onto the open expanse of leaves and grass.

He walked quietly under the Music Building portico on the edge of the north quad and sat down on a wooden bench underneath an enormous cedar of Lebanon, hoping the stillness of the place would help him think more clearly about the choices that might be facing him. He loved Evan, he loved his job, he loved Clarkeston, he loved being away from New York, he loved the friends he was starting to make. The threat that Evan's mood posed to all of these things had driven him anxiously into the night. If Evan demanded a move, he did not know what he would do.

He leaned back and looked out over the vast lawn to the wrought iron arches that marked the entrance to the college, and through which the distant lights of downtown Clarkeston twinkled over the river. After a while, the magic of his sanctuary began to settle over him. It was a place where problems outside his control, like Evan's wanderlust or his father's homophobia, lacked the power to upset him. He sat for a long time among the old brick buildings until he finally yielded to the call of the lights across the river. He walked the length of the quad and through the arches where he lingered for a moment to watch a bank of low clouds scud behind the dome of the courthouse and the steeple of the Methodist Church. Then he crossed over the bridge into town.

Main Street was bright and alive on Friday night. Every sign in town seemed to be turned on and the sidewalks teemed with bar-hopping college students and teenage townies who hung around smoking cigarettes in an unconvincing posture of world-weary boredom. John never drank when he was upset, so he skirted the row of taverns and dance clubs and headed for the Café Cappuccino where he found a more sober, but hardly

153

sedate, set of companions. He spent the next hour sipping a decaffeinated latte and reading the local arts and entertainment weekly that was distributed for free to every popular downtown locale. He found a different kind of peace among the buzz of the coffee drinkers, a comfort that came from sitting in the middle of the hive with nothing to do but enjoy observing its inhabitants. He failed, however, to notice that he himself was the subject of observation by the girl behind the counter. As he was finishing his coffee, she came over to his table.

"Do you want a free espresso? I screwed up my last order," the server smiled as she twirled her stringy brown hair.

"No, thanks. I'd never get to sleep." He instinctively returned her smile and she took his friendliness as an invitation to sit down. She pulled up a chair without asking if it was alright to join him.

"You know, I get off at midnight. You want to go get a drink when I'm done?" Her come-on was abrupt, but given the average level of sophistication of the male students in town, he figured that it probably worked with regularity. He was fascinated by her brashness and apparent invulnerability to a negative answer.

"No, thanks, I really need to get home, but thanks for asking."

"You're not gay or something?" She was not hostile, just curious and hoping to continue talking to the young man with the killer smile. Her matter-of-factness elicited his first laugh of the evening. "The cute ones always are, you know," she continued, extending her hand. "My name's Tish. I've seen you before. You come in sometimes after lunch."

"It's very kind of you to remember. My name is John." He made pleasant small talk with her for a few minutes before getting up. "I've really got to go. I'll probably see you next week."

"See ya."

He walked out of the coffee house and talked briefly with one of the Magistrate's clerks who was out celebrating the end of another week of probable cause hearings, discovery disputes, and warrant issuances. Clarkeston was beginning to feel like home, the kind he had long hoped to find. Growing up in suburban Ohio engendered no sense of belonging to a community, and his neighborhood in New York, the only other place he had tried to settle down, was in such a constant state of flux that he barely knew his neighbors' names, much less the names of the people who served him his coffee or whom he ran into on the street. He wanted to stay.

As he walked back through town and across campus, he weighed his commitment to Evan and his growing attachment to Clarkeston. It would be ridiculous, he thought, to choose a place over a person. But could he move without letting anger and disappointment ruin their relationship?  He realized that he was worrying over a decision that he might never have to face, but he had always been a worrier, the only boy in his elementary school to have an ulcer, at least until his mother explained that the world would not end if he got a "B" in geography. Convincing Evan to stay was the obvious course of action, but his partner was bullheaded and difficult to manipulate, prone to resist anyone's attempts to bend his will in one direction or another.  He was not even sure he should let him know how strongly he felt.

When he got back to the house, Evan was already asleep, barely able to manage an incoherent grunt as John slipped into bed.  "I want to stay," he whispered loudly.

"Uh, huh."

"In Clarkeston."

"Uh, huh."  Evan rolled over and started to snore moments later.

Well, that's a start, John thought.  Maybe if I whisper in his ear every night I'll get my way.  Then, he rolled over and slipped into a deep and dreamless sleep.

## 23

### Jorge Goes Home

Not until he was walking down the porch steps did Jorge remember his car was back at his apartment. For a brief moment, he considered asking Terri to drop him off on her way to the hospital, but he had a secret he wanted to keep from her, and he was not ready to talk about what had almost happened in the stereo room. The thought he was a coward crossed his mind, but he pushed it away. After all, the night is cool, he reasoned, and a long walk will help me clear my head. He strode briskly away from the old house and toward the highway to Atlanta, to the haphazard, non-descript part of town where he and hundreds of other students and young professionals found comfortable, if somewhat unimaginative, lodgings.

He had a lot to think about. Long before the party started, he had walked over to Monica's apartment near the entrance to the complex where they both lived. He knew that she was making tamales to bring to the party, so he dropped by with an offer to help. She set him to work at the sink while she chopped a couple of cloves of garlic.

"I saw you and Terri in the cafeteria the other day," Monica said after a few minutes of quiet work. "You two look very nice together."

"She's not my type." He spoke quickly, irritated by the hint in her voice that she would be pleased if he and Terri were a couple. It was one thing for Monica to have dumped him; it was quite another for her to push him on another woman.

"Sure, I understand. Tall, long blond hair, big chest. No, not your type at all." She smiled, and he was torn between despair and the gravity of her soul-swallowing brown eyes. He had begun a charade of cool friendship weeks before; now he ached to tell her that he still loved her, to remind her that *she* was his perfect type.

"Now, if she were about five-four, with long dark hair, brown eyes, and a perfect figure, then I might be interested." He dared to glance over his shoulder at her, but her head remained down, focused on her work.

"Yes, but then you wouldn't have a chance."

"Monica! Why do you have to be so cold?"

156

"As long as you keep pestering me, I'm going to be like a deep freeze."

"Pestering you?" Exasperation filled his voice. "I haven't said a thing in almost two months!"

"You may not have said anything." She looked up and chastised him the way a mother would a small child, "but I feel your puppy dog eyes staring at me all the time. What kind of man comes over and volunteers to peel vegetables anyway?"

He could tell that she was not really angry with him. At worst, she found him tiresome, but for a moonstruck young man who wished to inspire unquenchable passion, her attitude was difficult to accept. With great effort, he repressed his desire to tell her how he felt and forced a laugh.

"Well, first of all, I was talking about Julia Roberts. What an ego you have! And second," he said as he stood up, "if you do not want my help, I have plenty of homework that I could be doing right now." As if to reward his recovery, she asked him to stay, and they worked and gossiped until it was time to go to the party.

"Can you give me a ride?"

"Sure, but let me get something else on."

When she left the room, all of his energy left with her. It was exhausting to feign lightheartedness with a woman he longed to hold in his arms. As she disrobed and hunted through her closet just a couple of steps down the hall, he tried to remember the sweet curves of her body but could not conjure up the image he wanted. I'm an idiot, he thought. A wonderful blond is really interested in me, and a gorgeous brunette wants to be my friend. Most men would be envious, so why am I so miserable? While he waited, he picked a piece of paper and a pencil off the counter underneath her phone and started sketching out a short story. He frequently felt an impulse to write but had never been depressed enough to put pen to paper. *A brunette, a blond, a witty (tall) student, betrayal, anguish . . .*

"Are you ready?" she called from the bedroom.

"Let's go." He folded the paper into a shield that he pushed down into the front breast pocket of his shirt. Tonight I'm going to decide what to do, he told himself. I'm either going to commit to unrequited love, or I'm going to go after a voluptuous American girl with no regrets. He was certain of one thing--he was no longer going to wallow in indecision. But when the party was over and he found himself sitting on the swing with Terri, he realized that he had no will to decide. Maybe I'm the one who's been the Puritan, he thought to himself as Terri kissed him. He pushed the thought away and successfully kept it at bay until Arthur interrupted them.

When Terri returned with the news of Professor Henderson's fall, Jorge felt a guilty sense of relief, not because he lacked the desire to make love to her, but because he would have been unable if called upon. To his intense embarrassment, he had found her soft moans and the pressure of her body against him so stimulating that a sticky wet warmth now filled the space once occupied by his tumescence. When the opportunity for a gracious exit presented itself, he grabbed it and tried to sort his feelings out on the long walk home.

As he left the neighborhood and walked on the gravel shoulder of the broad thoroughfare that headed to Atlanta, he patted his shirt pocket and his mind wandered back to his story. He had vivid characters but no good ending. *After discovering his passionate affair with the blond, the jealous brunette begs for his love . . . After discovering him in bed with the blond, the angry brunette shoots them both . . . After discovering the affair, the bored brunette watches "Wheel of Fortune" . . . After shooting his load in his pants, frustrated author steps in front of a sixteen wheeler.*

The lack of stop lights on the edge of town allowed the traffic to whiz by at worrying speed, so Jorge walked as far away from the asphalt as he could, skirting the edge of the trash-filled ditch that separated the road from the parking lots lining his way. Only the gas stations and fast food restaurants were open, and he marked his progress by the bright beacons of their sodium lamps. In a dark stretch between a Magic Market and Dairy Queen, a car drove past him heading out of town more slowly than the others, before turning back toward him and parking in the lot of a furniture store directly in front of him, lights on and engine running waiting for Jorge to approach. He stopped walking when he was about fifty feet away.

"Hey, you wanna a ride?" He could not see who was speaking, but he could hear another voice deeper in the car snort with laughter.

"No thanks, man," he replied as confidently as he could manage, "I'm almost home." He stepped closer to the road, striding past the entrance to the parking lot as quickly as he could. He looked straight ahead as he continued on his way, but when he had taken no more than a handful of paces, he heard several of the car's doors open.

"I don't think so, asshole," the stranger's voice said. "You need to come with us." Jorge did not wait to see the men come after him. He sprinted quickly across the road, hoping they would not abandon their car in order to pursue him and figuring no Georgia redneck could keep pace with the speed of a soccer player.

As he crossed to the other side of the road he heard the doors slam and the car peel out of the parking lot after him. He headed for the gap between two buildings directly in front of him. If he could slip between them and into the neighborhood behind, he would be home free. Their car could not follow and he would lose them in the maze of streets or knock on someone's door and call the police. As he entered the alley, he looked up and saw nothing but chain link fence a dozen feet in front of him. The areas behind both buildings were protected by ten feet high fences that shared a common border, sealing off the end of the alleyway. He turned immediately but heard the tires of the car skid to a stop somewhere behind him. Ducking behind a dumpster between the buildings, he tried to choke down his growing sense of panic.

"Where'd the fucker go?"

"I think he went down the alley."

"Nigger or fuckin' beaner?"

"Don't really give a shit."

As Jorge listened to the footsteps of his pursuers crunching the gravel and broken glass at the mouth of the alley, he briefly considered hiding in the dumpster, but its mouth faced away from him and he would be caught if he tried to slip into it. He examined the fences that barred his escape. The business to his left was some sort of masonry firm; piles of tile and bricks sat on pallets behind the building. On his right, various sorts of heavy equipment, tillers, loaders, and panel trucks bore the trademark of a national rental firm. The fence protecting the bricks was topped by razor wire; the fence protecting the bushhogs was not. As the footsteps approached his hiding place, he took four huge strides to the fence guarding the rental store and furiously scrambled to the top just as his pursuers rounded the dumpster and saw him.

"Get him!"

Jorge dropped to the ground inside the yard with a painful slap to the soles of his feet. Hearing the fence shake with three new climbers, he immediately sprinted to the back of the storage area. He was only twenty feet away from the back fence and freedom when he discovered why the owners of the property felt no need to add razor wire to their barrier. A huge rottweiler lunged at Jorge from behind a Bobcat loader. With a violent twist that sent him sprawling, he narrowly escaped the jaws of the beast who skidded on the gravel and immediately turned back to Jorge with a deep growl and murderous look in its eyes. He held out his hands and walked slowly backwards.

"Good doggy," he whispered as he snuck a peek over his shoulder only to discover that he was too far away from the fence to make a quick turn and leap for freedom. As he lost eye contact with the dog, it barked and made a vicious rush for his throat. Instinctively, Jorge leapt to his right, grabbed the outside mirror of a sixteen-foot-long moving van, planted his left foot on the tire and catapulted himself up onto the hood of the massive vehicle. For a moment, he thought he was safe, but he suddenly felt himself slipping back toward the ground. The rottweiler had a tenacious grip on his pant leg and was using all of its 120 pounds to pull him back to earth. Jorge reached wildly for a purchase on the top of the truck, ripping out one of the windshield wipers until he finally got a hold of the lip of the hood where it met the windshield. He could hear the desperate scrabble of the dog's claws on the side of the truck as it tried to follow him up. He wanted to kick it with his free leg, but he needed it to maintain his purchase on the hood of the truck. He felt his fingers starting to slip.

"Eat 'em up dog!" Jorge heard his tormentors egging the animal on from the safety of the far side of the fence. None was stupid enough to enter the yard now that they knew about the dog. "Eat yourself some nigger ass!"

"Come on, rip the motherfucker up!"

The taunts renewed Jorge's determination, and he slipped his right hand deep in between the hood and the windshield, finally getting a solid grip on the wiper motor. By inching himself up, he brought the dog's head level with the oversized mirror that jutted out from the front edge of the driver's side door. While the dog's nails tap-danced a series of jagged furrows on the door's paint job, Jorge slid over slightly so that as he jerked his leg up a notch, the middle of the rottweiler's forehead hit the ragged nub of a bolt on the mirror assembly. The dog let out a squeal when it hit the metal shaft but continued to hold tightly onto Jorge's pant leg. He jerked the dog up again and a vicious cut blinded it with a gush of its own blood. As Jorge started to pull the dog up a third time, it let go and fell to the ground where it shook its eyes free of blood and paced angrily around the vehicle growling in pain and frustration. Jorge scrambled to the middle of the hood and sat hugging his knees to his chest as he watched his adversary circle the truck.

"Shit, man, the fucker got loose."

"Lucky fuck."

"He's not going to feel so lucky when the cops haul his black ass downtown in the morning for burglary." The shadowy figure laughed. "Hey nigger, maybe we'll come down to the station tomorrow and bail you out!" His three friends thought this was hysterical. "Yeah, we'll give you a ride home." After a few more insults, they sauntered back down the alley and drove into the night.

Although the safest course would be to wait out the night on top of the truck, Jorge knew that the young thugs were right. He was very likely to be accused of at least trespassing if he were found by the owner cowering from his guard dog. A glance at the damage done to the side of the truck further convinced him that he needed to find a way out of the lot. Unfortunately, the truck was just far enough away from the fence that Jorge could not be sure of jumping off and getting out of the dog's range before he was run down. The branches of a huge pecan tree beckoned over the fence from the backyard of a run-down house, but Jorge could not reach its limbs from the hood.

He looked behind him and saw that some of the branches were almost resting on the top part of the truck's storage compartment. Standing on the top of the vehicle's cab, he managed to pull himself onto the very top of the truck, fifteen feet off the ground and slightly below several promising limbs. Choosing the thickest one, he looped one leg over and sat on it like a horse, then slowly began scooting toward the trunk of the tree and safety. The going was difficult, and several times he almost lost his balance as he slid his legs gingerly over leafy offshoots that blocked his slide. Finally, he became stymied by a large limb directly over the chain link fence five feet below. As he tried to move his right leg past it, he slipped and found himself suspended upside down underneath the branch by his hands and the crook of his left leg. Instead of trying to right himself, he propelled himself underneath like an opossum toward the trunk. When he reached it, he let his legs down and stood on one of the lower branches where he dropped to the ground and caught his breath. This is where the paranoid landowner comes out of the house and blows away the Cuban, he thought to himself. But the yard remained quiet as he looked around for further trouble and walked quickly past the side of the house and onto the street.

Luckily, the quiet residential street paralleled the Atlanta highway almost all the way to his apartment complex. It meandered a bit through a lower-class neighborhood of cinder block and decaying wood frame houses, but Jorge was more than happy to keep to the narrow byway where overgrown bushes provided a constant opportunity to hide himself from passing cars. When it finally emptied into the thoroughfare, he found himself across from his complex and about a hundred yards past it. He waited several minutes, passing up several easy chances to cross until he could see no cars coming in either direction. Then he sprinted across the road toward the familiar parking lot. Just as he turned the corner, he heard a car behind him and pushed himself even harder, but it continued down the highway, leaving him panting, hands on his knees in front of the apartment's clubhouse.

"*Madre de dios*," he whispered after he caught his breath. He longed for the security of his apartment, but he was so full of adrenaline that sleep was impossible. He was headed slowly to his room when he noticed the light still on in Monica's window. His watch read two-thirty a.m. She's a night owl, he thought. Maybe it'll be easier to calm down if I tell her what happened.

After inquiring through the closed door who was there, Monica let Jorge in with a small gasp at his appearance. His pants and shirt were torn in several places; scrapes and bruises covered his arms. He looked at himself, realizing for the first time what a dirty and disheveled mess he was. "You should see the other guy," he murmured just before he collapsed on her couch.

## 24

### An Invitation


"I'm going to the hospital." John looked up and discovered Evan, sitting on the bed next to him, dressed and back from a morning walk. "You wanna come with me?"

"The hospital?" He rolled over, propping himself up on his right elbow and trying to shake away the cobwebs. "What the hell are you talking about?"

"I just got back from Henderson's house--I thought I'd bring her a peace offering of some gourmet coffee beans--and I met Arthur's sister coming out with a handful of books. I asked her what was going on, and she tells me that last night Henderson fell when she got out of her car. Apparently she's okay, but they're going to keep her in over the weekend to run some tests." He stood up. "So, I'm going to pay her visit. You wanna come with me?"

"No," John rolled on his back and looked at the ceiling with the realization that the leisurely sleep-in he had longed for all week was not going to happen. "But I will."

Evan called the hospital and learned that visiting hours lasted from ten until twelve, so they ate breakfast and shared a pot of coffee over a day-old New York Times. The morning was overcast and the view outside the large bay window was gray and gloomy.

"So why the hurry to offer the mea culpa?" John asked as he finished scanning the front page. Evan laid down the sports section and took another sip of coffee.

"Well, given the chance not to confront the dragon outside of her lair, I'd prefer to apologize before she gets back to work. Second, I'll earn some extra brownie points for visiting her in the hospital. You forget that lurking behind our little pissing contest is the fact that she's the senior member of a department that will vote on whether to renew my contract for next year, and maybe someday decide whether I get tenure or not. Oh, and we need to remember to pick up a Get Well card." The explanation got a chilly reception from John, who stared at his partner, arms crossed and eyebrows raised.

"Alright," Evan admitted in an exasperated voice, "and I feel guilty. I was a schmuck, okay? You don't need to rub it in."

"Just checking to see if you still had a conscience."

It began to rain as they drove to the hospital, so they pulled into the adjacent parking deck and tramped through the long glass corridor that connected it to the hospital. Dorothy had been moved out of the ICU to a regular room, and they found her reading one of the books Terri had bought. With her right arm immobilized, she had pulled the rolling dinner tray close to her chest, propped the book up against it, and was turning the pages with her left hand.

"What are you doing here?" She studied the two men carefully over the top of her reading glasses.

"I came to say I was sorry about last night." Evan mustered a tone of genuine sincerity. "John told me . . . this is him by the way, I don't think you've ever been introduced. He said that you couldn't help missing the concert last night." Dorothy and John acknowledged each other with a nod and turned their attention back to Evan, both keenly interested in his attempt at damage control. "Anyway, I've always been a hothead, and I let my temper get the best of me. That's no excuse, but I did want to apologize."

"Well, I'm sorry too. I really did want to attend the concert. I'm sure it was excellent. I'm looking forward to seeing the tape."

"The tape?"

"Yes. All performances are taped and kept on reserve in the Music Library. It's really surprising how much you can learn from watching yourself."

"I imagine it is." Evan's expression of despair showed that he had not known about the taping system. Dorothy enjoyed his discomfort for a moment and then changed the subject.

"So, this is your better half."

"Much better," John said as he reached over with a disarming grin and took her free hand, squeezing it gently while he spoke. "Nice to finally meet you."

"And it's a pleasure to meet you, John." She responded with a warm smile of her own. Ever since John could remember, older women had always found him irresistible. Maybe it was because he always smiled at them and listened carefully to whatever they were saying, or maybe it was the fact that, for some odd reason, he liked them too. "Are you also a musician?"

"No, ma'am. I'm the computer person over in the courthouse."

"That's wonderful. We could certainly use you in the Music Building. I hear there are all sorts of terrific things we could be doing, but the faculty don't even have computers in their offices yet."

"What a shame! In fact, I just got some really interesting music composition software for Evan last week. It lets you compose easily in any key you want and even suggests harmonies." John suddenly saw a chance to confront Evan's main problem with staying in Clarkeston. "Would you like a demonstration? You could come over for dinner next Saturday, and I could show you what it can do. That is, if you'll be out of here by then." He glanced over at Evan and hoped that Dorothy would not guess from the visible pulse in Evan's temple and his wide unblinking eyes that his smile and nod hid a horrified disapproval.

"I'd love to," she said. "I'm getting out Monday morning."

They made small talk for a couple more minutes until Dorothy's lunch arrived and Evan suggested they leave her to eat in peace.

As soon as the door shut behind them, he glared at John. "What were you thinking about back there?"

"What do you mean?" John said innocently, walking slightly ahead of Evan and refusing to look back. Evan stepped up even with him.

"You know what I mean! Dinner! Wasn't coming to the hospital on a Saturday and groveling at her feet enough?"

"I'm not quite sure I saw you actually grovel," he replied mischievously. "It will be good for you. You've been a real pain in the ass lately, and this will help chill you out. I'm sure Dorothy would agree with me."

"Pain in the ass!" He sputtered. "Dorothy would agree? If this were the Twilight Zone, I'd say that you actually like the old bat!"

"You know," he stepped into the elevator door ahead of Evan and turned to face him, "I do like her. She cracks me up."

## 25

### Dorothy's Last Rehearsal

In the weeks after Dorothy was discharged from the hospital, Louis noticed her tempos starting to lag, and he was torn between following her beat or the well-established rhythms that the chorus maintained out of habit. An unspoken tension between the group and its director slowly grew. The first week of rehearsal was not so bad, but by Thursday of the second week, everybody realized something was wrong. Unable to disguise the pain attending her every movement, she shifted uncomfortably in her chair, too distracted and exhausted to focus on fine-tuning the group's sound. On Friday, Louis arrived early for rehearsal in order to steal some extra minutes of practice time on the grand piano that sat in the corner of the room. As he played, he watched her walk stiffly to her chair, clenching the Beethoven score and a thin manilla folder against her side with her left hand. She looked ten years older than the woman who had taught him music history during the summer term.

"Hello, Mr. Coates," she said in a tired voice.

"Hello." He continued to play while watching her carefully over the top of his music. Her steps were so uncertain that he thought she might fall on her way to her seat, but she managed to make it before any of the choristers arrived to witness her struggle. She sat staring at the score as they began filing in several minutes later.

"Ms. Collingwood," she said as the choir was finally seated, "could you lead the group in warm-ups today?" Although the request was surprising, it was not unheard of. She occasionally let aspiring student directors warm-up the group and conduct short practice pieces, but the veteran accompanist had no plans to be a director that anyone knew of. Having watched Professor Henderson put the group through its paces hundreds of times, she had little trouble leading them through their exercises. The professor closed her eyes while the group sang and were it not for the stiffness of her posture, Louis would have thought that she had fallen asleep.

"Alright. Good. Let's start from letter A in the *Kyrie*." She held up her left hand (she had not used her right since the accident), but instead of cuing the music she dropped it down. No one breathed as they waited for her command. She slowly turned her head to Louis and nodded, signaling him to begin playing. The chorus started with him and sang through the section with Ms. Henderson sitting motionless in front of them.

"That was not too bad. Your entrances are still a little ragged." Her voice was weak, but Louis could see she still had the power to hold them with her eyes. "Yes, I know that I was not cuing you, but I shouldn't have to. The performance is less than two weeks away, and by now my presence should be virtually superfluous. By the concert date, you should not need a director at all. Why don't we declare ourselves finished for the week? I've got a horrible case of the flu to go with my bursitis and, to speak in the vernacular, I really need to crash. You go home too." The group seemed relieved by her explanation and offered no complaint about the chance to hit the campustown bars earlier than usual on a Friday afternoon. They filed out quickly until Dorothy was left alone with Louis and Debbie who talked quietly by the piano.

The two students watched her scoot to the edge of the seat, turn her body to the left and grip the top of the chair tightly with her left hand. She pushed herself upright and took several uncertain paces toward the door.

"Kids," she said, "could you come here?" Her distress propelled them to her. "Debbie, be a dear and take my score. Thank you. Now, Louis, if you would be so good as to pretend I'm an old lady and take my left arm. There you go . . . let's figure out a way to get me home. I really don't think that I can drive right now." They walked slowly beside her into the hall. Louis saw his teacher glance nervously in both directions to see if anyone was watching, but at 4:30 on a Friday afternoon, the building was nearly deserted.

"Do you want to go up to your office?" Debbie tried to mask the concern and worry in her voice. She knew her director well enough to know that any overt acknowledgment of her condition would not be welcome.

"No," she answered, "but I was wondering if one of you might be able to drive me home. I'm feeling woozy enough that it probably wouldn't be safe for me to do it myself. My car's also parked a long way from here."

"I don't drive."

"I've got my car," Debbie offered. "Why don't I pull up behind the building and pick you up there? That way you won't have to walk too far."

"You're a dear. If Louis will stay by me, we'll meet you there in a minute." Debbie walked off as rapidly as her short legs would carry her.

Louis and Dorothy moved slowly, hitched together like a terribly deliberate team in a sack race, their footfalls echoing quietly off the cool, dark halls of the stone building. He concentrated on matching her step exactly, accompanying each of her movements with the right amount of pressure and support.

"I'm sorry you're not feeling well, Professor Henderson." Being in such close contact with the person he respected most at the college, maybe in the whole world, was unnerving. She needed him and he was not used to being needed.

"Thank you, Louis. I haven't felt this bad since I had meningitis when I was a kid."

"I didn't know you had meningitis."

"I haven't even thought about it for years." Speaking took some effort, but it seemed to divert her attention from the fragile condition of her body. "The worst part was being quarantined. Once I was diagnosed, only my mother and the doctor were allowed in my room, and they were always dressed in hospital gowns and masks and gloves. I was only six years old, and I thought I was being punished for being sick. I desperately wanted to see my father, but he wasn't allowed in." Scattered rays of sunlight filtered softly through the trees as Louis pushed open the metal door that led outside to the loading dock. The tiny parking lot behind the building was limited to three disabled parking spaces and barely interrupted the urban forest that lined the eastern branch of the campus boulevard. Several cracked plastic chairs were surrounded by cigarette butts where the janitorial staff took their breaks. Dorothy led the way to one of them and sat down to wait for Debbie.

"Thank you so much for helping me Louis." She looked up at him and gauged whether he understood her need for privacy. "I find this very embarrassing, and I know I can trust you two not to tell anybody how weak I am." His expression told her he understood.

"I won't even tell Dr. Peterson." She nodded at the name of the well-known psychiatrist, unsurprised to hear that he was seeing someone. "Ms. Henderson, you're not weak; you're the strongest person I know."

They both looked through the trees for Debbie's car and before long they could see her shiny Honda turning into the lot. Louis helped Dorothy gingerly negotiate the steps down from the loading dock and eased her into the car, shutting the door carefully and standing back so Debbie could execute a quick turnabout.

"Could you come with us Louis?" Debbie asked. "We might could use you at the Professor's house."

"Okay," he said, trying to figure out how best to get into the two-door vehicle. Finally, Debbie got out of the driver's seat and pushed it forward so he could squeeze in. "I'll mash up my seat so you'll have some leg room."

Dorothy seemed to perk up a little during the ride and after getting out of the car with some help from Louis, she was able to walk on her own to the door of her house. She handed her purse to Debbie on the stoop. "Hold this, dear. I can't get my keys out one-handed." When she finally pushed open the door, a horde of cats rushed out to greet the threesome, mewling and crying as if they had not been fed for weeks. "Oh you pitiful beasts, we'll get you some food. Debbie? You all could do me one more favor before you go. These kitties would love a couple of cans of cat food. Could you open some up? There are some in the pantry next to the refrigerator."

While Debbie went to feed the cats, Louis followed Dorothy into the living room where she slowly lowered herself down on the couch. He did not know what to say. She was so different from her normal invincible self.

"I'm sorry you're sick."

"You already said that, Louis. Me, too." She gave a small sigh. "Having agreed upon my pitifulness, could I pick your musical brain for a momen?. You've been playing for Evan Roberts most of the semester, right?" Louis nodded. "Tell me what you think about him as a director. Is he good?"

"Yes, ma'am," he said after a moment's reflection, "he's very good."

"Could you elaborate?"

"Well, he's meaner than you are to the singers, but they pay attention to him. They've gotten a lot better than they were, but they're not as good as the college chorus." He thought about what he had said and decided it was right. He was uncomfortable talking about Roberts; he did not want to say the wrong thing about his mentor.

"He's meaner than me?" She seemed surprised. "I didn't think anyone was meaner than me." She was obviously impressed, and Louis was confused as to why someone would feel slighted by being called less mean than someone else.

"I don't mean he's more demanding . . . he just jumps up and down more . . . he gets in the choir's face, while you . . . ." Louis's voice trailed off, worried where his thoughts were leading him. He had never been taught to tell people what they wanted to hear. He noticed Debbie standing in the doorway and he gave her a distressed look.

"--while you just give us the death ray look," Debbie completed his sentence matter-of-factly. She was rewarded with a laugh from Dorothy and an awestruck look from Louis. "Don't you know that your eyes are

169

famous around town? I thought last week that you were going to burn the whole alto section to cinders with one glance."

"Death ray vision . . . that's the nicest thing I've heard all day." She smiled again and put her legs up on the couch in a posture of repose she would normally never adopt in front of her students. "Have you formed an opinion of Professor Roberts, Debbie?"

"His concert the other night was great, and I hear very good things about him from my friends in the group. Some other people don't like him," she added after a moment's hesitation, "but it has nothing to do with his directing ability." Dorothy gave her an understanding nod. "He's going to be an excellent director; it would be really too bad if folks around here drove him out."

"Well," Dorothy said, "perhaps we can do something about that." Debbie and Louis nodded eagerly in response. "Alright, why don't you two leave me to nap a bit. I'm very, very grateful for all of your help today, and I would be even more grateful if you two didn't mention my little disability. Okay?"

"Of course."

"Uh, huh."

"Good. I hereby give you each permanent immunity from death ray vision." They laughed and got up to leave.

"Are you sure you don't want one of us to stay for a while?" Debbie asked.

"It's alright. A friend of mine is coming over later." She looked back at the clock on the wall, "You can go." The two students left the house and closed the door quietly behind them.

"Do you need a ride home, Louis?"

"Well, I live a long way from here."

"Jump in then." Louis sat down in the front this time, still shaken from seeing his teacher in distress. "She really doesn't look very good. Does she, Louis?"

"No."

"Do you think we should call a doctor and ask him to go see her?"

"No," he said again, quickly this time, "no way." The decisiveness of his response was so out of character that Debbie was quiet for a moment, waiting for him to continue. He spoke deliberately, "You know, I think it was really hard for her to let us help her. She's a really strong person . . . She lives alone and spends all her time directing."

"You really like her, don't you?"

He nodded his head, thinking hard about what Dorothy would want him to do. "She's still the director. We should do what she wants."

"I think you're right. We should do what she wants." They rode in silence the rest of the way to Louis's apartment, concern for their teacher deflecting the anxiety that prevents people from being comfortable together in the absence of noise. When she pulled over in front of his apartment building, he thanked her but did not get out of the car. His experience that afternoon had been unsettling, temporarily eroding some of the barriers that separated him from his impulses. He stared at the dashboard and blurted out a decision before he could think about it.

"I think we should play together."

"You mean the four-hand competition?"

"Uh, huh."

"That's wonderful, Louis." She was genuinely excited. "We don't have a whole lot of time, but I'll bet we can still do it. Can we practice some this evening? Maybe meet at the third floor practice room around seven?"

"Sure," he replied, "but I gotta go now." He opened up the car door and got out.

"Okay, see ya!"

"See ya." He walked up to the apartment, mouth dry, heart pounding, palms sweating, but miles and centuries away from the salons of eighteenth-century Germany he used to dream about.

## 26

### Guess Who's Coming to Dinner

The next day, Evan sat in the kitchen watching John rinse two bags of dried beans in a colander. He had assigned John the job of cooking for Dorothy since he was responsible for the invitation.

"Have you spoken with her since you made this date last week?"

"No, why?"

"I don't know. I've been hearing some funny stories about her rehearsals. I'm not sure she's completely recovered from her fall. She probably should have taken more time off, but you know how tenaciously she hangs onto that group."

John failed to respond, and Evan wondered whether it would be a good time to mention that Syracuse had invited him and only one other person to interview on its campus. The invitation put him at war with himself. He felt guilty about agreeing to the interview without consulting John, and then angry at his guilt. Why shouldn't he look at other schools when things were going so miserably for him in Clarkeston? Even if things worked out in Georgia, he could never have any satisfying career so far away from the stages he had always dreamed of. Love shouldn't mean giving up your most fundamental dreams.

"So what are you cooking for us tonight?" He watched John move about the kitchen. Clarkeston was the perfect place for him, and Evan knew he was betraying his friend and lover. Why was John the one who could turn him inside-out? It was not just his looks. Somehow it was both thrilling and peaceful to share a life with someone who did not need a stage to be happy, someone for whom relationships always came first.

"It's getting cooler out, so I thought I'd make a spicy lentils and chorizo casserole with a Caesar Salad on the side."

"Well, she'll be making a joyful noise to the Lord in church Sunday morning."

"Could you be nice just for once?"

"I'm not nice. You should know that by now."

"Well, you can behave during dinner at least, and then you can leave us alone while I show her that software."

"Okay, okay I just don't trust her, that's all. But I'll be a good boy." Evan stood up and pushed his chair aside.

"We're going to have fun tonight."

"You're out of your mind."

While John continued with the dinner preparations, Evan worked in the den editing a collection of little-known English madrigals that he hoped would constitute his first publication as an academic. By six-thirty, the time appointed for Dorothy's arrival, everything was ready and John carried a glass of wine into the den where Evan contentedly studied a pile of manuscripts.

"Quittin' time." The cook held out a glass of chilled Valdepenas.

"Thanks." Evan took the glass and looked up from his work. "And thanks for cooking dinner tonight. You're better at doing the right thing than me."

"Maybe that's why you keep me around."

"Maybe."

The telephone rang, and John looked at his watch before walking across the room to answer it. He was dismayed to hear an exhausted and desperate voice on the other end of the line.

"John? This is Dorothy." She paused a moment and spoke with obvious difficulty. "I can't make it tonight . . . not feeling well. Sorry. I need to talk to Evan--"

"--I'll get him."

"No!" She paused again. "No. Just tell him to come over, okay? I need to talk to him." Then the line went dead. He looked at the phone and then at Evan before he put down the receiver.

"Don't tell me. She's getting more revenge by not showing up for dinner tonight." He finished his wine. "Well, I suppose that's only fair."

John sat down on the only other chair in the room, an old leather recliner he had found in the want ads. "No, she sounds really sick. I don't think she's faking it; she could barely talk." They sat with their own thoughts until John finally broke the silence. "She wants you to come over and talk to her."

"What!?"

"She said it was really important for you to go over to see her tonight."

"Shit."

"Calm down, I'll come with you and bring some dinner for her. She didn't sound like she could be doing any cooking for herself. Let's get our jackets and head over there."

They walked the three blocks to her home in silence, John holding a casserole dish in front of him and Evan carrying a small plastic container filled with a portion of the salad. It was a cool evening and so clear that the stars stood out brightly over the glow of the street lamps.

"It's really nice out." John looked up at the sky careful not to trip over the tree roots that broke up the sidewalk.

"Uh, huh."

"Why don't we walk down to campustown and have some pizza when we're done and save the lentils for tomorrow? They're always better the second day anyway."

"Sure." Evan turned up the sidewalk leading to Dorothy's front door. "Here we are." He took a deep breath and pushed the doorbell but got no immediate answer. Then he rapped his knuckles sharply on the wooden door and peered through the thin windows that ran parallel to it on either side. Seeing nothing but a dim light beyond the foyer, he knocked again and tried the doorknob. The door was unlocked. He looked at John with a shrug and stuck his head in the door. "Hello? Professor Henderson?"

"Come in," a voice called faintly from the room off the right side of the foyer. As they stepped inside, they were immediately assaulted by a phalanx of mewling cats who rubbed their furry cheeks against the visitors' ankles and followed the two men into the room where their mistress lay on the sofa, a heavy quilt pulled up to her chin.

"Placido! Luciano! Jesse! Leave them alone," she said in an exasperated voice to the cats. She looked up at John and Evan as if she were accustomed to receiving late night supplicants into her sick room. "You'd think they hadn't been fed all day."

"Where's Beverly?" Evan asked, picking up immediately on the operatic motive behind Dorothy's cat-naming.

"She's probably under my bed. She's usually scared of strangers."

"I was just kidding!" Evan was genuinely surprised and amused. "You mean there really is a Beverly?"

"Yes, and a Leontyne and Kathleen too. You won't see Kathleen, though. She's too good to hang out with the other cats." Evan laughed and Dorothy started to join him but her outburst was cut short by a paroxysm of pain that clouded her face.

"We brought you some supper," John said when the spasm seemed to have passed. He held out the casserole dish. "My world-famous lentils and sausage."

"That's very sweet of you." Her voice sounded a little bit stronger than it had on the phone. "But I haven't been able to eat anything for almost a week now." She looked much worse than she had in the hospital, face drawn and dark bags under her eyes. Her eyes maintained a reservoir of strength, but her body was deteriorating as they watched. "Why don't you two sit down?"

"I don't understand," John asked, "how your shoulder can ruin your appetite?"

"My guess is that I have some kind of tumor in my stomach now, too." She stared hard at both of them, daring them to express some sort of shock or surprise. "You must promise to tell no one about this, do you understand?" Evan gave a stunned nod; John's promise was in his eyes.

"Late last summer, I was diagnosed with an inoperable malignancy around my right collar bone. I went through a serious bout with breast cancer five years ago, and when the doctors told me it had come back in my bones and my lymph system, I decided not to let them fight it. They all agreed there was no hope of a cure, just prolonging my suffering. They also told me it would eventually spread. Even though my biggest problem is my shoulder, it's gotten bad in other places too." She gave them an ironic smile, "Starving's got to be a better way to go than cancer, don't you think? Right now, I don't even have the desire to eat."

Neither of them knew what to say. For a moment they could do nothing more than meet the fearless clarity of her eyes.

"Is there anything we can do?" Evan finally asked with a sidelong glance at John who immediately nodded. "After all we're just down the street."

"In fact, there is something you can do for a foolish old woman." Sadness and anger entered her voice for the first time. "I've spent the semester pouring my remaining energy into preparing a funeral mass for myself--"

"--the Beethoven *Missa Solemnis.*"

"Correct," she sighed. "Now do you understand why I couldn't let you have the College Chorus this semester? I know you thought I was being a bitch, but I couldn't very well tell you my secret, could I?"

"Why not?"

"I didn't know you well enough to be sure you wouldn't blab it around the music school. All I wanted was to prepare this last piece of music, enjoy one last performance, and then fade away without having to listen to the ritual moaning and wailing when someone around here gets sick. You see, I may be a bitch, but I'm not an unreasonable bitch." Evan laughed before he could consider whether his response was appropriate, but the expression on Dorothy's face told him it was welcome.

"Your secret's safe with me."

"No one will find out from us."

In the pause that followed her revelation, Evan looked around the room and surveyed the artifacts of a life lived around music. An enormous record collection occupied most of her bookshelves, the remaining space crammed with scores and biographies of various composers. More papers were piled on the bench and on top of the studio piano pressed against the far wall. A solitary black and white picture of a young man was perched between two stacks of music. Evan thought he looked familiar, but could not imagine how he might know the subject of the photo.

"Good, and one more thing," she said softly, "I'm too sick to conduct the Beethoven. Last week, I could hardly get through the rehearsals. I've got some really strong pills that take the edge off the pain, but they leave me so groggy that I can't think straight, and all I want to do is sleep. Even sitting and conducting with my left hand is too much. And if I don't take the pills . . ." She bit her lip hard and forced herself to take a deep breath. "I had to cancel the last half of rehearsal on Friday. I'm not getting any better, and these next ten days before the performance are going to be nonstop work. I haven't begun rehearsing the orchestra yet, and I haven't met with the soloists.

"You know, this is the part I usually look forward to the most, putting it all together, making that last push in a sleep-deprived blur. The feeling you get when the music starts and everything falls into place . . ."

She looked up at Evan and blinked back the tears. "I want you to conduct it for me. I watched the tape of your concert, and you worked wonders with those young men." She blew her nose and recovered her composure.

"I know this is a lot to ask. All I can promise you is that the chorus knows the notes. You'll have to do all the hard stuff. The orchestra meets for the first time on Monday evening and the soloists for the first time on Tuesday. After that, you've got a week to make it all work."

"Why me?" Evan asked, unable to comprehend the motive behind her request, "I mean, surely you know someone in Atlanta, or maybe even here in town, who could take over and do a good job."

"Evan, if I asked the director of the Atlanta Symphony Chorus, he would happily come down and substitute for me, but I want a colleague to do it." She managed a smile. "I've heard the story of your first rehearsal with the Men's Glee Club from about five different people now and, if you'll pardon the expression, you've got balls. I like that." She gave a weak laugh. "And you're a damn prickly person. I like that too. People have managed to put up with me my whole career. I'd be a damn hypocrite if I couldn't do the same for you. So, will you do it?"

"Of course." He looked down at the floor trying to control his emotions. "It would be a tremendous honor. It's more than I deserve."

"Alright, now don't go getting humble on me," she said with disgust. "If you're anything but a fire-breathing dragon next week, you're going to get eaten alive."

He suddenly looked up. "I've got an idea. I'd be perfectly willing to do all the prep work and let you conduct the performance yourself. You could rest all week and still get to do the piece."

"No," she shook her head slowly, "that would hardly be fair to you, and I couldn't do it anyway. I'm barely able to get to the kitchen and make myself a mug of tea, which is all I'm able to keep down these days. After ten more days of living on tea, I wouldn't be fit to do anything except totter onto the stage and fall off. And trust me, that is not how I want to be remembered." She sighed. "I'll be lucky to make it to the concert at all. But you know something? That group has been my baby for a long time. It will be interesting to see them try to walk without me." She was very tired now, looking as if she might drop off to sleep at any moment.

"John," she said with an effort, "reach behind you and grab that cardboard diploma box." He took a black cylinder from the top of the piano and handed it to her.

"Evan, I want you to have my set of batons. I've got a bunch of different sizes and weights in there." He opened the canister lid and peered in. "The damn things are so expensive that I can't stand the thought of them getting thrown out."

"But I can't take all your batons!"

"Don't worry." Her face broke into a mischievous grin, "I'm keeping my favorite troll baton. They can bury me with this one." She held up a wooden baton with a furry multicolored troll appended to the thick end. "The chorus gave this to me after we did a concert of excerpts from Wagner. He's supposed to be a little Niebelung."

After receiving assurances that Terri was going to look in on her the next morning, they got up to go home. Evan hesitated as he was leaving the room and then slowly turned around to ask her a final question. "You didn't out me for that first glee club rehearsal, did you?"

"No, but I think I know who did." She gave them a conspiratorial smile.

"Who?"

"Our dear department chair, Mr. Saunders. I overheard a couple of students talking outside my office when they thought no one else was around."

"That son of a bitch!" He slapped the door frame, for a moment too angry to speak. A thought occurred to him. "If he sees me standing at the podium to conduct the Beethoven, he'll have a heart attack."

177

"Believe me," she said with a smile, "that thought has already occurred to me."

They talked little on the way back home, overwhelmed by the scene they had witnessed. John headed straight for the kitchen when they entered the house. "Do you want me to fix you up a plate of lentils?"

"Wait a second, I've got to do something first."

"What's the hurry?"

"I'm going to call Gordon Samuels before it gets too late and see if he can come down and hear the performance."

# 27

## A History Lesson

"I'm not sure this is the sort of performance we can count to complete your degree," Gordon said doubtfully to Evan. "You didn't even choose the music, and besides I'm leaving for England the day after the concert."

"Look," the young director pleaded, "the soloist and orchestral preps are completely mine, and I'll have enough time with the choir to incorporate my interpretation of the piece. Shouldn't the condensed time frame and unexpected chance count in my favor? I'm working under real life conditions here."

He's got a point, Gordon thought. Unlike graduate students finishing their degrees, the world's great conductors never had a whole semester to concentrate on executing a single work with a single ensemble. "Alright, if I can get a flight to London out of Atlanta instead of New York, I'll come down and watch you."

"Thank you! And please let me pick up any extra fare you have to pay."

"Don't worry about it, I'm getting reimbursed anyway." He was about to hang up when he remembered what prompted Evan's call, and it finally sunk in that he was going to be seeing Dorothy again for the first time in thirty-five years. "You said Professor Henderson was ill. How sick is she?"

"Uh, she's pretty much laid up in bed for the next couple of weeks," Evan dissembled, remembering his promise of confidentiality. "She didn't tell me exactly what was wrong. Should I tell her you're coming?"

"No, don't do that," Gordon fumbled for an excuse. "If for some reason the performance is not qualifying, then it might be better if she didn't know that I was there and that you were under the gun." *And it will buy me some time to think about what to say to her.*

\* \* \*

It was ninety degrees and brutally humid on the day that Gordon and Dorothy moved in together. Like most homes in Champaign, Illinois, in the 1950's, their brick duplex was un-airconditioned, and neither of the young lovers brought a fan with them. Gordon spent much of the afternoon driving around trying to find a store which had not sold out its supply. He arrived back at his new home irritable and fanless to find Dorothy sitting on the couch sorting out a huge mess of sheet music while the boxes containing their kitchenware sat unopened on a counter.

"No one's got a fan until Monday," he said, putting a bag of groceries on the table. "but I did find us something for supper."

"Great. If you unpack the kitchen boxes, I'll whip us up something." After four and a half hours of driving from Chicago, two hours of unloading the car, and another two driving around in the fruitless search for a box fan, her offer to cook did not seem overly generous.

"I was kind of hoping the dishes would be unpacked by the time I got back."

"Oh. I'm sorry," she apologized and continued her sorting, making no effort to get up and help. "I just got caught up in these scores."

"So you expect me to do it?" Already feeling unappreciated for shouldering most of the heaviest physical labor under a scorching sun, Gordon's question was hostile and aggressive, a tone of voice that stiffened Dorothy's back.

"I'll be happy to do it," she said sweetly, "as soon as I'm done with this."

"Let me get this straight," his head was cocked at a scrutinizing angle, sweat dripping off his forehead onto the linoleum floor, "your priorities are: music sorting, first; pots and pans, second."

"I think as you get to know me you'll find that I consistently put pots and pans after music."

"Well, me too," he yelled, "but on moving day? When I've been busting my ass for ten hours on one peanut butter sandwich?"

She ignored him and looked down at her music. "I don't know how you can have an appetite in this heat anyway." She spoke with a note of condescension in her voice, the authority on hot weather. "We don't do much on summer afternoons in Georgia."

"Well, you certainly haven't done shit here today." Without waiting for a response, he stormed out to find himself some supper. Fortunately for their relationship, he had better luck finding food than fans, and after a salty fried fish sandwich and two glasses of fresh-squeezed lemonade at a nearby establishment called Deluxe Billiards, he returned home to find his boxes and suitcases unpacked, most of his things put away, and her boxes newly stacked next to the front door. Her music was nowhere in sight.

"This is obviously not going to work," she said as she emerged from the bedroom with a small suitcase.

"Yes, it will," replied the man with a full stomach. And over the course of the next three hours, he convinced her that two strong-willed people--two souls who loved each other beyond all comprehension--could weather the storms that sharing living space would undoubtedly bring. He did not know exactly where the speech came from, certainly not from experience, but it was passionate and earnest and made perfect sense at the time. And it worked. He would need to repeat various versions of it throughout the year as the couple struggled with the mundane sorts of conflicts that slowly fray the fabric of romantic love.

Both of them were sloppy housekeepers who grew up in neat homes where others had picked up after them. Neither liked to cook, but they lacked the resources to eat out often. They were both so focused on their work that they would lose track of time at the music school and inadvertently break solemn promises to be somewhere at a certain time. As a further drain on their limited reservoirs of patience and good will, the hot, sticky, buggy weather lasted well into September, rendering their apartment, including the bedroom, a place where body contact was to be avoided at all costs.

Ups and downs must be the lot of all relationships, Gordon concluded after a landmark day when they discovered a cool bath could make touching tolerable again. Thereafter they frequently retreated into the large bathroom tub to recover their balance. Eventually, they both grew more philosophical. In spite of the problems in their lives, the main core of their affection held together, bruised in places by the strong words both knew how to use in an argument, but essentially intact. By the end of the spring semester, they decided that although they both could imagine other people who would be easier to live with, they could not imagine being apart. They intensified their job hunting and planned to cobble together some sort of summer wedding.

\* \* \*

"Gordon, look at this." Dorothy handed him a letter she had just received in the afternoon mail. "The Atlanta Symphony Chorus is advertising a two-year postdoctoral fellowship that starts this fall. I know that nothing in Atlanta has interested you so far, but this looks fabulous: helping with auditions, running rehearsals, getting to direct the chamber chorus. And the pay's not too bad either. What do you think? All you need to do is send them a tape of your doctoral performance and a letter from your advisor."

"This does look good," he concluded after reading the letter carefully. "This really is perfect, and it's just two years. If we don't like Atlanta, then we can go somewhere else. But what would you do?"

"Some of the other jobs in Atlanta you didn't like sounded pretty good to me, especially the one at Emory. I'll just send them all my tapes, and we'll see what happens."

As summer approached, the rejections started coming in. The market for college and university jobs was extremely tight in the places where they were applying, and the community chorus and large church openings they inquired about demanded more experience than either of them had. A sense of desperation crept over the small duplex as they considered for the first time applying for high school jobs. Neither of them held any particular animosity toward teenagers, but they had been repeatedly told by their professors that once on the secondary school track, they would find it difficult to be taken seriously later for the jobs they really wanted.

"Maybe the thing to do is just move to New York, wait tables and volunteer with a group somewhere until something opens up," Gordon suggested over dinner one night.

"Why not Chicago?"

"Not nearly as many jobs, plus a glut of Illinois grads, at least according to Professor Schmidt. He also says even nonpaying work in New York will look great on our resumes, no matter where we apply later."

"I hear, *It's a Wonderful Town*."

"*The Bronx is up and the Battery's down.*"

"*If we can make it there, we can make it anywhere.*"

"Well, that settles it," Dorothy laughed harder than she had for weeks, "we'll coach the chorus for Bernstein's next musical."

Shared gloom is vastly better than suffering a frustrated ambition alone, and they managed to remain relatively light-hearted as their last semester came to a close and their summer wedding plans took shape without any jobs in sight. The sense of weathering the storm together ended, however, with the arrival of a letter from the Atlanta Symphony Chorus, a letter that was addressed to Dorothy. Gordon started to open the envelope, but when he realized he was not the addressee, he put it down and set it on the kitchen table. He grabbed a beer and started cleaning up the breakfast dishes, casting a glance back at it over his shoulder as he rinsed the last bowl. Then he sat down and took it up again. It was definitely the same distinctively styled envelope that the job

182

announcement had arrived in. He could not construct a theory of how the response in his hand came addressed to Dorothy. He wanted to open it, but had learned the hard way during the year how jealously she guarded her privacy. Instead, he opened another beer, turned on the radio, and sat on the stoop to wait for her.

He saw her walking slowly up the street under a canopy of maple trees. Her light cotton dress billowed in the same spring breeze that blew her hair wild about her head. When she turned onto their sidewalk, she flipped her hair back out of her face and acknowledged him with a smile warm enough to make the flower beds around him bloom early. Gordon offered her only a frown in return, waving her into the kitchen and handing her the envelope.

"Please satisfy my curiosity and open this." He sat down and studied her carefully as she gave him an anxious glance and slit it open. She read quickly and sat down on the other side of the table.

"I should have told you."

"Told me what?"

"Well . . . I sort of applied for the fellowship too."

"You mean you sort of made a copy of your tape, sort of got your advisor to write you a letter, and sort of mailed them to Atlanta?"

"Yes." She watched him carefully, not knowing what to expect. "I didn't think I'd get it."

"Well, it looks like you did." He cast his eyes downward. He guessed she was studying him, probably wondering what sort of verbal retribution he might deliver. He refused to look at her and stared absently at a loose thread hanging from the seam of his right pant leg. Although he admitted pangs of jealousy and disappointment, it was the overwhelming sense of betrayal that paralyzed him. He had wondered perversely on occasion how he would react to finding her in bed with another man. Would he attack her lover? Attack her? Quietly slink from the room before he was noticed? Now he had his answer. He would just sink slowly to the floor and wait.

"It's the only real job either of us has gotten so far, Gordon," she tried to explain. He did not respond. Nothing short of a direct question could raise his head. "You could apply to one of the other jobs in Atlanta, like I did."

She started to stand up. "Why don't I get the job descriptions?"

"Don't bother."

"Why not?"

"I'm not going to Atlanta," he said bitterly. "I never wanted to live there, you know that. The only reason I was even willing to consider spending any time there was because this job looked so great." He looked at her and saw how the future would be, and he was gripped by an impulse to contrast her betrayal with a dose of magnamity. "It is by far and away the best chance either of us is going to get. You should take it."

"Of course, I'm going to take it." She looked at him uncomprehendingly. "Gordon, I can understand why you're pissed off--I should have told you I was applying. And I even understand why you're not happy for me, but there's no question that we have to go to Atlanta now, right? You'll find something. I know it."

"I already found something," he said as he got up and walked to the door, "but I just lost it." The previous day, Gordon would have followed Dorothy anywhere. But as he finally looked up at her across the room, he did not recognize the woman he saw. The conflicts they endured throughout the semester had taught Gordon something about her single-mindedness and determination, but the woman who stood before him now was too cold, too strong, too willing to look right past him.

As he walked down the steps and onto the sidewalk, he paused for a moment and listened. The door stayed shut. No apologetic voice pleaded with him to return. He crossed the street and distanced himself swiftly from the house. She'll have to decide, he thought, between this job and me.

No further job offers arrived and Dorothy made her choice. When she committed to the job in Atlanta, and he decided to try his luck in New York, they stopped talking about a summer wedding. Eventually they stopped talking altogether. By the time Dorothy's parents came to help her move, he was already on his way.

* * *

As Gordon looked for his travel agent's phone number, he noticed the pile of love letters still laying in his waste basket. He stared at them a long time before pulling them out. I have no idea what to say to her, he thought. Music's a safe subject. Maybe she can help me figure out why I don't really care anymore. Maybe when she looks at me she'll remember who I am. He looked at the letters again. If she's wise, he thought, she threw hers out long ago. If she's wise, she's lived her life without regrets.

# THE CONCERT

# 29

## Getting Ready

The doctor who saw Dorothy in the emergency room after Terri's party had said, *No aspirin. It thins the blood and makes a hemorrhage in your shoulder or neck much more likely. Of course*, he had added, *this IV we're hooking up is dangerous too. The fact you're dehydrated actually alleviates some of the pressure on the walls of your arteries, but we've got to get some fluids in you or . . .* His voice had trailed off, and the painkillers had prevented her from completing his sentence with an ironic twist. She wondered why old Dr. Burton had never mentioned the dangers of aspirin during their weekly meetings or when he had seen her in the hospital after her fall. But why should he mention it? Given his knowledge of her condition, he probably guessed (and quite rightly) that a death caused by massive internal bleeding was preferable to the bedridden purgatory endured by his other cancer patients. The young doctor was handsome and energetic, but she preferred the intuition of her crusty personal physician.

As the concert grew closer, the pain grew more intense and varied, and her appetite for solid foods gradually disappeared. Her diet consisted of several large glasses of sweet tea and a milkshake each day. Her bones ached, and her lungs felt stiff and inflexible. She was still mobile, but she felt like every joint in her body was rotten with arthritis and every muscle fresh from a fifteen-round battle with Muhammad Ali. Although Doc Burton stopped by her home once a week to check on her, she did not complain to him about the pain or lethargy. She had a favor to ask him and was afraid that he would not grant it if he perceived her to be too weak.

\* \* \*

Although he was exhausted from spending the weekend with a copy of Dorothy's heavily annotated score of the *Missa Solemnis*, Evan's first rehearsal with the College Chorus went decently well. He took Dorothy's advice and told them that he was only going to run practices until she felt well enough to come back, explaining changes in the music under the pretense that he was just following orders. He would have made more adjustments to the text were he starting from scratch, but his approach to the piece was basically compatible with hers. He was able to put his imprint on the choral sections of the work without requiring the group to make too many additional markings and erasures in their scores. Since she had not yet rehearsed the solists, he was able to shape those lines with greater freedom, although some of his choices were constrained by what Dorothy had told the choir to do.

The group was well-behaved, but they sang as if they wanted to impress him more with their mastery of the piece than with their ability to follow his precise directions. At times, he felt like he was directing a recording, that his presence did not really influence the sound the group was producing. But when he admonished them to get their noses out of their scores and pay attention, he encountered resistance, much like a three-year-old will offer when told not to do something by an adult other than his own parents. They'll have to get used to me fast, he thought, or rehearsal is going to become a battle they will not enjoy losing. All in all, he was hopeful for the choir--at least they wanted to work and were committed to the piece. The necessary trust would somehow have to emerge before the concert.

Preparing the orchestra was a more serious worry. Given the lateness of his assumption of the role of director, he was stuck with the instrumentalists that Dorothy had chosen. Even though they were a very able group, mostly junior and senior music majors with a few good community musicians filling out the ensemble, they were not used to playing together. The level of talent in Clarkeston was not high enough to fill out all the sections with master performers. He discovered early in the first rehearsal that the second violins would be a problem, along with a bassist whose mind tended to wander when he was not playing and two trombonists who found it impossible to tune to each other.

"Okay, not too bad," he lied after listening to the group run through the first couple dozen measures, "but this is Beethoven's *Solemn Mass*, not his *Mass for Dying Cats*. The second violins must not go flat, not even a little bit. This is not Webern or Berg—if the note you're playing against the first violins sets your teeth on edge, then the chances are excellent it's the wrong one!" Everyone but the second violins laughed until he took aim again.

"And my bass . . . excuse me, what's your name again."

"Brian."

"Good. Now, Brian, you're giving us a wonderful sound. Not a wrong note in the bunch, beautiful, but do you think you could play them in time? I'm not waving my hands about trying to take off and fly around the room. I'm giving you the beat! If you follow it, everyone else will too." He looked at the rest of them briefly before starting again, letting them know that their sins would not go unpunished. The uneasiness of those who had not spent enough time pouring over their scores before the rehearsal was palpable. "Right. Now, let's go over the beginning one more time . . ."

By the end of the brutal session, several members of the ensemble asked sheepishly whether he would be willing to schedule an extra rehearsal. When he saw most of the others in the group nod in agreement, he smiled for the first time that night and told them that he had already reserved a practice room precisely for that purpose. "Wonderful! As my alcoholic friends tell me, realizing you need help is the first step to recovery."

* * *

John's parents were to arrive the day before the concert, and he could not decide whether to tell them about his relationship with Evan at the beginning of their visit or at the end. If he told them as soon as they arrived, then he would not get the benefit of any positive feelings about Evan that they might develop beforehand. On the other hand, if he told them at the very end, then he ran the risk of their leaving without having the chance to calm down and get used to the idea.

"How's this for a plan," Evan suggested, finally taking pity on his anxious lover, "let them see us together for a day or so, sleeping in separate rooms of course, and then spring it on them when they're more used to the fact of our living together. We'll still sleep apart after the big announcement, and they'll understand we're not trying to throw anything in their face."

"What if they hate you?"

"Oh come on, what are the chances of that?" Evan was much more confident than John of his ability to turn off his acid wit at will. "I'll charm the socks off them."

"You couldn't charm the socks off a barefoot hooker, but your basic idea is pretty good. I suppose that step one is just letting them get used to us. After that, who knows."

Even with a plan of action, John could not keep his parents' visit off his mind. All he could see were the negative consequences of shaking up their world: stress, anxiety, disappointment, anger. He anticipated no great relief from telling his mother and father. After all, he had long ceased requiring their approval in order to be happy in his life. Strangely

189

enough, Arthur, who seemed to have a whole theory of personal secrecy, was excited for him.

"Sometimes when you reveal your true self," he tried to explain over a pitcher of beer at the Wild Boar, "it's like saying *I love you*. Telling someone who you are shows enormous trust; you lay yourself open and risk all kinds of judgment. That's what makes it an offer of love." Although Arthur was one of the more compelling bar room philosophers John had met, he was unsure whether he wanted to believe him. Any theory that made risk sound good was entirely suspect.

\* \* \*

Terri had not seen much of Jorge after the party. When she saw him reading in the coffee shop, she wasted no time in bringing him a Cuban coffee, a warm smile, and an invitation to the concert. "Dorothy wants me to spy on Professor Roberts and report on how well he conducts the piece."

"What is it again?"

"The Beethoven *Missa Solemnis*." She was disappointed to discern no excitement on his face. "I've never heard it before, but she says it's going to be good. My brother's singing in the chorus."

"When is it?"

"A week from today, next Wednesday night." He thumbed his textbook. She wondered what was wrong with her usually bluff young friend. "I don't know. I've got a paper due that Friday. Let me see what I get done this weekend, and I'll give you a call."

She decided not to make a joke about his Protestant work ethic. The way he's partied this semester, she thought, he must be way behind. She had a roommate in college who always saved her work until the last minute. Although she usually managed to pull out good grades, she was hell to live with during the last two weeks of a semester. She reached out and touched his hand. "I had a really good time on Friday night."

"I'll let you get back to work. Call me."

\* \* \*

After the night of the party, the choice between Terri and Monica became a choice between two sorts of worlds Jorge might live in, two sorts of people he might grow into. To choose Terri would mean continued assimilation in the Anglo world, a world that produced the sort of racist pricks that had chased him after the party. She would probably not make unreasonable demands on him, but inevitably there would be

190

compromises with the part of him that wanted to stay pure *Cubano de Miami.* Someone like Monica would give him the chance to maintain his cultural and linguistic heritage, to discover the magic center of his grandfather's stories and make them come alive. Monica had even hinted he had a chance. Horrified by the tale of his pursuit and impressed by his stoic and vivid recitation of the event, she had softened her heart a little. She had not taken him to bed, nor even kissed him passionately, but she had used words like *patience* and *time* in a way that led him to think that he would have another chance with her.

He spent the days after the party catching up on his schoolwork and avoiding both of them: Monica because he did not want to push his luck and upset the fragile rapport they had established; Terri because he knew that eventually he would have to let her know that their flirtation was over. After the awkward meeting in the coffee house, he was forced to think about what he should tell her. They had gone too far on Friday night to pretend nothing had happened. Her invitation to hear the Beethoven provided an obvious opportunity, so after a day's contemplation, he called her and accepted. I should explain things to her before the concert, he thought, and then we can go together as friends.

* * *

Sitting next to Debbie on the piano bench was difficult for Louis. First, there was the substantive matter of how much space she occupied once she settled herself onto the seat. Far more distracting was how wonderful she smelled.

"I'm glad to see you're human, Louis! You came in a whole measure late there." He blushed when he realized his mistake and turned an even deeper shade of red when he realized he had been paying more attention to her perfume than the sheet music. She darted a smile at him and turned her attention back to the music when she noticed his embarrassment. "I don't think I could stand to play with someone who was perfect. You want to start from measure 55?"

"Okay, sorry."

"Don't worry about it! I've made three dozen mistakes and now you've made one. Perfection is too high a goal for us; let's give up on it. I know I did long ago!"

"It's hard to play together," he replied, "but I sorta like it. It's like accompanying a singer or playing a concerto . . . you've got to really pay attention to what the other person is doing."

"I think it's even harder," she said. "There's a contrast between a piano and singers or an orchestra that you can play off of, but we're on the same instrument. We've got to really stick together." He nodded and tried to turn his attention away from the mellifluous sound of her voice and the sweet scent of her porcelain skin.

\* \* \*

"If you can't make it to the concert," Evan told Dorothy over the phone, "the public radio station is going to broadcast it live. The station manager called and told me that they've been broadcasting your concerts for years."

"Yes, they've always been very supportive of our programs. The better performances sometimes get replayed on the Atlanta affiliate." She tried to sound fresh and cheerful, but his afternoon phone call had awoken her from a fitful sleep on her sofa, and she took a moment to compose herself. She originally planned to take a cab, slip into the concert at the last minute and listen from the lighting booth behind the top balcony of the Watkins Center auditorium, but now she wondered whether she had the strength to pull it off. "You know, the thought of lying here and listening to it on the radio sounds very tempting. Thanks for reminding me."

She desperately wanted to see her chorus one last time, especially if she could hide herself away from the view of the audience. She wanted no tearful farewells in front of her students, but if she could say good-bye from a distance, she would feel more ready for the end. This need was all that remained of her fear of dying. All other emotions had been conquered in musical metaphor: She was a work carefully prepared by the great Composer, with a beginning, middle, and an end, and it was up to her to make each part as beautiful as possible. Her life's opus should not be marred by a coda discordant with what came before it. It was a horrible disappointment that she could not end by conducting the Beethoven, but there had been something unexpectedly pleasing in passing the baton to Evan and she felt the integrity of her work was still intact.

That just leaves this aching body, she thought, and as soon as the concert is over, we'll see about that.

\* \* \*

"That fuckin' faggot's going to be directing a concert at the Watkins Center next Wednesday."

"So?"

"Why don't we make sure he gets a proper welcome to Clarkeston."

"Like what?"

"I don't know. Let's talk to Wes. He always has good ideas about how to deal with niggers and faggots."

* * *

The extra orchestra rehearsal, and the time the terrified members of the ensemble spent practicing on their own during the days preceding it, worked wonders for the group's sound. Unfortunately, the situation with the soloists was far from settled. The tenor developed laryngitis and backed out the night before their first rehearsal, while the soprano insisted on over-singing, wilfully refusing to blend with the remaining members of the group. Evan spent hours on the phone talking to friends of friends in Atlanta until he could find a replacement for the tenor. By all accounts, the new tenor was very good, but he would only be able to come to a single rehearsal—the one held the night before the performance. The soprano remained a problem.

"I assure you, Evan," her voice dripped with condescension at the young academic who in her eyes lacked a sufficiently established musical reputation, "that I will sound fine on the night of the concert." Slightly built with a pinched face topped by a crown of frosted brown hair, only her attitude fit any soprano stereotype.

"Sophie," as he spoke her tanned and windburned face adopted a mask of studied boredom, "you sound wonderful now, but you're overbalancing the other singers. Look, I know it's easier to sing high notes loudly, and I realize that this piece has the reputation of being a real screamer, but I don't think we should let Beethoven's little hearing problem get between us and what could be some very beautiful music. I've toned the choir and the orchestra way down, so the soloists need to take the volume down a couple of notches too." She did not seem to be paying attention, so he tried to simplify his message. "Sophie, this is going to be the quietest performance of the *Missa Solemnis* ever. Period. It is a *solemn* mass, after all."

"Certainly," she said and then continued to sing at precisely the same volume as before, much to the irritation of the bass and the alto. Evan eventually stopped directing, sat down in a defeated posture and listened to the trio make its way through the rest of the section. Louis looked over at him, but Evan indicated that he should keep on playing. Then, he noticed the music coming from the piano getting softer and softer, gently encouraging the trio to sing more quietly. Eventually, the instrument was completely inaudible unless the singers kept to no more than a *mezzo-piano*, exactly the volume Evan wanted for that part of the piece. For the rest of the rehearsal Sophie fought intermittently with the piano, but singers have no prerogative to direct accompanists, so Louis's strategy gradually began to pay off, and in the process Evan discovered why she preferred singing *forte* whenever possible.

"Sophie, that's much better, much, much better." Not perfect, Evan thought, but at least the screaming has stopped. "Look, I know, your tone gets a little straight when you sing *piano*, and you even went a tiny bit flat once or twice, but I vastly prefer that to a heavy sound in this section. If you just let it float, we'll be in great shape . . . alright, let's take it again from measure 126." After the two and a half hour rehearsal was over and the soloists had scurried off, Evan walked over to the piano.

"Thank you for getting them to quiet down. It didn't occur to me to use you to dampen the sound." As usual, Louis was looking down and shuffling his papers as Evan spoke. "Sophie sure is a piece of work, isn't she?"

"All she needs," he said, looking up from the piano at his professor, "is to pay attention to what's going on around her."

\* \* \*

When Gordon got on the plane at LaGuardia, a gray sleet was falling from the sky, coating all of New York in a grimy, frigid slush. Two hours later, he emerged into a bright sunshine that was baking Atlanta well into the fifties. He had not been south for years, and the mildness of the day softened his heart to the region and even to the idiot who programmed "Winter Wonderland" on Hartsfield Airport's muzak system. He looked around and, as promised, Evan was waiting for him.

"How was the flight?"

"Boring, but worth it just to see the sun for the first time in two weeks." He shook his favorite student's hand. "I'm already feeling better about agreeing to your cockamamie scheme. These three days will recharge my batteries a little bit before getting over to England. I love it there, but it doesn't get any more winter sunshine than New York." Evan took the heavier of his two carry-on bags, and they walked briskly down the concourse.

"Did you check any baggage?"

"Unfortunately. I'm leaving straight from here, so I've got three months worth of stuff with me." After they collected his bags and loaded them in Evan's Volkswagen, they sped off through the piney woods of northeast Georgia on the ninety-minute trip back to Clarkeston. "Thanks again for picking me up. Those shuttle buses always make me queasy."

194

"Well, I've got no classes or rehearsals this morning," Evan explained, "and I know we need some time to talk about the performance." Part of Gordon's evaluation of Evan was based on his intended interpretation of the piece and his defense of the choices he had made. They spent the entire trip arguing about the proper approach to the *Missa Solemnis* and to Beethoven's choral works in general.

"In theory, ratcheting down the volume is a great idea. That would allow the remaining forte sections to really stand out, but how are the sopranos and tenors going to sing all those high notes softly? You could be setting up a huge train wreck here. Are you sure you don't want to play it a little more conservatively this time out?" He looked at Evan and noticed that the odometer read seventy mph just as a highway sign told him that they were in a forty-mph zone.

"You're the one who's always telling your students to take chances! And besides, Dorothy agrees. She toned down a lot of stuff even before I got to the score, and she thinks that the chorus can do it. Remember, we got some nice young vocal chords in there."

"How is she, by the way?"

"Not too great, but I'm going to let her speak for herself. She's a pretty private person," Evan said carefully as the car hit the outskirts of Clarkeston.

"That's funny," Gordon replied without thinking, "she always seemed pretty open to me, maybe even too honest sometimes." They pulled into Evan and Dorothy's neighborhood of neat brick houses and shady, manicured yards. "Not the shy, retiring type, I'm afraid, at least not when I knew her."

"That's not what I meant." He gave Gordon an inquisitive look. "She'll still get in your face, but she does have some secrets she keeps. You'll have to pry them out of her yourself." Evan turned into the driveway of a small bed-and-breakfast that stood midway between his house and campustown. He parked the car and opened the trunk. "Just how well do you know Professor Henderson, anyway?"

"Pretty well." As Gordon spoke the years sloughed away, uncovering vivid memories of snow storms, breezes off Lake Michigan, and macaroni and cheese dinners in the cozy duplex. He had thought about Dorothy much of the flight and how he would feel when he saw her for the first time. He turned to Evan and decided to take his own advice on risk-taking. "I know her well enough to think that I was a fool not to marry her thirty-five years ago."

Apart from the stunned look on his face, Evan made no response. He picked up two of Gordon's bags and carried them to the foyer of the house. The handsome building was one of the few two-story wood frame houses in the neighborhood, predating the residences surrounding it by fifty years. After Gordon checked in, they went up to his room.

"Here, I drew you a little map of the neighborhood and how to get to campus from here. It's all an easy walk." Evan put the sheet on top of an antique dry sink set against the middle of the wall. He leaned over the map and pointed. "I'm just down the street, and Professor Henderson is three blocks farther down from me, around the corner, right here. I'll drop you off back here after we eat lunch, and then I'll go off to teach my class. You can rest, or maybe visit with Professor Henderson, until it's time for the four o'clock rehearsal that you wanted to attend." He stabbed his finger at the map one more time. "And by the way, there's a florist right here, on the edge of campustown about four blocks away."

\* \* \*

"What a lovely place, dear!" John's mother, Joanna, was thrilled with everything about the house, from the curtains in the living room, to the brightly painted cabinets in the kitchen, to the quilt-covered queen-size bed in the guest room where she and Hal would be staying. "Why, maybe we should just spend our whole vacation here." Knowing that both her son and his father would be equally appalled, she did not even bother checking their response to her suggestion. "Just kidding, dears."

She was a well-groomed pharmacist in her mid-fifties, still proud enough of her trim legs to wear skirts that ended significantly above her knees. Although her hair was streaked with gray, she kept it stylishly trimmed and casually pushed back with a pair of designer sunglasses. She sometimes joked among her tennis partners at the Whispering Pines Country Club that she sold drugs for a living; her sense of humor might have been one reason why she never quite fit in there. Her husband, Hal, might have been the other. He was a surly high school principal, one of the rare men whose personality improved significantly when he drank. He perpetually looked like he had just emerged from a stormy parent/teacher conference. They loved each other madly, and no one really understood why.

The couple arrived late Monday afternoon having left Ohio before sunrise (John could not remember a single family vacation that did not start in the dark). Evan was not due home until seven, so he had plenty of time to settle them in and field their questions about the neighbors, the town, and Georgia.

"I'll bet you don't have any black families in this neighborhood." His father looked out the guestroom window as if he expected to see a hooded Klansman galloping down the street.

196

"Uh, actually we've got two families who live just around the corner and another down the street." In a city with a forty percent black population, John would have expected a few more, but he was not about to point out to his father any defects in his adopted home town. "How many do we have in our subdivision back home?"

"None that I know of, but that's not the point," his father blustered, "and they'd certainly be welcome if they moved in." Since race relations were second only to homosexuality on the list of subjects he avoided discussing with his father, John turned their attention to the weather and questioned them about how much snow they had left behind in Ohio and how lovely it was to see them on a sunny day in December when the daytime temperature was unlikely to dip below fifty.

"Why don't you show us where you and Evan sleep, sweetheart," John's mother asked, confirming her status as mistress of the malaprop. A quick look at her failed to reveal whether she was just being sloppy or going on a fishing expedition.

"This is where I'm sleeping." John showed them the study with its pillow-covered day bed--his as the result of a lost coin flip. He took a few steps down the hall. "And here's the master bedroom." All signs of dual habitation had been carefully disguised.

"I hope you're paying less rent since you're stuck with the smaller bedroom," his father grunted.

"I never thought about it that way. We don't spend much time in the bedroom." John felt his mother's gaze upon him, and he hustled them back to the kitchen for a cup of coffee and some donuts he had bought earlier that morning. "This should hold us until dinner. We'll eat when Evan gets back."

\* \* \*

"We can go to the concert if you still want to." Jorge's phone call surprised Terri while she was making a batch of cookies with Maria. "Why don't we meet at that Italian place next to the Wild Boar? I'd like to talk a little before we go."

"Sure, you want to meet around six o'clock?"

"Okay, see you there." Even before he hung up, she started wondering what he wanted to talk about. He was usually so breezy about their relationship that the simple phrase *like to talk a little* sounded portentous. She hoped that he was coming to the same conclusions as she, that they needed to spend more time together, that their frictionless friendship and strong physical attraction had blossomed into something deeper. "Love you too," she whispered into the dial tone, just to see what it would sound like.

"Who was that?" Maria asked through a mouth full of cookie dough.

"Oh, nobody. Hey, don't eat all that dough or there won't be any cookies for Dorothy!" Even as she fussed at the little girl, she knew that Dorothy would show little interest in the cookies. She baked to show she cared and to have something to snack on during the extended hours she was spending at the little house in College Hills. The cataloguing was long finished, but she continued to visit, reading aloud or talking about their mutual acquaintances while her friend rested on the sofa. She slowly became aware that there was no one else who was willing, or whom Dorothy would tolerate, to witness her passing.

"I got a mysterious call from Jorge today," she announced when she arrived at Dorothy's house. "He wants to go to the concert with me, but he also says he *wants to have a talk* beforehand."

"Maybe he wants to break up with you," Dorothy picked her head off her pillow. "That would be a horrible thing to happen. I want my funeral to be the only bad memory you have of Clarkeston."

"God, you're morbid!" She did not know whether to be outraged or amazed by her friend's attitude. "And, may I ask you: break up what? We're not even dating, so I'm not sure we can officially break up. Leave me alone with my fantasies, okay?"

"Bah, you don't need fantasies, you need a man. I just don't want to see you with a broken heart."

"Don't worry about that. I'm not stupid enough to lose my head over somebody on a vacation, and if I were, I'd be smart enough to set my sights lower than Señor Jorge."

They sat in silence for a moment, enjoying the sunlight streaming in through the large picture window. The trees were mostly bare now, allowing far more natural light to enter the house than ever did during the summer. For Terri, whose memories of winter in Iowa consisted of interminable days under a roof of gun-metal clouds, the association of December and light was especially marvelous. When she went to the window to pick up Dorothy's empty tea glass, she noticed a neatly dressed and handsome older gentleman turn up the sidewalk toward the front door. She walked into the foyer and waited for him to knock.

"Good afternoon," he said politely, "I hope I've got the right house. I'm looking for Dorothy Henderson." He looked vaguely familiar, carrying himself with the air of a Hollywood leading man from a generation before, like Gregory Peck or David Niven, graceful and distinguished. Terri could not quite place where she had seen him before. His blue eyes twinkled expectantly at her.

"You've got the right place, but let me check with her," she replied, "she hasn't been feeling well."

"So I've been told." He pulled a small bouquet from behind his back.

"Is someone there, Terri?" She could hear Dorothy struggling off the couch, and she walked through the vestibule to tell her about the unidentified stranger. Dorothy was standing next to the sofa with a grimace on her face. "Might as well let 'em in. I need to stretch my legs anyway." The visitor must have heard her, because a moment later he popped out from behind Terri, flourishing his roses and an enormously warm smile. Terri, still puzzled, did not have to wait long for Dorothy's response. "Oh God," she heard her murmur, just before she hit the floor in a heap.

\* \* \*

As he sat studying in the cafeteria, Jorge thought he recognized the voices of three frat boys sitting two tables down from him. He could not be absolutely sure, but the tallest of the three sounded just like the ringleader of the gang that had pursued him after the party. He strained his ears to hear what they were saying in between the guffaws they half-heartedly tried to stifle. All he could make out--and then only because of their vicious emphasis on the initial sibilant of the words--was *faggot*, *fucking faggot*, and *Sanders*.

\* \* \*

"I don't think you have to do or say anything special, Louis," Dr. Peterson told him calmly at the end of their session on the day before the concert. "The anxiety of romance is not worth the trouble. Take it from me, I've been married twice." When he saw the shock and disapproval on Louis's face, he was quick to add, "And number two is still going strong after twenty-two years."

"I don't even know if I like her like that." Debbie was the first real friend he had ever had, and it was hard to sort out whether he had other feelings for her and whether those feelings were appropriate. "I just want to let her know that I think she's nice, but whenever I try to say something nothing comes out."

"Well, don't say anything then." The doctor seemed delighted that his patient had made such a promising friend. She sounded unlikely to be

199

an ice-cold heartbreaker if he did develop a crush on her. "Here's an idea. Arrange to meet her after the concert for ice cream and give her some silly gift for singing well. Nothing expensive or symbolic, like a ring, but something goofy, like a musical pair of socks or a Beethoven t-shirt, something to let her know that you appreciate her and think about her, but nothing that openly threatens romance." Louis thought for a long time before replying.

"That's okay. I can do that." His face brightened as he stood up and the doctor got his reward for playing father in addition to psychologist. "Dr. Peterson, I better go. I've got to do some shopping."

* * *

When Dorothy came to, she opened her eyes and saw the concerned faces of Gordon and Terri looking down at her. She blinked hard, but they did not go away. As self-awareness and memory returned, she realized her head was resting on something soft. They must have put me back on the sofa, she thought as she peered back up at Gordon and studied his face with a frown. "You got old."

"But you're just as beautiful as ever," he said with a laugh as spontaneous as any that had passed his lips in months. He gave her hand a squeeze. "Are you okay? You really hit the ground pretty hard. I must be looking pretty rough if I can knock people to the ground. Or maybe it's just my breath."

Years before, his sense of humor had broken through her defenses and convinced her to give away her heart for the first and only time in her life. Apart from a little gray hair, he was just as handsome as he was as a graduate student. "So, who told you that I'm croaking?"

She watched the color drain from his face as he looked quickly at Terri who did not meet his gaze. "I'll go make us some tea," she murmured.

"Did Terri call you? I've sworn her and everybody else to secrecy, but she's such a romantic." She gestured at the top of the piano. "Ever since we found your picture, she's been dragging stories out of me about our years in grad school. You'd think she's planning to write a book."

When she pointed out the picture, Gordon slid off his perch on the sofa and walked over to the mantel. He picked it up and examined it closely. "Good lord in heaven, I don't remember being that skinny."

"Or that handsome?"

"In a Don Knotts sort of way."

"Au contraire, everyone who looks at that old picture wants to know who that handsome young stud is. I don't think they can quite

200

believe that a fussy old bitch like me could ever have carried on with him." She reached for the picture and studied it. Then, she gave it back to him. "You know, you really don't look too bad."

"Thanks." He paused. "About what you said before . . ."

"It's alright. I'm not going to carry on a vendetta against whoever told you I was dying."

"No. No one told anything!" Surprise and distress were evident on his face. "Evan Roberts invited me down to see if we could count directing the Beethoven toward completing his doctoral degree requirements. I told him that I knew you, and he told me you were sick-- which is why I brought flowers--but he didn't tell me . . . didn't say anything about your condition."

"Oh shit." She sighed, and he sat back down next to her, folding his hands uncertainly in his lap. He was very still for a minute, and she wished that she could read his mind. Would he understand after all of the years and a lifetime of unshared memories that she did not want sympathy, just respect?

"What . . ?" He struggled to phrase the question.

"Cancer. What else?" He took her hands and held them. Neither of them saw Terri peek around the corner and then quietly leave by the back door. Finally, he let out a deep breath and wiped away a single tear with his right hand.

"So, did you ever write that opera about the courthouse?"

"How wonderful of you to remember! I don't think I've ever told anyone else about that . . . You know, I've written bits and pieces here and there but I never really had the time to try and pull the whole thing together."

"Could you use this, uh, leave to complete it?" He could not suppress his instinctive desire to make lemonade out of lemons.

"Not enough time, darling," she replied in a voice devoid of self-pity. "I'm afraid I'm a bit closer to the end of the road than it might look." Her acceptance took him aback, and he turned his head away from her in an attempt to hide his emotion.

"If you turn this into *Terms of Endearment*," she protested, "I'm gonna puke. Let me explain right now that this house is a Grieving-Free Zone. Only four people know about my condition: Dr. Burton wouldn't cry if you ran over his mother. He knows how to get pissed off at his sick patients, but he's incapable of shedding any tears. Evan knows, and I'm happy to admit that he turns out to be quite a mensch, as you New Yorkers say. Terri, whom you just met, was the first person I told, and just like the daughter I never had, I can assure you she is tough as nails." The authentic scowl on her face helped him pull himself together.

"If only to avoid being ranked below my own student, I'll abide by your rules." He diverted their conversation away from her illness. "Tell me about the kind of music you've been doing here recently. I hear talk about you once in a while from other southern directors at choral conventions, but my information's pretty spotty. They all respect you, but claim you avoid being seen anywhere outside Georgia."

"I float in a pretty small pond down here, but there's always been so much to do. Years ago, when the College Chorus first started to sing the way I wanted them to, I lost all desire to conquer New York or Chicago or Boston. I just wanted to hear them do it over and over again."

"I've got the *King David* recording you did last year. It's wonderful! Do you ever take them on tour?"

"Hardly ever. I can't stand arranging hotels and meals and making sure nobody's been left behind. I'd rather schedule performances here or in Atlanta and let people come to us."

They talked for the rest of the afternoon about the music they loved to direct the most, the difficulties of building and maintaining a first-rate choral program, faculty politics, students who had gone on to promising careers and numerous other professional experiences they shared even though they lived almost a thousand miles apart. They deliberately avoided any talk of personal relationships and Dorothy's illness. Just before four o'clock, he looked at his watch and realized that he had to leave.

"Damn, I've got to go. Do you feel well enough to go out for dinner?" She shook her head and he realized for the first time that she was far sicker than she appeared at first glance. "What if I brought something back here? I've got almost two hours between the last orchestral rehearsal this afternoon and the beginning of the dress rehearsal this evening."

"That would be nice," she said with a tired smile. "And Gordon, could you do me another favor?"

"Sure, anything."

"Could you come back here after the evening rehearsal too? I'd love to hear how it went . . . and hear more about you too."

"Are you sure you want to stay up that late? I probably won't be back until 11:00 p.m."

"I'm afraid that I'm not sleeping much these days." She paused. "It would be nice to have some company."

"No problem. I could even spend the night if you want."

"Gordon, you lovely man! It's been such a long time since anyone's said that to me!"

*  *  *

The dress rehearsal of the Beethoven in the Watkins Center inspired confidence in no one. Evan thought the biggest problem would be keeping the ensemble singing quietly, but volume control turned out to be the least of his worries. The choir, soloists, and orchestra all found the space so acoustically live that they were not tempted to over-sing or over-play their parts. The hard surfaces of the hall in front of the them and the curved shell of teak-veneered walls behind them made each performer acutely aware of what he or she was doing. Unfortunately, heightened consciousness sometimes leads to musical paranoia and musical impotence.

"It's sounds different in here, doesn't it?" He spoke with confidence to calm down his singers. "Don't be eaten up by doubts because now you can hear yourself and all the other vocal and orchestral parts so much more clearly than back in the rehearsal room. It's distracting, and that's where the pitch problems and the sloppy entrances are coming from." And, he thought, because the orchestra sounds like shit. "Let's take it again from the beginning of the *Gloria*."

By the end of the evening he was exhausted and the ensemble was defeated. Every time he fixed a problem, another erupted, sometimes in places which had been played through cleanly a dozen times before. When the second violins were finally beaten into submission, the oboes decided to go out of tune and the French horn seemed unable to get through five measures without splatting some ungodly dissonance that sent a shiver through the whole orchestra. Although the choir eventually remembered their notes, all the sections were consistently weak in their entrances, and every screw-up from the orchestra seemed to dampen their enthusiasm for singing the piece. Thank goodness for the soloists, Evan thought. They weren't great, but they were professional. The new tenor was the only one having significant problems.

Depressed and tired after the rehearsal, Evan was in no hurry to get home, especially since more trauma undoubtedly awaited him there. Hours earlier, the long-dreaded family dinner had started off surprisingly smoothly. Evan had not arrived too late, and he enjoyed talking to John's mother and father. His mother was an energetic and eccentric character who played off his laconic father in a British sitcom sort of way. All was well until Evan assumed wrongly that John had chosen a lively moment in the conversation to breach the subject of sexual orientation to his parents. Hal had mentioned in an offhand way that every musician he had ever hired in his school had been an "incredible fruit."

203

"Dad, I'm not sure that's the most respectful thing to say in front of a choir director." Hal looked at Evan and screwed up his face. Evan looked at John and thought he saw an invitation to plow ahead.

"You see, sir, I'm a bit fruity myself." He had never come out to anyone in quite that way before, and the horrified expression on John's face told him that he had totally misread his cue.

"Oh well, I'm sure that's perfectly fine, isn't it dear." Joanna addressed her husband in an especially cheerful voice, trying to cut short any further opportunities for him to display his homophobia.

"I never said they weren't damn fine musicians." He frowned at his wife and nodded meaningfully at Evan. "And I must say that I never had a single problem with any of 'em. They always toed the line. Of course, you'd have to in a public high school or you'd be out in a flash." He jerked his right thumb over his shoulder. The other three at the table stared in fascination at Hal's impromptu disquisition on the difficulty of being a gay high school teacher. He took this as a sign to continue.

"I imagine it must be different at a university, though. A little looser, maybe? But then again, we are in the South."

"Well, I certainly don't feel free to skip down the quad, hand in hand with my lover." Evan took a sip of his wine, happy just to go with the flow at this point. John would have to decide for himself whether to stay on the sidelines.

"Especially if it were one of your students, I'd imagine."

"Hal!"

"Dad, it wouldn't be one of his students," John slowly rose from the table. "It would be me." At his interjection, Evan heard Joanna's fork clatter down to her plate, and Hal's head dropped as he feigned an intense interest in the condition of his cauliflower.

"But we wouldn't be skipping together, for heaven's sake," John continued with a hint of desperation is his voice. "We live very discreetly. We're happy here, but it's hard to keep things hidden from everyone all the time . . . that's why we finally decided to tell you. I hope you can both understand that."

"No, I don't understand why you had to tell us. We would never have said anything." Hal was not making eye contact with his son. "Not a word. We would have had a nice visit and then gone to Florida and everything would have been just fine. Just like it was before." With that, he got up deliberately from his chair and walked out of the room. When Joanna heard the front door shut a moment later, she ran out after her husband.

"You did the right thing," Evan gave John a look that counseled common sense. "They'll snap out of it soon enough. It's just going to take them a while to accept what they've obviously suspected for a long time." John responded with a deep sigh.

"At this point, I'll settle for them just coming back."

* * *

As soon as Gordon got back from watching Evan run the final rehearsal, Dorothy opened up the door to the past, and they were both sucked swiftly in.

"I don't even know if you're married." Dorothy sat propped up against some pillows on the sofa. Gordon sipped a glass of wine as he faced her in a faded wingback chair.

"I was married to a very nice woman named Helen for twenty years. We got divorced about ten years ago." Dorothy did the math in her head.

"Gordon! How stereotypical. You divorced your wife at fifty? Did you at least wait until the children were grown?"

"I haven't mentioned any children." Gordon blanched under her steady gaze. "Oh, alright. I have two wonderfully talented daughters. And you're quite right to guess that I did not abandon them when they were little. Claire, the youngest, was already at Eastman when we were divorced. I'm not totally stereotypical, though. I didn't leave her for another woman."

"Why then?

"God, this is going to sound cold, but I think the marriage was over in the first year. There was just no passion there." Dorothy gave him another disapproving look. "I don't mean in the bedroom. I don't know quite how to explain this . . . she never understood anything about music, so she never understood anything about me. We couldn't have a decent conversation about what I cared about most in the world." He smiled at her. "You set the bar pretty high." She ignored the compliment.

"Good lord, Gordon. How do you tell someone that after twenty years of marriage?"

"You don't. You just feel like a schmuck. It actually might have been easier if I were involved with one of my students."

"That's a situation I've managed to avoid so far." Dorothy rolled her eyes and he laughed.

"Well, I've recently sworn it off. I'm afraid I haven't been a very good boy over the last couple of years. I probably have turned into a bit of a stereotype." He contemplated his wine glass and twisted it in his hand. "What's funny is I was just breaking up with someone when Evan first called me to complain--"

"Hah!"

"--to talk about his job. Since then, I've pretty much resolved to stick with my own age group. It's ironic that Helen's been much happier than me since the divorce. She got married to an architect in Connecticut who's just perfect for her. She's too nice to tell me that I did her a favor, but that's pretty clear whenever I see them together."

"That must make you feel better about the divorce."

"I guess it does, but it makes me wish that I had something more in my life." He looked at her and finished his wine. "Boy, that sure sounds pathetic. It's probably just one of those turning sixty things."

"Well," Dorothy commiserated, "turning sixty definitely stinks. I just concentrated hard on the next concert and managed to distract myself most of the time. Think of it this way, now we're both having affairs with the same lover: Ms. Music."

"I don't know," Gordon said, "the way I feel when I stand at the podium these days, I think maybe I divorced her too."

## 30

### A Mass for Dorothy

After Gordon's arrival, Terri stayed away from Dorothy's house for the rest of the day so the two old lovers could have some time alone. She waited until the following morning to check up on her friend. Over the previous weeks, she could tell that Dorothy was in more and more pain. When she stopped eating, Terri knew that one day soon she would visit and find the sick woman in such a desperate state that an ambulance would have to be called to take her to the hospital. Since cats cannot phone, Terri knew she would be the one to make the call.

She let herself in through the side door into the kitchen planning to make a pot of tea. When she flipped the light on, she was startled to find Gordon sitting at the table with a coffee mug in his hand.

"Good morning!" He stood up and extended his hand. "Nice to meet you again under less dramatic circumstances." Given the amount of adrenalin rushing through her veins, she wondered whether their meeting really was less dramatic.

"Nice to see you again too. Is Dorothy still asleep?" Gordon had already brewed some tea and made himself completely at home. Terri suddenly felt like she did not belong there.

"Yeah, she finally drifted off a couple of hours ago after she took a couple of extra pain pills." He shook his head in amazement. "She's still as stubborn as a mule. I think she held off on the pills just so she could talk to me straight-headed."

"She never says anything, but I think she's in an enormous amount of pain." Terri tried to think of something else to say. She liked Gordon, but the new sense of intimacy in the house made her feel uncomfortable. "Well, I usually check on her in the mornings, but it looks like you've got things under control. Tell her I stopped by. See you at the concert tonight, I guess."

"See you there! And thanks for being such a good friend to her. I don't know what she would do without you."

"She the greatest, but I suppose you already know that." He studied the bottom of his cup.

"I do now."

* * *

John got up early to make his parents a breakfast of pancakes, bacon, scrambled eggs, toast, hash browns, and freshly ground gourmet coffee. He was in the middle of his preparations when they appeared, not in bathrobes, bleary-eyed after a rough night's sleep, but freshly showered and ready for the road.

"Get a cup of coffee and sit down." John was happy to play gracious host since he had no idea what he would say if he sat down at the table with them. "The pancakes are almost done, and I got center-cut bacon, just the way you like it."

"Why thank you dear," his mother replied as he poured out two cups of black coffee, "you didn't have to go through all this trouble."

"Yeah, we could have stopped at Shoney's on the way out of town."

"Out of town? You're not leaving, are you?" John did not know whether to be relieved or appalled. He settled for hurt.

"I'm afraid your father hears those lush Florida links calling him, and he's antsy to get down there." John flipped his pancakes over and stepped back.

"That's not it and you both know it." He sounded more determined than he felt. "Look, Evan and I are both working all day. You've got a gorgeous sunny morning to spend at the botanical gardens. Then, you could go downtown and have a nice lunch. I've got you tickets to tour the Ridgely Plantation in the afternoon. Most of all, I really want you to stay for the concert tonight. It would mean a lot to me if you both would come." John watched his parents and judged from the way they were squirming that they felt precisely the way he did as a child when they chastised and cajoled him. They never let the pressure off when they wanted him to crack, so neither would he.

"I know I've disappointed you, but that doesn't mean you have to disappoint me too. Please say you'll stay just one more night?" Joanna gave Hal a questioning look and nodded her head hopefully at him.

"Alright," he finally said with a growl, "but this so-called nice restaurant downtown better have something decent on tap. If this is a dry county, I'm out of here."

* * *

208

For the first time since he had met Terri, Jorge arrived somewhere early. The waitress at the newly refurbished Ristorante Milano had time to seat him in a quiet corner of the restaurant, light the wax-laden Chianti bottle candle that towered lopsidedly in the middle of the table, and bring him a glass of wine before Terri walked through the door. She was dressed for the concert in a long black skirt and a simple violet blouse. The ensemble set off her green eyes spectacularly. He stood up and wondered if he was going to lose his nerve.

"Boy, you sure dress up nice!" She admired his neatly pressed jeans and dark linen jacket. He offered her a chair and when he sat back down, she pushed the candle aside so they could see each other.

"And you look quite lovely yourself." He tipped his wine at her but refrained from taking a sip until the waitress had brought her a glass. She responded by handing him the tickets, explaining that she did not have a purse to match her outfit.

"I haven't been here since they remodeled." She took a quick glance around. "The place looks pretty good." Three weeks earlier, the restaurant had been a pizza dive.

"It's an improvement." They made small talk for a while. She inquired about the status of his term papers, and he learned what she knew about the concert they would be attending after dinner. The food arrived just before the first awkward silence grew too big to ignore, and Jorge diverted his attention to his pasta, digging in with more enthusiasm than he really felt. Halfway through the meal, he wiped his mouth with his napkin and noticed her staring at him.

"I'm sorry," she was blushing and smiling at the same time, "but I was just wishing that one of my girlfriends from back home would suddenly walk in and see us here together. I'd introduce you and go: *Ta, we must be off to the concert.* The whole town would be talking for weeks." Jorge looked back down at his food. He needed to say something to her or the whole evening was in danger of spinning out of control.

"I'd also be glad to have one of my friends from Miami walk in. I could tell him how wonderful you are and, of course, he could see how pretty you are tonight." This was pure agony, but he blocked out her beaming face and plunged ahead. "And he would think I'm crazy to tell you that we can't keep seeing each other like we have been . . . that this is just too much for me right now." He saw the blood drain from her face and her shoulders sag. "And you would hear him tell me that I'm an idiot and a complete fool."

"No, Jorge, I'm the fool." She looked like she would cry for a moment, but then she gave her head a violent shake, swirling her thick blond hair around her shoulders. "I'm the one who's convinced herself that you were going to fall in love with me. God, I'm so embarrassed! I finally got up the nerve to throw myself at you last Friday. I really thought that I'd read you right, that you wanted to be something more than just my coffee buddy." She shook her head again. "I even convinced myself that there wasn't a look of relief on your face when I told you that I had to go to the hospital to see Dorothy. I pretended it was disappointment." She drained her wine and looked fiercely at him. "Jesus! And self-pity is even more disgusting than lovesick delusions."

"That's not it, Terri." He fumbled for the right words, a desperate need for understanding in his eyes. "I've made a commitment to myself that can't include you, a commitment to Miami, to my language, to my grandfather . . . to who I really am. I just don't know how to fit you in." He knew he sounded insincere.

"Just like I can't fit into size six jeans?"

"No! Listen, you're extremely attractive--"

"--don't bullshit me--"

"--I'm not bullshitting you." Jorge struggled for a way to let her know that she was desirable, that her green eyes and light hair and creamy complexion still confused and disoriented him. He could not stand to see her consumed with an emotion as debilitating as self-pity. *Oh shit, here goes.* "You remember Friday night and that look you thought might be relief?" She braced herself for more bad news. "It was relief, but not like you think. You see, you got me so excited while we were making out that, uh . . . I sort of finished before we could get started. No woman's ever done that to me before."

"But if you're really attracted to me," a look of total incredulity spread over her face, "and we get along great, then what's the problem?"

"We're still friends," he tried to explain again, "the problem is that I know who I am and what I want to do--"

"--and I know who I am," she put her napkin on her plate and got up to leave, "a foolish dental hygienist from Iowa and that's where I'm going back to." He watched helplessly as she walked out of the restaurant without looking back.

* * *

Louis felt strange as he walked to the Watkins Center. Professor Roberts wanted him there early to help with warm-ups, but once the orchestra, choir, and solists were ready to perform, he was to exit backstage and find his seat in the audience. It was not a bad feeling. He looked forward to being able to concentrate on the music without

210

worrying about playing, but he wished that the strangers sitting next to him would know that he had played a part in preparing the work they were hearing.

He was one of the first to arrive, so he sat down at the piano to work on a sonata that he was preparing for Herr Gabel. As the choristers slowly filed in, he noticed that they each took a sheet from a stack of papers piled on the end of the instrument. He stopped playing (earning one emphatic "Don't stop!") and took a copy for himself. It was the program for the concert, listing Beethoven and *Missa Solemnis* in large bold letters on the front with Professor Henderson's name and the Clarkeston College Chorus and Orchestra just underneath. He opened it and looked for his name among the dozens of choristers and instrumentalists listed in the middle pages. With a frown, he flipped over to the back and found nothing but the names of the donors and sponsors of the event. He was about to toss the program back on top of the piano when someone tapped his shoulder.

"Look on the front, you dodo," Debbie whispered in his ear. He did and noticed his name and "rehearsal accompanist," right under (and in the same size type!) as the concertmaster's name.

"See you at Jack-the-Dipper after the concert," she reminded him as she left to take her position on the risers.

\* \* \*

"Shouldn't you be getting dressed?" Dorothy looked at the clock on the mantel and then at the casually clad Gordon sitting next to her.

"I've still got an hour until the concert starts. Are you sure you don't want to try and come with me?"

"Absolutely! Even if I felt like I could walk up all of those stairs to the Watkins Center, I couldn't sit in one of those seats for two hours. I won't have everyone's last memory of me be a sick, doddering old woman hanging onto some man's arm for dear life." She wanted to see the performance, but the fear of a pathetic swan song was a formidable deterrent.

"Not to mention that all the damn pain pills I've been popping are loosening my grip on my tear ducts. I'd probably blub through the whole performance. God, what a thought."

"I understand."

Maybe he does, she thought, and she remembered the night before. After the initial shock of being alone together for the first time in thirty-five years, they quickly slipped back into comfortable familiarity. Although she had been involved with several men over the years, he still

211

knew many things about her that no one else did. Once she realized Gordon's charm was genuine, that the years had softened his rough edges, she found herself trusting him as much as she trusted Terri. And history and age made him an even better listener than her adopted daughter. When she heard him talk about his own life, she knew he trusted her too. He talked about his marriage and the string of failed relationships that followed, and he admitted that, like her, he had never again experienced anything like the magic they shared in graduate school. No great love stood in between him and Dorothy.

"Do you have any regrets?" she asked as she lay in her bed, dark eyes glistening in the light of a small table lamp. She was extremely sensitive to any movement of her bed, so he had pushed a chair close enough to touch her hand or run his fingers through the thick, graying hair she had let down just for him.

"You mean apart from your abandoning me?"

"Yes, was that your Waterloo?"

"Hiroshima is what it felt like." He laughed. "Letting you go was a mistake, but I got two terrific daughters in return. I've made worse bargains. I really wish you could meet them! You could use Rachel in your choir and Claire in the violin section right now. What about you? How come you never married? I can't believe that there weren't dozens of suitors beating down your door."

"Beating their heads against it, more likely." She sipped her tea and gave him an ironic smile. "You've got to remember that I moved back to the South in the 1950's as a twenty-six-year-old with a doctorate, a career, and left-wing politics. In spite of my devastating looks and charm, I was not exactly the belle of the ball. And I really sealed my fate by moving from Atlanta back to a town like Clarkeston where everyone meets their mate in high school. I married Clarkeston College and had hundreds of children, none of whom stayed for very long, but some of whom cared enough to let me teach them something."

"Any regrets at all?"

"No," she squeezed his hand and met his gaze straight on, "not anymore."

They spent the night together in her bedroom, returning again and again to memories of the first Christmas they spent together sheltered from a snowstorm that changed their lives. Toward dawn, when the novelty of his presence was no longer enough to distract her from the pain, she took a double dose of her medication and slipped into an oblivion that she was not sure she wanted to return from.

When she awoke the day of the concert, it was almost noon, and she was so stiff that it took her almost twenty minutes to crawl out of bed.

She stumbled into the bathroom to take a shower and inspected herself naked in the mirror, horrified by what she saw. She had lost so much weight that her skin looked three sizes too big for her bones. Much of her body was discolored, legs a sick, chicken-skin yellow, shoulder and chest a bloody, bruised raspberry. So much of her body hurt that she found it difficult to separate the places that radiated a dull ache from those that generated a sudden snap of pain if she moved wrong. She felt her gorge rise, and leaned over the toilet with sudden heave. When she picked herself off the floor, she resolved to call Doc Burton and ask him to meet her the next day.

She and Gordon spent the afternoon of the concert talking, and at his insistence, listening to some of the recordings that the College Chorus had made under her direction. Although she had something critical to say about each performance, the admiration in his eyes was genuine. By the time they finished listening to excerpts from the performance of Honegger's *King David* which she had directed the previous spring, it was time for Gordon to leave and judge his former student. "Dorothy, that's the best recording I've ever heard of that piece. It's incredible."

"It's probably the only recording of it you've heard. That's why it got picked up by TelArc, there's hardly any others out there."

"Shows how much you know. I've got three different recordings at home and I've heard most of the others. I'll stand by my rating. What you did was just magic."

"Well, thank you. I didn't realize you were a connoisseur of obscure French choral works." She watched him closely while he tied his tie and slipped on his jacket.

"Are you sure you'll be alright alone?"

"Just get out of here, for heaven's sake!" He gave her a peck on the cheek and slipped out the front door. Once he was gone, she got up slowly and switched the stereo to the channel that would be broadcasting the concert. On her way to the kitchen to fetch a glass of tea, she picked up the phone and called the doctor.

* * *

Stepping up to the podium to address the singers an hour before the doors opened, Evan took a deep breath and began to preach his gospel one final time.

"Okay guys, by now you've figured out that Professor Henderson is too ill to direct this wonderful piece tonight, but she assured me that she will be glued to the radio. Many of you have sung for her for many years and know how much she's meant to the program here--how in many ways she *is* the choral program." He had their undivided attention. "I want you to sing this for her."

He put the choir through a vigorous body warm-up, making them stretch, rotate shoulders, massage and pound on their neighbors' necks and backs. Then he started them humming scales quietly, slowly pushing them to the top of their range. "We are not going to sing through any of the sections of the mass right now," he told the surprised group. "You know the music cold. I'm only worried about two things. First, and most important, volume. That's why we'll spend almost the entire warm-up doing vocal exercises. Singing this as quietly as I want, and as quietly as Professor Henderson expects, will be more vocally demanding than anything you've ever sung.

"Second, some of your entrances are a little tentative. During the last ten minutes or so, Louis will give us a few short preps, and we'll make sure we're all getting in together at the trouble spots." With one glance, he seemed to meet the eye of everyone in the chorus. "Alright, let's get to work."

He put as much passion into the warm-up session as most directors did during a performance, demanding that they sing in a voice that sent pure vowels floating gently to every corner of the Watkins Center. The expression on his face showed them how much he cared about the sound, how all of them would sink or swim together when he raised his baton and the music started. By the time the chorus had run through the entrance to the last section, the orchestra had seated itself, and he sent the singers backstage with a curt nod. He saw Louis linger at his instrument as long as he could, finally disappearing when the doors swung open and the crowd started trickling in.

* * *

Gordon was stunned by the size of the audience. Every seat of the large auditorium was occupied and not just with friends of performers or music majors obliged to bring a program back to class to meet an attendance requirement. Given the wide variety of people sitting around him, it was clear that the town had claimed Dorothy as its own. With the whole of New York City to draw on, Gordon doubted he had ever attracted such packed and excited audience. And Clarkeston has how many people, he wondered, thirty or forty thousand? Neither his conversation with Dorothy nor her wonderful recordings had explained how she could have no regrets about hiding her talent in a southern backwater.

214

"Ladies and Gentlemen," Evan turned and addressed the audience as soon as the polite applause and puzzled whispers that greeted his entrance subsided. "My name is Evan Roberts, Assistant Professor of Music at Clarkeston College, and it is with great sadness and disappointment that I must announce Professor Henderson is too ill to direct tonight's performance of Beethoven's *Missa Solemnis*." He cast a quick glance at the radio booth to make sure that his remarks were being broadcast.

"But her chorus stands ready to sing for her nonetheless, courtesy of WCCR," he gestured to the technician in the back of the auditorium and paused. "And since it's uncertain when Professor Henderson will be able to direct this group again, I was hoping that we might show our appreciation, not only for the enormous effort she has made to prepare this piece, but also for what she has meant to Clarkeston over the last thirty years." He began to applaud and before he had struck his hands a second time, the choir was on its feet clapping madly and stomping on the risers. The enthusiasm on stage, however, was immediately overpowered by the response from the audience, as the crowd rose as one and sent waves of endless thunder reverberating back and forth across the auditorium.

I wish I could see her face right now, Gordon thought to himself as he stood whistling and clapping until his arms hurt. Why didn't she tell me? She must have just assumed I understood, that my experience as a director paralleled hers. I'm afraid not, Dorothy. I'm afraid you still have something to teach me. He looked at Evan cue the orchestra, and for the first time in several years, he longed to be the one behind the podium.

\* \* \*

When the applause finally died down and the audience began to seat itself, John heard his mother stifle a snort of laughter as Hal whispered in her ear. "What was that about," John leaned over and asked her quietly. She considered her reply and then repeated his father's exact words. "Your father said: *At least he didn't marry an asshole.*"

John stared at his mother for a long moment.

"Does that mean you'll stay a little longer?" Joanna nodded affirmatively, Hal rolled his eyes and gave a small sigh of resignation, and John leaned back in his chair with a lightness of being he had not felt since he was a small boy.

\* \* \*

215

When Terri emerged into the cool December night choking with embarrassment, she had no clear idea where she should go. Unless she wanted to retrieve her ticket from Jorge, attending the sold-out concert was not an option. And even though Arthur would be sorely disappointed, she doubted that she could sit in a crowded public auditorium for two hours. Being alone was equally unappealing, so there was no question of returning to the house and waiting for Suzanne to return from the concert. She eventually trudged away from campus and into College Hills. As she approached Dorothy's house, she saw Gordon driving away and sighed with relief that no one but her friend would see her in such a miserable state.

She knocked on the door and walked in to find Dorothy perched on the sofa, sipping a huge ice tea and eating a small pile of aspirin gel-caps, one at a time. She squinted at Terri.

"What are you doing here, darlin'?" Terri opened her mouth to respond, but her tears did the talking as she dropped to the floor next to the sofa and laid her head in old woman's lap. Dorothy stroked her hair and tried to piece together what had happened. She did not wait until Terri's sobs subsided.

"Here's my guess: Jorge presented you with a diamond ring and begged you to marry him, but you told him he wasn't good enough for you." A moan broke its way through the tears. "No? Hmmm . . . you forgot about your date with Tom Cruise and when Jorge walked in all hell broke loose." Something like a snort of laughter followed. "No? Then I'd have to guess that he dumped you." Terri moved her head. "I knew he was too good-looking not to be a shit."

"Well, you might have told me that before, you know," Terri sniffed, looking up and wiping her face with her sleeve.

"I'm just kidding, sweetheart. He seemed like a perfect gentleman the times that I met him." She handed her a couple of tissues from the box she kept on the window sill. "You want to tell me what happened?"

Terri explained what had transpired in the restaurant. In response to Dorothy's prodding, she described Jorge's attempts to convince her that she was not the problem, that some internal conflict stymied an otherwise plausible match. "You know," she admitted, "I'm not even that mad at him. I'm just so embarrassed . . . and I feel so stupid and foolish."

"Maybe he's telling the truth," Dorothy suggested when she had heard the whole story.

"Huh?"

"Maybe it really is difficult for a militant Latino to take a green-eyed-blond Anglo as a wife. One thing's for sure, you must have touched him in some way. That story he told you about Friday night . . . if it's

216

true, then you can consider yourself one hell of a hot babe. Even if it's not, he must have some strong feelings about you to invent something that embarrassing just to make you feel better." Terri rested on the floor as she considered the lifeline her friend was trying to throw her. They sat without speaking until the radio announced the beginning of the concert "live from the Watkins Center in Clarkeston, Georgia."

They were both surprised to hear the program start with the sound of Evan's baritone voice announcing the change in directors, and Terri forgot her own misery when she felt Dorothy's hand squeezing her shoulder tighter as his speech went beyond the mere technicalities of the substitution. When applause exploded through the speakers and shook every corner of the room, her first impulse was to turn around, but the grip on her shoulder told her not to look back. As the roar of the audience intensified, she blindly reached over her shoulder and took Dorothy's hand in her own, staring straight ahead at the stereo while she held it tightly to her cheek. She knew without looking that Dorothy's face too was streaming with tears, tears knowing nothing so important as friendship, tears singing there are many kinds of love.

* * *

Jorge sat at the empty table with two concert tickets sticking out of his front pocket and wondered how to spend the rest of his evening. He did not want to attend the sold-out concert, which meant that he should return the tickets to the box office so someone else might use them. Well, maybe I can do one thing right tonight, he thought. After five minutes in the ticket line he felt a tap on his shoulder.

"Jorge? Where's Terri? I thought you guys were going to sit with me." He turned and saw a dark-haired woman looking very uncomfortable in a navy blue maternity dress. He had forgotten that Suzanne was sitting with him and Terri. He flushed a deep red as he tried to explain what had happened earlier.

"Uh, we didn't have a very good dinner," he stammered. "I tried to tell her that we should go to the concert as friends, and I made a horrible mess of it. She ran out of the restaurant, and I'm sure she doesn't feel like coming anymore." His feelings were written plainly on his face. "It's all my fault, but I thought the right thing to do was to turn in the tickets." He saw Suzanne scrutinize him carefully, judging the degree of culpability in the lines of his face and in his eyes, trying to determine whether he was being honest or deceptive.

"Don't turn them in," she finally said. "Come sit with me—I don't want to waddle into the auditorium all by myself."

He did not feel like sitting through two hours of Beethoven, but he felt guilty about Terri and owed some courtesy to the gracious woman who had twice invited him to her home. He forced a smile as he took her arm. "It would be my pleasure."

To his surprise, he found himself enjoying the concert in spite of his mood. The standing ovation for Professor Henderson was astonishing, and the chorus and orchestra carried that excitement and passion into their performance. He had just begun to lose himself completely in the music when he felt another tap on his shoulder. "We have to go now," Suzanne whispered. He responded with a confused look. "My water just broke." He opened his mouth, but nothing came out for a moment. "Of course," he said, "let's go." Good luck put them close to the end of a row in the back of the room, and Jorge slipped into the aisle and watched her make her way toward him with surprising dignity. He took her arm as they walked the short distance to the exit doors and into the lobby where they met with an astounding sight.

Two well-dressed students were standing by the double doors far to the left of Suzanne and Jorge. One of them was carefully slipping the tip of an antenna in the crease between the doors, while the other was looking nervously around the lobby. As the lookout saw them, he grabbed the shoulder of his friend and whispered anxiously in his ear. Before Jorge puzzled out what was going on, a third student seemed to appear out of nowhere, rushed past him across the room and knocked the first two away from the door. While the two dazed victims struggled to their feet, their assailant ignored them and leapt onto the electronic device, stomping it repeatedly against the floor. The two, now fully-recovered and enraged students hammered him with blows to his head and body. Jorge pulled Suzanne behind a pillar and peered around its edges, torn between his impulse to break up the fight and his duty to Suzanne. He was relieved from making a decision by the appearance of a security guard who intervened with nightstick and handcuffs and dragged the three boys off to a room behind the ticket office.

"I think that lets us off the hook for the moment, don't you?" Suzanne nodded wide-eyed at his summary of the situation, and they headed gingerly for the exit from the lobby. "Boy," he exclaimed when they emerged into the cool night air, "who ever said that classical music was boring?"

Suzanne insisted that he drive her car slowly on the way to the hospital. This was not her first child, she explained, and she could tell that the baby was coming in a matter of hours, not minutes.

"I can get checked in by myself," she said as they pulled into the emergency entrance to the hospital, "but could I ask you one more big favor? Could you go back to the Watkins Center and tell Arthur where I am? Don't do anything dramatic, just wait until the concert is over, find your way backstage and let him know to come over here."

"Sure, no problem." He got out of the car and walked over to the passenger door to help her out. By the time they had taken a couple of steps toward the hospital, a nurse met them with a wheelchair. Although it felt awkward to leave her in the care of a stranger, he knew he should go find Arthur.

When he arrived at the Watkins Center, intermission had concluded but the performance was still far from over. He peered at the enraptured audience through the small window set in the auditorium door and decided to wait in the lobby until the performance was over. As he looked for a place to sit, he noticed the security guard interrogating the three young men in the back of the ticket office. The one who had initiated the confrontation sat with his head sagging miserably, handcuffed to a chair, while the other two, also cuffed, talked animatedly to the guard. Jorge walked over to the door and knocked on the glass to get the guard's attention. The guard opened the door and stepped out.

"Officer, I saw what happened with those three in there." He carefully explained what he and Suzanne had witnessed.

"So you say it was the weird kid who attacked the two frat boys, and it was them who were holding the remote control?" The guard's expression indicated he had heard a different version of the story. "And your friend saw it, too? Where's she?"

"In the hospital having a baby, but I'm sure she'll confirm that it was those two." He pointed through the window at the two students he had overheard talking in the cafeteria a few days before. "They were holding the device that the other kid destroyed."

\* \* \*

When the guard unlocked his handcuffs and brought him back out to the lobby, Louis was sure he was going to be taken to the police station. Then he saw the Hispanic man who had been hiding behind the pillar, and he dared to hope that he would not be blamed for the bomb that was sitting just offstage in a brown paper bag.

"Okay Harpo, this guy says you attacked those two in there when they started waving that remote around. Is that right?" Louis had been unable to speak more than a couple of words since his arrest. Between being beaten and handcuffed, and the sheer frustration of listening to the other boys claim that the remote control was his, he had been driven

219

toward catatonia. He struggled to respond to the guard's skepticism; it was like trying to run through thick mud.

"How come you tackled them?" Jorge posed his question in a more sympathetic voice.

"I think they put a bomb by the stage," he finally stammered. "I think they were trying to set it off."

"A bomb?" The guard instantly became wary and nervous. "Can you show us where it is?" Louis nodded and led them down the corridor past the dressing rooms, the Green Room, the backstage bathrooms, and into the shadows of the area just to the side of the performers. As they walked closer to the stage, the sound of the music grew louder and louder. The hardwood partitions that formed the sides of the stage were open to the chorus and orchestra at two recessed niches, angled so that the audience could not see in. As the music rose to a crescendo, Louis pointed to a chair sitting in one of the recesses. A large paper grocery bag lay on the floor underneath it, mouth open and facing out to the space in between the orchestra and the chorus.

"How did you know this was here?"

"I'm the accompanist for Professor Roberts, the director." He pulled the program out of his pocket with pride and pointed to his name. The guard leaned over to hear him better. "After the warm-ups were over, I had to go to the bathroom really bad. When I got finished, the concert had already started. I saw those guys putting the bag under the chair. They didn't see me, so I followed them up to the lobby. When they got out the thing with the antenna, I figured they were going to set off a bomb."

The guard seemed to believe him but had little notion how to respond to the possibility that an explosive device sat a mere fifteen feet away from him and within close range of hundreds of others.

As the guard pondered the proper course of action, Louis saw Professor Roberts motion the choir to open up on the final section and sent waves of pure emotion crashing across the auditorium. The look on Evan's face was ecstatic, as if he had found complete fulfillment in that moment of making music. The orchestra and singers were not merely his tools; they were fused with him and the audience in a transcendent bond that Louis had never witnessed before. With sudden and complete clarity, Louis realized that if he returned to Clarkeston in thirty years he would find Evan standing behind the same podium.

The security guard crossed himself and walked slowly to the chair. He put one hand gently on top of it and dropped to his knees, craning his head around to look inside the open bag. As the music climaxed, Louis feared the violent reverberations thundering from the stage would set off the bomb. He dropped his head so he would not have to watch.

A long moment later, he felt the Hispanic man touch his shoulder and point at the guard walking toward them with a bag in his hand and a cryptic look on his face. "Let's go back up to the ticket office."

As they turned to follow the guard back up the stairs, the music ended and an ovation erupted immediately from the crowd. Louis instinctively hunched his shoulders against the sound, half-expecting pieces of the ceiling to come raining down on them from the uproar. The noise was even louder when they got to the lobby and was still audible even after they ducked into the ticket office. When the door was shut behind them, the guard gave the two handcuffed boys a disgusted look and emptied the contents of the bag onto a table.

"My son got a plastic car exactly like this for Christmas." He pointed at the bright pink, remote-controlled convertible emblazoned with the title FAGGOT-MOBILE. "He just didn't decorate it quite so creatively." He shook his head and turned to Louis and Jorge. "I'll need to take your formal statements."

"Could we do it later, sir," Jorge said urgently, "I've got to tell someone in the chorus that his wife is having a baby--"

"--and I've got to talk to someone too," Louis added with equal force.

"Alright, I'll hold them here until you get back. There's no reason for y'all to be inconvenienced on account of assholes like these two."

"Thank you, officer!"

"Thank you!"

Jorge and Louis hurried back down the corridor into the middle of the mayhem that had broken out backstage. The choir and orchestra pressed around the soloists and Evan. Everyone was talking at once, congratulating Sophie on her delicate touch, praising the superb blending of the quartet and chorus, hailing the masterful direction and risky vision of their director. The performance had bridged the divide between instrumentalist and singer, as orchestra and choir intermingled seeking unnecessary confirmation of the quality of what they had accomplished together. Ten minutes after the last standing ovation had finally ended, the Green Room was still empty, its refreshments tempting no one while a mass of tuxedos and black dresses crowded the area immediately beside the stage unwilling to leave until the last bit of magic had faded.

After scanning the crowd on tiptoe, Jorge spotted Arthur on the far side of the stage and pushed his way through to talk to him. Standing at the mouth of the corridor on the edge of the sea of musicians, Louis saw a mixture of joy and worry animate Arthur's face before he started wading back through the crowd. As he looked for Debbie, he nervously fingered a thick wad of tissue paper in his pocket and pulled it out to check whether the two porcelain figures inside had been broken. He had taken Dr. Peterson's advice and bought Debbie a whimsical salt and pepper shaker set: two china cats, one dressed in a tuxedo sitting at a piano and the other dressed in a fancy gown, molded so that she could perch on the piano to sing. He unwrapped them slowly and was relieved to discover that they had survived intact.

"Those are so cute!" Debbie exclaimed as she squeezed next to him. "Where'd you get them?"

"Here," he pushed them awkwardly at her, "they're for singing so well." Despite hours of agonizing, he had been unable to script an acceptable speech for presenting her with the two figurines.

"They're lovely." She gave him a quick peck on the cheek. "Thank you so much! Now, are you ready for some ice cream?"

"Uh, I sort of have to make a statement to a policeman upstairs." He spoke to his shoes, unable to hold her curious gaze. "It's a long story—"

"No, it's not." Jorge was eavesdropping as he and Arthur passed by on their way up the corridor. "He's a hero. That's all there is to it. Now, if you'll excuse me, I've got to take this man to the hospital." Debbie looked in wide-eyed astonishment at Jorge, and then gave Louis a questioning look, but all he could manage in response was a Gallic shrug of his shoulders.

* * *

When the applause finally faded, Terri got up and turned off the stereo. Before she could turn back around, Dorothy closed her eyes and tried to hear the music once again above the sound of clapping still ringing in her ears. For a moment she was able to recapture the profound sense of peace that had come over her during the performance. She had expected longing or regret, maybe even bitterness and jealousy as she heard Evan direct her choir, but instead she had felt a sense of relief from a burden she hardly knew she was carrying. The mass had reminded her that she was not the music; she was not responsible for it. She and Evan and the choir, were only instruments playing their parts. And when she was too tired to play any longer, the music did not stop. It continued and continued in glorious, godly harmony.

She opened her eyes and realized Gordon would be home soon, and for the first time since she was small child, she wanted to be taken care of, if only for one more evening. Listening had given her the knowledge that

222

she did not, and could not, control the music. When the time came to embrace or reject that wisdom, to stand alone and fight or plunge into an uncertain future, she found herself falling back into the arms of her friends. She was done making music, but she listened to its message, to its story of connection and community, of tears and forgiveness.

Terri tidied up the room in anticipation of Gordon's return, waiting to speak until Dorothy seemed ready. When she came back from the kitchen with two mugs of hot tea, Dorothy propped herself more upright on the sofa.

"Thank you, dear." She took a small sip. "At the risk of sounding banal: What did you think about the concert?"

Terri laughed. "I think it was wonderful, of course. It got me thinking about so many different things."

"Like what?"

"Like what I'm going to do the rest of my life."

"Oh, just trivial stuff like that. Are you going to stay here?"

"I'll stay for a while longer." Terri squeezed her friend's hand. "I'll go back to Iowa eventually, but not to the damn cornfields. I'm going to spend some of my money and get a nice place in Iowa City, close to the campus. I want to start taking some classes again, and I'll get to more concerts than I did when I was working on my degree." She gave Dorothy a smile that nearly broke her heart. "And who knows, I might even visit the Spanish table that used to meet every Thursday afternoon."

GOING HOME

# 31

## Coda

Gordon and Evan arrived triumphantly from the concert to toast Dorothy with a bottle of expensive French champagne, and they talked deep into the night, celebrating the performance and Dorothy's role in it and sharing with her the strange story of two hooligans' foiled attempt to disrupt the show. Terri managed to find some snacks in the kitchen, and when it grew too late, discreetly let Evan know that he should make his exit with her and leave the two old friends alone.

"Shall I see you tomorrow?" She leaned down and kissed Dorothy's cheek.

"Oh, I'm sure you will. But if you don't, I hope you won't forget this evening."

"I couldn't if I wanted to."

Evan, full of champagne and feeling invulnerable, impulsively added a kiss of his own. "I'll never forget it either."

"Good lord," she chastised the two young people, "get out of here before someone suggests a group hug and I get sick on the floor. Go on now and leave me alone with this beaten-up old musician for a little bit." When the door finally clicked shut, she turned a tired head to Gordon. "I guess he passed?"

"With flying colors."

"I suppose with a great recommendation from you, he'll soon be off to greener pastures."

"I don't think so. He told me he was turning down a job interview from a very good school up in Syracuse. He says he's going to stick around here for a while." She smiled at the thought of another uncompromising director carrying on her tradition of controversy and independence. Suddenly, a wave of exhaustion and pain held off too long by adrenaline crashed down on her.

"Could you get me about ten pain pills and a big glass of tea," she asked in a shaky voice.

"How about two? Doubling the dose is probably okay."

"No, give me three. That's what I took last night and I'm still around." When he returned from the kitchen, she swallowed the pills and stood up with a groan. "Thank you, dear. Now, why don't you tell me some nice stories while I try to get to sleep."

As she lay down in her bed and the pills finally took hold and began to dull the edges of her pain, she listened to Gordon's warm voice and wondered whether it was really time to leave, whether life might not have a few more wonderful surprises in store for her.

In the morning, she awoke to pain so intense that she could hardly breathe. Every bone and joint ached with a white-hot intensity that begged for the kind of medication only a hospital could provide. With a tremendous effort, she got into the clean blouse and skirt she had chosen for her appointment with Doc Burton, and slipped an envelope she had prepared the day before into her purse. She found Gordon in the kitchen drinking tea.

"Good morning!" he rose and embraced her gingerly, "you look especially nice this morning."

"Thank you, I've got an appointment with my doctor." As she started to elaborate, the phone rang and she brightened to the sound of Terri's voice on the other end of the line. "Good lord, what a night! Let me get a pen . . . alright. Nine pounds, two ounces, three-thirty a.m., Cynthia Dorothy Hughes-Garfield. That sure is a mouthful . . . no, I don't know what to say . . . good-bye."

"I gather you have a new namesake in town," Gordon ventured as she hung up the phone.

"I guess I do." She was surprised and flattered by the news. "One of my singers and his wife had a baby last night. Apparently her water broke at the concert. Imagine that!" Before she could finish the story, a wave of nausea hit her, and she sat down until it passed. When the room stopped spinning, she looked up at the clock. "Could you drive me to the airport in fifteen minutes? Doc Burton is going to give me a ride today in an authentic World War One Fokker biplane." Gordon looked at her like she had lost her mind.

"I'm feeling especially good," she lied and quickly swallowed a handful of aspirin before he could object, "and this may be my last chance to accept his invitation. He's been trying to get me up in his damn plane for years." The doctor had been extremely dubious when she called him the day before, but she described her condition in glowing terms, "must be some kind of temporary remission, Doc," and insisted that she was healthy enough to fly. He grudgingly acquiesced, and she agreed to see

228

him after the flight for an examination and serious discussion of what he referred to in his inimitable style as "end-term treatment options."

As she sat in the passenger seat of Gordon's rental car sipping sweet tea, her worst fears played themselves out in her mind. In one scene, Doc Burton looked at her and refused to take her up in the plane, leaving her to the uncertain remedy of an overdose of pain pills, and in another, she gave in to the temptation of asking Gordon to stay until she could die in his arms. She banished the first with a reminder of the trump card she kept to play on Doc Burton; she banished the second with the foreknowledge that her cancer would not permit a romantic death room scene with friends and family gathered close, but rather a technology-ridden, drug-hazed, memory-annihilating mess of a departure.

They followed Burton's directions to the parking area behind the corrugated metal building where the private planes were stored. The doctor had already pulled out the Fokker and was carefully checking the operation of its rudder and wing flaps. When he saw his patient, he made one final adjustment and climbed deliberately down out of the plane. As she expected, the doctor and Gordon took an instant dislike to each other. "Sorry, Dorothy, but I've only got room for one passenger, unless maybe this gentleman knows how to fly vintage aircraft," Burton said in lieu of a polite greeting.

"That's okay doctor, I feel safer just staying here on the ground, but I'm not really sure Dorothy is up for this either. Do you think it's okay?"

"I wouldn't fly this thing if I didn't think it was safe," he growled. "I'm retiring next month—Dorothy here is about my last patient—and I'll be flying to air shows all around the country. It's safe, alright."

"No," Gordon looked tentatively at Dorothy, "you misunderstand. It's she that might not be in good enough shape to fly." The doctor grunted and looked hard at Dorothy.

"Maybe I should check her out first," he used the same tone he would to discuss his plane.

"Can we talk for a moment, Doc?" Dorothy reached over and grabbed Doc Burton's arm, pulling him to the far side of the plane. "First of all, I'm not some kind of equipment that needs to be checked out. I can make my own decisions without the help of two clueless men—"

"—and second," he interrupted, "you don't look very strong to me, and these planes do pull a lot of g's. An examination is not a bad idea." She had no choice now but to play her ace in the hole.

"David," she called him gently by his Christian name for the first time in twenty-five years and looked directly into his eyes, "you've been in love with me for how long? Twenty years at least?" He sputtered and turned bright red, the illusion that his unrequited passion was his secret alone completely shattered. "Couldn't you do just this one favor for me? Just this one time, forget you're my doctor." Stunned and disoriented, he stammered his acquiescence.

"Sure . . . sure, let me drag the stand over so you can get in." While he went to get the large aluminum stepladder that helped open-cockpit pilots and their passengers to slip into their seats, Dorothy walked back to Gordon fighting to maintain her composure.

"We're going up right now," she squeezed him tightly with her good arm. "Don't worry. I'll be okay." She heard the doctor call for her and embraced him as tightly as she could. "I love you, Gordon."

"I love you too." Caught off-guard by the intensity of her declaration and the tears welling in her eyes, he said no more before she turned and walked away.

She smiled and waved to him after Doc Burton started the engine. As the Fokker began to pull away, she reached into her purse, pulled out the envelope and tossed it at Gordon. The back draft from the propellers blew it past him into the parking lot, and by the time he retrieved it, the plane was soaring in the pale blue sky over Clarkeston. He watched until it faded from sight and then sat on the hood of the car to await her return, gently tapping the envelope, simply addressed "Gordon," against his thigh. After a few minutes, his curiosity got the better of him and he opened it. With some confusion, he recognized the handwriting as his own, the ancient date at the top right corner marking it as one of the love letters he had written Dorothy during the first summer they had spent apart. He read the three pages through, tears streaming down his cheeks long before he got to the final page and the brief message she had scrawled, "I kept them all."

* * *

Dorothy thought that she might have to dare Doc Burton to demonstrate some of his acrobatic flying skills, but even the most basic maneuvers pressed upon her with roller coaster force. When he banked sharply to give them a sparkling view of the city, she was pushed especially hard against her seat harness and felt something give in her shoulder. A sudden warmth exploded inside her chest as the fragile aneurism finally burst. I was right, she thought with an odd joy as she leaned over to take a final look at the town and school where she had spent most of her life, it really doesn't hurt. Then, unable to hold up her head any longer, she closed her eyes and was no longer flying in an ancient biplane, but sliding on a suitcase down a snowy hill into the white haze of flurry swirling street lamps.